MURDER IN MATERIAL GAIN

ANNE CLEELAND

ARTEMIS
PRESS

For Charles Francis Feeney, who gave away billions in secret; and for all others like him.

PROLOGUE

*H*e watched her from the second-story window, as she played with Edward in the garden. He loved to watch her, but rarely had the opportunity, nowadays. It was one of the reasons he liked to come here.

She was so much better, near fully recovered, and it was an immense relief—not that he ever doubted she would right herself; she was extraordinary. On the other hand, it would be a long while before he forgave himself; he'd been so consumed with rage that he'd lost sight of other important developments, and he mustn't allow such a thing to happen again—he had much ground to make up, so that it could all be set to rights.

He'd put protections in place, and apply pressure to mend-up the problem—no easy feat, in light of the promise that he'd made, the first time they'd met. No matter; he'd welcome the challenge. It was an interesting dilemma, and it would require careful handling.

He turned to his piano, so as to contemplate his next move.

CHAPTER 1

*D*etective Sergeant Kathleen Doyle was in the process of discovering that doing "good works" wasn't all that it was cracked-up to be, although if she were any decent sort of person she wouldn't even notice that being all kindly to the less fortunate was such a monumental pain in the neck. She wasn't, and it was, which just went to show you that the nuns were right, and she was nowhere near sainthood.

At present, she was standing in the cafeteria that served the minimum-security side of the Wexton Women's Prison, and trying to helm her first Bible study session. She'd a dozen prisoners who were participating in the class, and the lesson today was supposed to be about the false idolatry of greed. Unfortunately, the lesson didn't seem to be resonating very much, with the aforesaid prisoners.

"I don't get it," loudly declared a middle-aged woman, whose name-label on her prison uniform identified her as "Harrison". "This farmer-fellow sounds plenty smart, to me."

Nonplussed, Doyle wasn't certain how to respond—mainly because she wasn't someone who'd ever pictured herself in the role of a teacher-of-anything, and let this be a reminder as to why this was. They were studying the Parable of the Foolish Farmer, who'd worked hard to store-up his bountiful crops, only to unexpectedly die, and therefore never enjoy his wealth.

"I think the point of the story is that you're not supposed to devote yourself to gettin' rich," Doyle explained. "You're supposed to devote yourself to God, instead."

"He didn't *know* he was going to die, though," the prisoner pointed out in a practical manner. "None of us does —may as well get rich in the meantime; God doesn't pay very well."

Several of the other women in attendance laughed and expressed their general agreement. "You may as well try to get rich," a second prisoner, named Charbonneau, spoke up. "You're going to die, eventually, either way." Charbonneau was younger than Harrison, and a bit more posh than the other prisoners who were present.

"I wish *I'd* known," Harrison, the first prisoner, replied in a bitter tone. "Stupid old cow, to pull through."

"Now, Harrison, it was only your bad luck." A prisoner named Smythe then explained to Doyle in an aside, "Her maiden aunt had a stroke, and they thought she was going to die, so Harrison, here, drained her bank account. But then the aunt pulled through, and once she realized what had happened, she reported it to the police."

"Can you believe it?" Harrison exclaimed, very put-upon. "She called the coppers on me, even though I was family."

"Oh," said Doyle, who continued nonplussed.

"*Stupid* old cow," Harrison repeated. "She turned everyone else in the family against me, too."

"Including Harrison's husband," Smythe added, in another aside to Doyle.

"He left me high and dry, the bastard," Harrison agreed, very much affronted. "All on account of her—shows you where his loyalty was. I should have gone over to the hospital and put a pillow over her face, just to make sure."

Several of the others cackled with great merriment, and Doyle tried to restore order as best she could. "We're not supposed to murder, or covet, or steal," she explained. "There's important rules about it."

"Tell that to the Warden," Harrison offered, with a sly expression.

"Well, you wouldn't be able to inherit from your aunt anyway, if they could show that you were the one who killed her," Charbonneau offered, as cold comfort. "Better to set it up to look like a suicide, or an accidental overdose."

"Wait a minute—I should take notes," Harrison joked, and lifted her pencil.

"You should indeed; better luck, next time," Charbonneau replied, and everyone laughed.

Doyle lowered her gaze to her lesson plan, because her scalp had started prickling, which was what it did when her intuition was prodding her to pay attention. Irish by birth, Doyle had a fine-tuned perceptive ability, which allowed her to read the emotions of those people around her, and in particular, she could usually tell when someone was lying. She wasn't certain why her intuition was acting up in this instance, though—save that Charbonneau was more irritated with Harrison than she was letting on. Not to mention that advice about the best manner and mode for murder didn't seem a very appropriate topic, for a woman who'd landed herself in a minimum-security prison.

A hand went up from the back of the room, and Doyle was happy for the distraction. "Yes?"

"If you please," asked the prisoner, a young Haitian woman named Marcelin, "What is a 'silo'?"

"It's where they store things, on a farm," said Doyle, a little vaguely, since she wasn't completely certain, herself.

"It's a big, erect tube—looks a lot like a man's willie," Harrison offered, which sent everyone into peals of merriment again, save for the young Haitian woman, who only bent her head.

"Please," Doyle called out, over the noise; "I wouldn't want to cancel the class."

This turned the trick, and everyone immediately quieted down; class attendance meant good-behavior points, and good-behavior points meant a reduction in a prisoner's sentence.

Doyle had decided to volunteer at the Prison Ministry, because she'd been reminded, lately, that she wasn't doing enough, so to speak, on the "good works" front, and that she should devote more time to charitable endeavors. This residual guilt came, no doubt, from the fact that she'd a working-class background, but had somehow managed to marry the famous Lord Acton, so that she was now rich— although exactly how rich was not something she knew or cared to ask; she only knew that Acton seemed plenty rich.

As a matter of fact, at the present time, they were living "in residence" at Trestles, Acton's hereditary estate, instead of their usual London flat—mainly because they were in sore need of a restful holiday. Christmas had come and gone, though, and Doyle had decided it was all a bit *too* restful;

she'd never got the hang of being idle—what with that working-class thing, going on—and so when one of her friends had suggested that she volunteer to teach a class, here at the prison, she'd willingly accepted.

And it was a shrine-worthy miracle that her husband had acquiesced in this plan. He tended to be over-protective—especially since she was currently in her second trimester of pregnancy—but he'd made no objection, and had only requested that she limit her students to those who were in for minor crimes, and who'd shown exemplary behavior.

And so, Doyle now found herself in the unlikely role of study-leader, tasked with teaching basic religious principles to a room full of unruly women, who'd landed here by virtue of not having the slightest interest in basic religious principles.

Dr. Okafor, who was the friend who'd suggested that Doyle teach the class, had warned her that—because of the "good-behavior" incentive—she shouldn't expect too much, in terms of genuine interest from her students. "But some women do hear the call," the African woman had advised, in her placid manner. "And often they will sign-up for the remedial reading class, as a result."

In fact, apparently this wasn't so very unusual—that a prisoner who took a Bible study class then became inspired to learn how to read, so as to be able to read the stories for themselves. Marcelin was just such an example; she'd been trafficked into the country, and then had taken to petty crimes and prostitution to support her drug habit—Doyle had seen this story play out a million times, during the course of her police work.

Apparently, the subdued young woman had shown only a desultory interest in her surroundings or in the other prisoners, until one day, a few months before, when she'd reluctantly attended her first class. The lesson had been about the Samaritan Woman at the Well—an outcast, who was found to be worthy by the only opinion that mattered—and from that time forward, Marcelin had been a fixture in any and all classes offered, and was determined to learn how to read.

Once she'd regained everyone's attention, Doyle made a mighty attempt to return to the subject at hand, even though it didn't seem to be resonating very much with her audience. "It's the same as worshippin' a false idol, if you are so bent on makin' money that you neglect everythin' else."

Harrison scoffed, "Easy for you to say; you lot are making money, hand over fist."

A bit disconcerted, Doyle hastily demurred, "No—not me; that's my husband."

Harrison raised her brows. "Oh? Who's your husband?"

Oh-oh, thought Doyle. During the training class, it was emphasized—many times over—that a volunteer should neither give out nor listen to personal information, being as many of the prisoners were very good at manipulation. Not to mention that the last needful thing would be to disclose that her husband was a Scotland Yard Chief Inspector.

"He works in the city," Doyle offered vaguely. She then added, "He works very hard," just so they didn't think him a member of the idle rich. Hopefully, none of them would put two and two together, and look up a photo of Trestles, which could have been the dictionary entry for "hereditary estate owned by the idle rich."

"No; I meant you're making plenty of money, here at the prison," Harrison clarified, and gave Doyle an arch look.

With a knit brow, Doyle disclaimed, "No—no, this is a

volunteer position," and then hastily reminded herself that she wasn't supposed to be speaking about personal matters, and she should probably try to get the discussion back on track.

"You must stop teasing her, Harrison," Charbonneau suggested with some irritation. "Or else she'll never want to come back again."

"All right, all right," Harrison replied, and cast a knowing look at Charbonneau. "Touchy subject, I guess."

I wonder what that's all about, thought Doyle; Charbonneau's telling Harrison to button her lip, and Harrison's giving it right back to her again.

"Please; continue," Charbonneau suggested.

After ducking her head to review the lesson plan, Doyle advised, "We're supposed to have a discussion about when we've seen this in our own lives—people who are so focused on money, that they forget about the more important things."

"My father," Smythe offered immediately. "He left us, because he didn't want to have to support us, and then he went off and married a chippy, instead—spent all his money on her, and left us high and dry."

As this particular tale hit very close to home, Doyle offered, "Well, he doesn't sound like he was much of a father to begin with, and so it may have been for the best, in the long run." A bit belatedly, she realized that the woman was here, in prison, and so this may not have been the most reassuring thing to say.

With great relish, Smythe replied, "Well, it definitely wasn't the best for him; he'd been telling the chippy some porky pies about how rich he was, and so she killed him, to inherit the money he didn't have. And it all came back to bite her; he'd forgot to change his insurance beneficiary, and so my mum got the money, and the chippy got nothing. My mum was that chuffed about it."

"The chippy couldn't get the money anyway, if she was the one that killed him," Charbonneau reminded her.

"Oh, she was never caught," Smythe readily admitted. "But we all knew she killed him, just the same."

"Didn't the police look into it?" Doyle asked, rather dismayed by this recitation.

"Of course, they did—he was poisoned," the other replied. "But she was a posh little chippy, and so they weren't about to throw her in gaol."

Doyle would have expressed her outrage at this implied insult to the justice system, save for the fact she was well-aware there did appear to be a different set of rules for pretty young women. With this sad fact in mind, she decided she could make no rejoinder—and besides, she was supposed to keep the fact that she was a police officer under wraps.

Harrison offered, in her obnoxious way, "I wish I was a posh little chippy; then I'd never have to do any work, to fill-up my silos." She then turned to Charbonneau, and added, with heavy innuendo, "Charbonneau, here, can tell us all what that's like."

Hiding her irritation, Charbonneau replied, "Not really; instead you find yourself servicing a lot of silos, instead."

Hearing this ribald jest, all of the participants—save Marcelin—launched into peals of merriment, and once again, Doyle tried to call the class to order. "Ladies, please; we won't have time for the Old Testament tie-in, about the Wells of Isaac."

"I prefer silos, myself," declared Harrison, with an arch look.

Amid the renewed riotous laughter, Doyle decided it

wasn't so very terrible—they all seemed to be enjoying the class, at least—and so perhaps she should temper her expectations, and give poor Isaac short shrift, this time around. First, however, she had to rein-in Harrison, who was in the process of reciting an off-color joke to her willing audience.

"Ms. Harrison," Doyle called out; "please quiet down."

In response, the unrepentant prisoner held up a just-a-moment finger to Doyle, and then concluded, "—and I've lost my braces, besides!"

As laughter once again erupted, Smythe offered to Doyle, "We're not what you're used to, I think."

Since Doyle couldn't admit that she was, in fact, well-used to criminal types, she only replied, "I'll sort it out, don't worry."

"It's surprising that you are here, at all," Charbonneau offered.

"I'm happy to be here—truly," Doyle replied in a hearty tone.

"Only because you can walk out the door," said Harrison, in her loud manner. "We'd all like it a lot better, too, if we could just come and go. Isn't that right, Charbonneau?"

"Shut up, Harrison," said Charbonneau. "You're annoying."

CHAPTER 2

*A*fter a post-lesson conference with Dr. Okafor, Doyle exited out the prison's main entrance, and emerged onto the pavement, where Acton promptly pulled up in the Range Rover. Her husband had waited outside in the car, because he was someone who didn't much like people fawning over him, and the Warden, here at the women's prison, tended to fawn over him.

"How did it go?" he asked, after he'd settled her into the passenger seat.

Doyle blew out a breath, and then admitted in all honesty, "I think I wasn't prepared for the general attitude, in there, Michael. I was supposed to talk about the Parable of the Foolish Farmer, but everyone seemed to think that he should be applauded, and that greed was a virtue, instead of a sin. But mainly, they wanted to joke about how the farmer's silos were phallic symbols, which seemed off-topic."

He smiled slightly, as he pulled the car away. "Now, there's a new take, on an old story."

She chuckled, and lifted her palms to press them against her eyes. "Mother a' Mercy, I wish you'd been there to keep order, Michael—although on second thought, they'd have probably rioted outright, if you were there." Doyle's husband was a handsome man; tall and dark—not to mention he was unfailingly polite and well-bred, which were characteristics that greatly appealed to women who rarely interacted with men who were unfailingly polite, and well-bred.

In an encouraging tone, he offered, "The audience may not have been as receptive as you would like, but surely you can hope that a seed was planted."

"We're back to sexual innuendos, I see. You're just as bad as they are."

Acton chuckled, and raised a hand to the guard at the gate, as they turned onto the main highway. With a pleased smile, the guard brought his own hand to his brim, but Doyle inwardly winced, because the Wardens at the prison would no doubt be made aware that the illustrious Lord Acton had been on-premises, but had hid in his car rather than go inside for a ceremonial greeting—usually Acton was careful about such things, when dealing with government middle-managers. The system needed its bureaucrats in order to function, and no one was more aware than Acton that the bureaucrats needed to be flattered, on occasion.

She watched the road ahead for a few moments, before confessing, "The class was a crackin' disaster, more or less, and don't think that I don't appreciate how you never say 'I told you so', even though you always tell me so. You're the next thing to a saint."

"So, I keep telling you," he teased.

She sighed, and turned to review the scenery out her side window. "It was all a bit dauntin', truth to tell. But I should go back, because I shouldn't be such a baby, and also because I should do some follow-up on a professional level. There was a woman in the class named Charbonneau, and I wouldn't be a'tall surprised if she's a murderess, even though she's in on a minor charge."

To her surprise, her husband readily informed her, "The evidence was inconclusive, in her case, and so she's in on involuntary manslaughter. No doubt influenced by the fact she was represented by Sir Vikili."

Doyle raised her brows, because Sir Vikili was a top-shelf defense solicitor, known for handling well-heeled villains. "She did seem posh—especially compared to the others. She must have money."

"Yes. She is a CI."

Doyle turned to stare at him in astonishment. *"She* is?" A CI was a Confidential Informant; someone who regularly rubbed elbows with criminals, and who would be paid to pass along tips to the police, on the quiet.

And, if this was the case, oftentimes the police would look the other way if a CI was dabbling in crime, depending on how valuable their information tended to be. If the CI was passing along information about high-level villains, then it was important to keep them in the thick of things—just as it was important that the CI's cover be protected. The CI was risking their life, by being an informant—no one tolerated a snitch—and this was no doubt why Charbonneau was willing to spend a short sentence in a minimum-security prison. It helped with her credibility, and she would be trusted by the crooks all the more. Not to mention she could snitch on whatever information she picked up in the prison, itself; oftentimes cold cases were solved because prisoners liked to gossip about their other misdeeds.

Thoughtfully, Doyle said, "If she's a CI, that would explain her attitude, then. I'd the feelin' that she was—she was *wary* of me, I suppose is the right word. It made my antennae quiver, a bit."

Her husband listened to this pronouncement with all the respect it deserved; he was well-aware of her perceptive abilities—in point of fact, she'd told him about them the first day she'd met the man, which was a testament to how much she'd trusted him, right from the start. In turn, he respected her intuition almost more than she did, and together, they'd put more than a few villains in prison.

"Did she say anything in particular that gave you alarm?"

Slowly, she shook her head. "No; nothin' I could focus on —although she did say she was surprised I was there, so mayhap she knows who I am."

"Very possible," he agreed.

Doyle was semi-famous, because she'd jumped into the Thames to save a fellow detective, and the media had subsequently puffed her up as a hero. It was ironic, in a way, because before she'd jumped off the bridge, she was semi-famous as Acton's unlikely bride, with everyone checking their watches to count how long it would take for the man to come to his senses. After she'd been deemed a hero, though, everyone instead thought him very discerning—to have recognized her merit, before anyone else had.

With a knit brow, she tried to explain what had caught her attention. "She was needlin' another prisoner named Harrison—or, more properly, Harrison was needlin' Charbonneau—and there was somethin' there—somethin' between them that seemed a bit ominous to me, even though it looked as though they were just jokin'. And Harrison made some reference to the Warden's makin' money, hand over fist, which made Charbonneau change the subject, quick-like."

He tilted his head and warned, "You mustn't make any reference about Charbonneau's role as a CI; not to her, nor to anyone else."

"Oh, I know I mustn't, Michael. Thank you for givin' me the head's up, though."

He paused. "She was recruited to the CI Unit as a result of her association with Philippe Savoie—just so you are aware."

Doyle raised her brows. "Fancy that—Savoie's bein' useful, for a change." Philippe Savoie was a well-known underworld figure, although to be fair, Doyle had the feeling the Frenchman had scaled back his operations, ever since he'd moved to London. He and Doyle had a long history together, mainly because he'd saved her life, on a best-be-forgot occasion. Twice, actually, if you counted another best-be-forgot occasion, that coincidentally featured Wexton Prison.

And, as a result of these harrowing experiences, Doyle and Savoie were friends, of sorts—despite the fact that a Scotland Yard DS shouldn't be rubbing elbows with a criminal-syndicate kingpin. There seemed to be a silver lining, however, and Doyle liked to think that it was her influence which had caused the notorious Savoie to mend his criminal ways, and put his feet on a better path. He'd moved to London, where he and his young son experienced nearly a day-to-day interaction with Doyle's own household, between the school, and playing in the park, and she liked to think this busy new life left him little time for following his former questionable pursuits.

It was an amazing turnaround, truly—and a testament to the power of redemption—to think that the Frenchman's life had undergone such a dramatic change, all thanks to the fact that he'd come to the fair Doyle's rescue in a dilapidated hallway, one fine evening.

Acton's voice broke into her thoughts. "Harrison is in prison for larceny-by-trick."

Doyle made a wry mouth. "Yes—I heard the story, and it's a corker, believe you me. Tell me, husband; do you know chapter-and-verse about *everyone* at Wexton Prison?"

"I know chapter-and-verse about everyone who will come into contact with you, and I won't apologize for it."

This was only to be expected; her husband was very protective of her—a bit over-protective, truth to tell, only see how he was willing to lurk about in parking lots—and he'd a rather alarming history of going to great lengths, in his over-protectiveness.

He was a complicated man, was Acton, and it was only after she'd married him that Doyle began to discover exactly how complicated. Although he enjoyed a sterling reputation with the public as a solver-of-crimes, she'd begun to realize that much of his reputation was the result of his own manipulation of evidence, so that the appropriate blacklegs would be sent off to prison with no further ado. And—even more troubling—on occasion, he would see to it that any blacklegs who might escape justice altogether were simply made to disappear from sight, never to be seen again.

Once she'd come to the shocking realization that the illustrious Chief Inspector was something of a vigilante, she'd worked very hard to pull him back, and had tried to impress upon him the importance of following the rule of law, like they were supposedly sworn to do. And—although she'd achieved some measure of success—nevertheless, she knew that he only indulged her; if push came to shove, he wouldn't hesitate to swing a mighty sword, if he thought it necessary—the same as his ancestors. He'd murder-in-the-blood, being as how the House of Acton had a long history of looking after itself, and ignoring any paltry constraints like the rule of law.

And, to be fair, there were times when his over-protectiveness did seem a blessing, and let this serve as just such an example; he'd carefully researched her prison-class and its attendees, before he'd allowed her to walk into a potential hazard.

She reached for his hand. "I appreciate you, Michael—I truly do. I'm glad you told me about Charbonneau's bein' a CI, but she may also be a murderess, and mayhap the CI Unit doesn't realize it."

"Or perhaps they do," he offered, in an apologetic tone—the tone mainly because he was well-aware that Doyle tended to see things in black-or-white, with little room for shades of grey. He offered, "I could look into it, but be aware that double-jeopardy may apply."

Doyle nodded. Under the law, if a defendant was tried for a crime and found not guilty by a jury, the Crown couldn't re-try them on the same charge. It was one of the reasons they had to be certain they'd a decent case to present to a jury; the prosecutors only got the one chance. "Still and all, I should follow up, a bit—sound her out, somehow."

Acton offered in warning, "You must be careful about confronting her, Kathleen."

"Of course, Michael; 'careful' is my middle name."

She was teasing him, because she tended to act first, and think later. He was just the opposite, of course, which was probably why they made such a good team. She acted on impulse, trusting her trusty instincts, and by contrast, he was always careful and deliberate, moving the chess pieces around so that the villains didn't even realize he was coming after them, until they were well-and-thoroughly trapped.

"I'm determined to go back in, so no tryin' to talk me out of it. Besides, I shouldn't be craven, and turn tail after my first go. I've only got to make sure the next lesson-plan has nothin' to make a sex-joke out of."

He smiled. "Right, then."

They rode along in companionable silence for a few minutes, until he mentioned, "Savoie would like to make a visit with his son—apparently, you've offered an invitation."

A bit guiltily, Doyle admitted. "I did, indeed—I told him he could bring Emile to ride the horses." Pausing, she asked, "We do still have horses, right?"

"We do."

"How many?"

"There are four, at present."

He was amused, and she admitted, "I should know these things, I suppose. I rode that one, once—the grey one."

"Buckle."

"And you have a black one, who jumps over fences."

"I do."

Suddenly alert to a potential hazard, she turned to him. "Please don't teach Edward to jump over fences, Michael—I will have your solemn promise." Their small son tended to be a bit reckless, and it was a wonder he was still in one piece.

"I won't; at least, not yet," he equivocated.

She sighed with resignation, and leaned her head back against the head rest. "I suppose that goes along with his bein' a nob—poor Edward. He has to learn to chase foxes, and say 'hip, hip'."

"Fox-hunting is illegal, now," her husband noted, "but I may have to encourage him to say 'hip, hip'."

She smiled at his teasing. "I'd warn you not to crush his spirit, with your nob-ways, but I think his spirit is uncrushable."

"I would agree."

"Well, he'll be thrilled to see Emile, who's a fellow 'uncrushable'. Small wonder that Savoie can't seem to find himself a nice girlfriend; it would take a stout-hearted woman, to take-on Emile."

"Again, I would agree."

Suddenly alert, Doyle thought she caught a nuance to his tone, and turned in surprise. "What, Michael? Never say Savoie's seein' someone?"

"Not that I know," he replied.

This was the truth, and so Doyle returned her gaze to the road ahead, thinking that she must have misunderstood something. "I suppose that's not a surprise; he's mightily devoted to Emile, and not likely to let anyone else divide his attention away from the boyo. I think Munoz found that out, the hard way."

Detective Sergeant Isabel Munoz had dated Savoie for a time, which was not necessarily a prudent course to chart. In fact, the only reason it hadn't seemed to affect the girl's career path was the undeniable fact that Savoie was allied with Acton, in some mysterious way, which was another nettlesome subject that was best avoided. Aside from his vigilante tendencies, Doyle's husband tended to dip his fingers into underworld doings on the sly, so as to increase the fortunes of the House of Acton, with no one the wiser. And yet another shocking thing—on the unending list of shocking things—was the fact that Doyle entertained the strong suspicion Acton was allied with none other than Philippe Savoie, in some of those questionable doings.

And—in a strange way—his criminal tendencies made her feel almost sorry for her husband, even though she shouldn't approve of lawbreaking on any scale. Acton had his demons, poor man, and his schemings seemed to be his way of beating them back.

In truth, she was cautiously optimistic that his demons had been tamed a bit, ever since the man had married his unexpected bride, but she knew they were still there, lurking 'neath the surface, and ready to bite him hard, given half a chance. His parents were a nightmare—his father had died under horrific circumstances—and she surmised that, on some level, it comforted him to gather-up as much power and riches as he was able. A psychiatrist would probably say it was about maintaining control, when for so long he'd had none; Doyle didn't know much about psychiatry, but she'd picked up a thing or two, from a psychiatrist she knew.

But—as the Foolish Farmer had discovered—it was a losing game, to try to control the uncontrollable, and so there could never be an end to it. Doyle, of course, had a far different perspective than her husband, being as she grew up poor, and had necessarily learned this lesson long ago.

Her husband's voice interrupted her thoughts. "How does Tommy?"

She smiled. Tommy was their second son, due in a few more months. "Tommy is hungry."

CHAPTER 3

hey drove down the long, graveled drive to
Trestles, with its huge, ancient trees lining the road
on either side, so that their branches almost formed a canopy,
overhead.

It was a beautiful place, and—due to some shrewd
maneuverings, by several previous Lord Actons—it had
managed to stay afloat, even when so many other hereditary
estates had gone bankrupt, and had to be purchased by the
National Trust. The founding of Trestles dated back to
Norman times, and over the centuries, the various
generations had made improvements so that it stood as it did
at present—a great, drafty barn of a place, with various
outbuildings and rolling lands that stretched out as far as the
eye could see.

Doyle knew that Acton loved Trestles—probably the thing
he loved most, next to her—and he seemed to draw a great
deal of satisfaction from being here. Doyle, however, tended
to have mixed emotions, whenever they were in residence;

her working-class sensibilities shrank from so much grandeur, and she always felt a bit out-of-place. And of course, there were the stupid ghosts—heaps and heaps of stupid ghosts.

As part-and-parcel of her perceptive abilities, Doyle would see ghosts, on occasion, and sometimes a ghost would visit her dreams, to give her some helpful insight on a problem she was experiencing. She rarely saw the ghosts outside of her dreams, however, save for here at Trestles, where they abounded—no doubt because so many generations were tied to this ancient place. They hung about in the high rafters, and were generally an annoyance, because they seemed very much entertained by the upstart Irish Countess, and her ability to see them. On the whole, they were a raucous bunch, and often quarreled with each other over past grievances and slights—apparently there'd been some war about roses, of all things, and feelings still ran high on the subject.

In truth, Doyle didn't much like having to contend with the Trestles ghosts, and it made her visits to the place all the less enjoyable. Although lately, there'd been one ghost in particular who'd caught her eye; a little black boy, skinny, and about five years old, if Doyle was any judge. He seemed very shy, and tended to hang back, watching her from afar. She'd never noticed him on previous visits, and wondered about his role in Trestles' history. There were not a lot of black people in this area—although Adrian, their driver in the city, had told Doyle that his family had lived in the nearby village for many generations. Mayhap the little boy was a distant relation to Adrian's family.

The little boy's ghost wasn't in evidence today, as they pulled up to the front entrance, and a footman leapt to open

Doyle's door under the watchful eye of Hudson, the Estate Steward. Doyle wasn't well-versed in how an army of servants operated, but she was aware that Hudson acted as their major-general, and oversaw everyone so that Acton didn't have to.

And, as was always the case, Reynolds waited within the doorway to take Acton's overcoat, because apparently the footman was not worthy of such a privilege, and Hudson himself was far too important for the task. Reynolds was their own butler from London, and he'd been all too happy to come along with them to Trestles, since he admired it almost as much as Acton did—making constant references to the glories of its history to Doyle, who wasn't necessarily the most appreciative audience. In truth, it made her a bit uncomfortable, that—in an odd way—Reynolds seemed so proud to be subservient; that he very much identified with being a servant to a great family—or at least, a great family, as far as he knew; he didn't know the ghosts like she did, after all.

She'd mentioned it to Acton, once, who—as could be expected—couldn't quite see her point. "He is being well-paid, for a job he very much enjoys," her husband had noted in a practical manner. "It is not as though he is an indentured servant."

"I know," she'd replied, struggling to explain. "But it seems so strange, to me, that he—that he *glories* in a life of service, and to people who aren't even related to him."

Acton, rather gently, observed that ordinarily, she would admire this very trait in a stranger. "I believe the reason you feel uncomfortable is because, in this case, Reynolds serves you."

Trust Acton, to get to the nub. "Aye," she'd admitted slowly; "I suppose that's exactly it."

Her thoughts were interrupted when they crossed the foyer, and their young son broke apart from his nanny and pelted over to her, shrieking like a banshee so that the ghosts in the rafters scattered like doves.

Doyle laughed, and bent to return his heartfelt embrace. "You never even wince, Hudson. I wish I had your nerves."

"Not at all, madam," Hudson replied with a small smile, but nevertheless directed a glance at Callie, the nanny.

Callie was quick to take the hint, but Doyle smiled her away, as she took Edward's hand. "It's all right, Callie—I've missed him, too. How was your mornin'?"

"It went very well, madam. We went out to the pond, to catch frogs."

"Lots of frogs!" Edward shouted excitedly. "They jumped, when they saw us!"

Doyle kissed her son soundly, and said to Callie, "Please tell me you didn't catch any."

Callie laughed. "No, madam—the frogs are a bit too quick for him, as yet. And it was wet work, so we came back inside, to have cocoa and biscuits in the kitchens. Cook let him stir the chocolate."

"Cook let me stir," Edward affirmed, very happy because he thought the cook was the next thing to a goddess—a plump, kindly sort of goddess, but a goddess, just the same.

The young nanny was well-familiar with the Trestles servants, being as she was from the local town, and had started out as a maidservant here, herself. She'd then been recruited by Acton to help them out in London, since Mary— their usual nanny—was due to have her own baby, at any moment. Callie had proved to be an excellent stopgap; the girl was perfect for her new role, vivacious and pretty, and always patient with Edward, who could be quite the handful.

Trust Acton to make a shrewd choice, Doyle thought; after all, he'd chosen Reynolds, too. And it was no surprise that he was careful in his choices; she and Acton were necessarily very private people, and therefore it stood to reason that he'd be very exacting about who would be allowed access into their lives.

"I envy the both of you," Doyle said to Callie. "Save for the frog-huntin', of course. Has he had lunch?"

"No madam; we were holding out for your return."

"We will dine, then," Acton said to Hudson.

"Very good, sir," the Steward replied, with a barely perceptible nod of his head. *"En famille?"*

"Yes, please."

"This way, if you would, madam," said Hudson, and indicated the route to the dining room with a respectful gesture.

Doyle dutifully followed his formal invitation, despite the fact that their routine was exactly the same every lunch-time, and she certainly knew her way to the dining room. Apparently, the formalities must be observed between Acton and Hudson, or the world would come crashing down around them.

"I hope there's sausage!" Edward called out in anticipation.

"Certainly, young sir," Hudson agreed, with a measured response.

CHAPTER 4

The next morning, Doyle was making a circuit in the back garden with her son and Callie, because even though the weather was cold, the boy needed to work off some energy or he'd be bouncing off the hallowed walls, and turning poor Reynolds' hair grey. This new resolution had started several days ago, when the boy had managed to break a bowl that was on a fireplace mantle—some old Chinese thing—and the butler had nearly wept with remorse.

Therefore, even though Edward could always run up and down the long gallery, Doyle decided she'd best not take any chances with the ancestral portraits, and so she tried to take him outside for at least an hour every morning, so long as the weather permitted.

As they walked along the graveled paths between the flowerbeds, faint notes from a piano could be heard, coming down from the second floor, and Edward paused to point a little finger toward the windows overhead. "Da!" he exclaimed.

Acton was playing his piano, the notes pouring out as he played some complicated melody which always seemed to be his preference; some Russian composer—Doyle had forgot the name. She wasn't one for music appreciation—unless it was an Irish gig, of course, which was the best kind of music, since it was made for dancing.

"He's very talented," Callie offered.

"He is indeed," Doyle readily agreed. "And he loves that piano."

Truth to tell, it always made her a bit uneasy, when Acton played the piano; it was as though he retreated within himself, and became almost unrecognizable to her. Which was a strange thing to think; after all, that was Acton's usual mode and manner—to retreat within himself. His fair wife was allowed the occasional glimpse within, but those moments were few and far between, because Acton guarded himself like a fortress.

She couldn't complain, of course, being as she was a fortress in her own right, and didn't dare let people within, either. For the millionth time, she thanked God fasting that they'd managed to find each other—although that was mainly Acton's doing; he'd bundled her into marriage with hardly a whisker's pause 'twixt the proposal and the ceremony. Which was just as well, all things considered, and trust Acton to come up with just the right strategy to accomplish his aim.

Still and all, there was something about the piano that seemed to emphasize his solitary nature, and as they continued their walk, Doyle shook off these rather unsettling thoughts, and asked, "How's your family, Callie?"

The girl made a wry mouth. "They're pestering me to stay here longer—they miss having me at home."

"Well, they'll have to have a tug-of-war with Edward, and he's a mighty little boyo, so I'm not sure who'd win."

Callie laughed, and Doyle continued, "And who's to blame them, after all? My own mum couldn't bear the thought of bein' parted, and so she pulled-up stakes, and moved to London with me—not that I minded; neither one of us could contemplate missin' the other. But it is a wrench, to face your future head-on, and know that things won't be the comfortable same that they've always been."

The girl nodded. "I think that's part of it; they've no children besides me, and it's a big change for them."

"They'll just have to be patient, and wait for grandchildren, then."

Callie laughed. "Another subject, that comes up a lot."

They started to head back toward the back-entry door—it was a bit too cold to stay out for long—and Doyle asked casually, "How's our Adrian? Is he home, still?" Adrian was their driver in London, and Doyle entertained the shrewd suspicion that the young man entertained warm feelings for Callie.

"He is, Lady Acton. In fact, I saw him in Meryton, only a few days ago."

Doyle had the sense that the girl was hiding her amusement, because she knew exactly what Doyle was hinting at. Stop it, Doyle commanded herself; you've had absolutely no luck, when you've tried your hand at matchmaking. Let nature take its course—if these two are slated to be together, they will get there, all on their own.

"Oh—oh, Lady Acton—if you have a moment!"

They turned to behold the portly figure of Father Clarence, puffing a bit, as he caught up to them at the back portico. "Good morning, Lady Acton, Miss Callie. I've just come up from the Dower House, and I was wondering if I could seek your permission. Lady Acton. The Dowager suggested that I make a tour of the Slough Field; there may be some old growth trees that might be useful as landmarks, for my map of Lancastrian times."

"Have at it, Father," Doyle easily replied, and thought it was just like Acton's mother to bestow permission where it was not hers to give.

Father Clarence was the Roman Catholic priest in this area —not a plum assignment, as RCs were rare as hen's teeth— and Doyle had made his acquaintance at a funeral, last year, when the man had—rather unexpectedly—fallen into the good graces of Acton's mother.

The Dowager Lady Acton was a very difficult woman who was heartily disliked by her son—although to be fair, she was heartily disliked by everyone else, too, with the result that she'd been relegated to living in the Dower House toward the back of the estate, so that Acton didn't have to see her very much. Doyle always felt a bit guilty about this—she and her own mother had been very close—but since the woman tended to stir up trouble, it was probably for the best. The thoroughly aristocratic Dowager despised her thoroughly Irish daughter-in law, but she'd been minding her manners, lately, because Acton held the purse-strings, and he wouldn't hesitate to thrown his mother out on the street, if she so much as looked cross-eyed at Doyle.

To everyone's astonishment, the unassuming Father Clarence had become a favorite of the Dowager's—so much so, that she invited him regularly to dine at the Dower House, with the unfortunate result that he'd gained quite a bit of weight, in a fairly short space of time.

The priest was nice enough, but Doyle found him to be

rather tedious—not to mention a bit foolish, besides. As a case in point, the Dowager had recruited him to write her memoirs, and—rather than think this the vain, silly project that it was—the priest had developed an outsized fascination with Trestles' history. As a result, he was now intent on a brand-new project; creating a compendium of the estate's history during the Lancastrian period—whenever that was. It sounded hideously boring, not to mention that such a history probably featured regular beat-downs of the pesky Irish.

As the priest paused to catch his breath, he cast his gaze out toward the far fields with a knowledgeable eye. "I have tried to sketch a preliminary map, but there isn't much to go on, since many of the maps from that particular era were destroyed by the fire, during the Glorious Revolution."

Absently, Doyle corrected him, "No—everyone thinks that's what happened, but it was truly the fault of a maidservant, who was careless with a candle. This lot laid low, during the Glorious Revolution, bein' as they were making bushels of money tradin' with the Dutch."

"Oh? I suppose that is certainly an alternate explanation, Lady Acton," the priest replied in an indulgent tone. "Although the twelfth Lord Acton's letters do mention the attack by hostile forces as the cause for the fire."

Doyle refrained from explaining that the twelfth Lord Acton had good reason to come up with another story, since he'd been away, visiting his mistress, whilst his poor wife was tasked with putting out the fire. Instead, she listened patiently as the priest launched into a recitation of the twelfth Lord Acton's mighty deeds, and reflected that he would probably be very surprised to hear that the fellow had died of having his man-parts cut off by an angry husband.

Behind the priest's back, Callie pantomimed that she'd

take Edward in, and Doyle nodded; she wouldn't mind ducking out on Father Clarence, herself—he was never more tedious than when he mounted his hobby-horse—but she felt a bit sorry for him, and he was a consecrated priest, after all, so she'd best be polite.

To divert his narrative, she interrupted to ask, "Have you had a look at the archives, Father?" The original keep, here at Trestles, had been transformed into an archives room, where another eager beaver had once launched into a project to research Trestles' history. Matters hadn't worked out very well for her, though.

A bit flustered, the priest admitted, "I did ask for permission, but Lord Acton would rather not allow access—which I don't blame him for, in the slightest," he hastily assured her. "I am certain the documents are quite fragile, and I am no expert, of course."

Good one, Acton, thought Doyle; the last needful thing was to have this fellow underfoot, and Acton had no qualms about being rude to anyone, even a priest.

To Doyle's disappointment, Father Clarence then picked up the train of his narrative, once again. "In truth; the twelfth Baron is merely one example in the estate's history; the Trestles nobility showed amazing courage, during Lancastrian times."

But this was an accolade too far, and Doyle made a skeptical sound. "I don't know, Father; I think mainly they were using the war as an excuse to murder their enemies, and seize a bunch of sheep. And land, too—they didn't hesitate to take everythin' away from the neighborin' estate, as soon as someone named King Hal gave them the all-clear. They were nothing more than a pack of reivers, who happened to hold titles." She paused. "And they didn't treat their wives very well, either."

Very much surprised by this recitation, the priest lifted his brows, and offered diplomatically, "Oh—oh, I may have to respectfully disagree, Lady Acton—I do think the eighth Lord Acton was a loyal Lancastrian. And I suppose we cannot be certain, either way, since all eyewitness accounts have been destroyed. "

Mentally, Doyle sighed, and made no argument; it seemed evident that the Dowager was manipulating the history-struck priest in a masterful way—the woman had a dearth of lackeys to boss around, nowadays—and this fellow seemed very persuadable.

And so instead, she decided to change the subject so as to delve into the puzzle of the shy little boy, who she'd glimpsed, watching her. "Did the earlier generations transport any Africans, here?"

Hastily, the priest shook his head. "Oh no; the House of Acton was always much opposed to the concept of indentured servitude—and its Barons spoke out in Parliament quite often, on the subject. It was strongly felt that loyalty could not be purchased in such a way."

Doyle made no rejoinder, since she'd seem plenty of purchased-loyalty during her work as a detective, and oftentimes that loyalty was purchased at a very paltry price. Money—and love, of course—tended to be the prime motivators for murder.

Although, when you thought about it, it was never "love" in its true sense, but rather thwarted-love, that inspired people to kill one another. And, since greed was just an outsized love of money, greed was thwarted-love in its own way, too. It all came down to love of false idols, just like she'd been trying to explain to the prisoners with such little success —it would be a much better lesson just to have them walk in a detective's shoes, for a couple of days.

With half an ear, she listened to the priest expound about the glories of the past for a few minutes, and then thankfully took her leave.

CHAPTER 5

*O*nce inside, Doyle was making her way toward the informal dining room, when she was hailed by a familiar figure—Melinda, who she'd met a few times before, here at Trestles. Melinda was the daughter from one of the neighboring estates, and she'd had a youthful affair with Acton, back in the day—she was about his same age, which meant she was some years older than Doyle. Languid and thoroughly aristocratic, the woman nevertheless seemed good-hearted, and Doyle had always found her amusing—as though she were a completely different species from the fair Doyle, and with a completely different world-view.

"I've invited myself for lunch," Melinda explained candidly. "Although Reynolds did his utmost to throw me out."

Doyle laughed. "I don't mind, Melinda—as long as you don't mind Edward's table manners, which are a bit hit-and-miss."

"Acton's playing, I hear."

"Yes, he should be down, shortly, if you'd like to say hallo. I think he loses track of time, when he plays."

They went to be seated in the informal dining room, which was deemed "informal" because the table was only about ten feet long, and was decorated with only one silver epergne. Doyle had developed a routine whereby Callie would help mind Edward for the morning's activities, but then the girl would be released to go home, so that Doyle could lunch alone with her husband and son. The two of them would then put the little boy down for his nap—it was far too easy to hand him off to servants, in this great barn of a place, and to forget that they were an ordinary family. Well, maybe not exactly an *ordinary* family, but they should at least make the attempt, for Edward's sake.

As Doyle began to cut-up Edward's sausage, she asked, "How are you, Melinda?"

Melinda nodded her thanks to Reynolds, as he very correctly set a plate before her. Doyle hid a smile, because it was clear to her that the servant didn't much like Melinda, but you had to look carefully, because the signs were very subtle.

Melinda made a vague gesture. "The usual. Are you pregnant, or just gaining weight?"

Doyle smiled. "Pregnant. Another boy."

The other woman paused to chuckle. "The title is secure, then—poor Stephen."

She referred to Acton's second cousin, who'd been Acton's original heir, back when Acton was a confirmed bachelor. Sir Stephen had sustained a heavy blow, when the title-holder had unexpectedly married the youthful Doyle, and so the man had promptly conspired with the Dowager to put paid to said marriage. They didn't succeed, of course;

MURDER IN MATERIAL GAIN

they'd severely underestimated Acton, and you'd think that they—of all people—would not have done so. Not only was Acton not someone to be manipulated, he was also the grand master at turning the tables, which they'd eventually learned, to their great sorrow.

As she helped her son with his cup, Doyle admitted, "I can't muster up a thimbleful of sympathy for Sir Stephen; greed makes people do terrible things."

"I'll pretend I didn't hear that," said Melinda, as she addressed her meal. "Greed is my major motivation, in pursuing my next husband."

This was of interest, and Doyle glanced her way with a smile. "You've a likely prospect, then?"

"Indeed, I do."

As nothing further was offered, Doyle prompted in amusement, "Can't you say? You're being very mysterious."

In her languid manner, Melinda shrugged her thin shoulders. "It's early days, still, and I don't want to jinx it."

Doyle thought she detected a nuance in the woman's tone that made her antennae quiver, and so she warned, "Don't antagonize Acton."

"Oh—as well I know; not to worry. In fact, I am so dedicated to my cause, that I'm taking instruction from Father Clarence."

Doyle paused to stare at her in surprise, as Melinda had never struck her as someone with any kind of religious bent —not to mention the woman seemed too lazy, in general, to embark upon such a project. "Well—well, that's wonderful, Melinda."

Melinda smiled at her reaction, and warned, "Don't tell Stephen; he thinks this Clarence fellow is an idiot."

"Sir Stephen doesn't know about your husband-prospect, then?"

"Definitely not. I tell him as little as possible, at all times."

Since the subject had come up, Doyle ventured, "I hear Sir Stephen keeps visitin' the Dowager, over at the Dower House, and I have to say it makes me uneasy. It's never good for family peace, when those two get their heads together."

"I wouldn't worry," Melinda said in her off-hand manner, as she lifted her crystal wine glass. "Neither one of them is as clever as they think they are."

"They can't hold a candle to Acton," Doyle agreed. "And hopefully, that lesson has been well-learned."

"You would think," Melinda agreed, and then eyed Edward benignly, as he stabbed at a cherry tomato with wild abandon, which caused it to roll off his plate toward her.

Doyle confessed, "I was thinkin' of settin' you up with Tim McGonigal, but it appears I'm a step too slow. He's a nice, kind man, and he'd let you lead him around, and be happy for it."

Melinda chuckled. "You know me only too well, Kathleen. It was a good thought; he's plain-vanilla, but he makes good money. Not as much as my prospect, though, and so I shall stay the course." She sighed with regret. "Of course, Acton's got more money than *anyone*, and it's a *shame* we didn't wind up together."

Doyle couldn't help but laugh. "Not a shame for *me*, Melinda."

"Oh—oh, right." The other woman waved her hands in a vague apology. "Sorry."

They ate for a few minutes, and Melinda then asked, "How's your nanny—did she stay in town? Talk about plain-vanilla."

"Yes, Mary's still in London. She didn't make the trip, because she's due to have a baby at any minute."

"Good luck to her—she's too nice for her own good," Melinda remarked. "And how is Callie working out, in her place?"

"Faith, she's workin' out wonderfully. Edward adores her."

"We saw frogs!" Edward declared happily, as he abruptly raised both hands over his head, which sent another tomato flying.

"They went frog-hunting, at the pond," Doyle explained, as she bent to retrieve the errant tomato from the floor.

"Yes. I was spying on them, yesterday, on my way over to the Dower House. And I hear Lizzie Mathis has landed on her feet."

Doyle smiled at the trace of incredulity in the woman's voice. "Indeed, she has; she's married Thomas Williams— remember him, from the funeral?"

"I won't soon forget," Melinda declared, and put her elbows on the table, so as to cradle her glass between her hands. "He's *yummy*. I'd never have believed Mathis could manage it."

Since the reason Lizzie Mathis had "managed it" could be laid squarely at Acton's door, Doyle made no comment. In truth, her husband had a better record at matchmaking than she did, which was all kinds of surprising—Acton was not someone you'd suspect was romantically-inclined. Although —more correctly—it was not that Acton was romantically-inclined, so much as he'd paired-off Williams with another one of his loyal henchmen, so as to keep him out of trouble.

Faith, when you thought about it, it was very similar to how his own ancestors had operated, all the way back to the

Trestles knight, who'd married a woman so as to obtain an advantage over his enemies. The medieval knight's ghost was another one who'd barely tolerated Doyle, at first—being as Acton's foolish love-match hadn't brought power or riches to the House of Acton. Nonetheless, the knight had teamed up with the fair Doyle, on occasion, so as to outfox the evildoers, and Doyle now felt he carried a grudging sort of respect for her. That, and she'd given birth to an heir, which was top o' the trees, in his medieval mind.

"He's out of her league," Melinda declared. "I imagine he'll be ripe for an affair, in no time."

Recalled back to the subject at hand, Doyle warned, "Well, Lizzie and Williams have a baby, now, so keep your sights firmly on your new prospect."

Melinda smiled in assurance. "Don't worry, I will. You will be *amazed* by my dedication."

At this juncture, Acton appeared in the doorway, and apologized for his tardiness. "Melinda," he said, with a polite nod. "How are you?"

"*De trop*," she replied easily, and then rose to glide from the room with no further ado.

CHAPTER 6

*E*dward offered his father a rather crushed cherry tomato, which was accepted with good grace as Reynolds promptly appeared to serve Acton his lunch.

"We are to have no unvetted visitors," Acton said briefly.

Before Reynolds could make a reply, Doyle said with some exasperation, "Faith, Michael; what do you expect him to do—take her down in a choke-hold? And Melinda's harmless, after all."

"I beg your pardon, sir," Reynolds said to Acton, with a remorseful little bow. "She was in, before I realized."

"Stop it, you two," Doyle exclaimed impatiently. "I'm sittin' right here, and I can make my own decisions." Some months ago, Doyle had experienced a violent altercation with a suspect, which was one of the reasons they were staying here at Trestles; Acton wanted her to rest, and take it easy. He couldn't understand, of course, that she found "taking it easy" more stressful than keeping herself busy, hence the compromise about the prison classes.

Doyle continued, "And please don't blister Reynolds, Michael; Melinda was over at the Dower House, and came in through the back."

"I see," said Acton, but Doyle intercepted the glance he gave the servant, which inspired Reynolds to retreat in an uncharacteristic hurry, and which left Doyle to say crossly, "I'm not a *baby*, Michael."

"Mum," said Edward a bit worriedly, and he handed her a piece of sausage, since he was all out of cherry tomatoes.

Doyle blew out a breath, and smiled at her son, as she tactfully placed the mangled bit of meat on her plate. "I'm sorry, Michael—I shouldn't snap at you; I know you mean well."

"No—the fault is mine. Forgive me, Kathleen."

"Nothin' to forgive," she said easily, and leaned to kiss her husband, so that Edward wouldn't be anxious. "You over-worry, and I overreact, followed shortly by fisticuffs."

"Fisticuffs," said Edward, although because he couldn't pronounce his f-sounds very well, it came out "tittycupps."

"Even better," said Acton.

Doyle laughed, and leaned to kiss her son also, for good measure. "Tell me why you're worried about Melinda, of all people."

"Lately, Melinda has been meeting with my mother and Sir Stephen."

At this news, Doyle hastened to assure him, "Well, that may sound ominous, but there's a harmless explanation; she goes over there to take instruction from Father Clarence."

Acton paused in surprise. "Does she, indeed?"

"Indeed, she does," she teased him. "It's the eighth wonder of the world, but apparently she'd got her eye on a rich husband, and religious conversion is part of her strategy."

"Interesting," he observed, and bent to continue his meal. "I hadn't heard."

"Well, she's bein' a bit mysterious, so mayhap he's controversial, or somethin'. He has money, though, and that seems to be the main driver." Doyle paused. "I feel a bit sorry for her, to be reduced to such plottin'. I wonder how she makes ends meet?"

He glanced over at her. "She knows she has only to ask, and I will help her." He paused, and then admitted, "I have done so in the past."

"Well, that's very generous of you, Michael. I do think—in her own way—that Melinda means well. And my hat's off to her, if she can suffer through Father Clarence's instruction; Mother a' Mercy, but that man could bore the hind leg off a donkey—although I shouldn't speak ill of a priest. I had to talk with him for a bit in the garden, yesterday, and he's got a mighty bee in his bonnet about Trestles." She glanced over at him, and added, "The same as a few others, I could name."

"Careful," he warned, with a small smile.

"In fact," she continued, "he's so invested, that he's writin' some hideously borin' account of Lambcaster times."

"I believe it is 'Lancaster'," he corrected, almost apologetically.

"Oh—is it? Well, 'Lambcaster' would be more appropriate, since everybody was stealin' herds of sheep, back and forth—apparently, wool was worth a lot of money, back in the day."

Surprised, he lifted his gaze to hers, and couldn't help but smile. "You astonish me, Lady Acton."

Button your lip, my girl, Doyle reminded herself. Acton always grew a bit uneasy, when she spoke of the ghosts, here, and what she gleaned from them. She'd best mind herself, or he'd lock her up indefinitely, and then the ghosts would drive her mad in truth, like that story about the man who kept seeing his father's ghost, and went mad—although Doyle wouldn't as much go mad, if she saw her father's ghost, as she would throat-punch him, instead. Twice, just for good measure.

"What's that famous story?" she mused aloud. "The one with the castle, and the murders, and the vengeful ghost."

"Father Clarence's History of Trestles?" he asked, teasing her.

She laughed aloud. "Good one, Michael, only this one's a bit more famous—you know the one, with the poison, and the fellow holdin' the skull."

"*Hamlet*?"

"Aye, *Hamlet*," she agreed. "I read it in secondary school—now, there was a slog to end all slogs. The teacher felt it was somethin' like, and that we should all identify with mopey Hamlet, but none of us were much impressed. He loved to hear himself talk, you could tell—always so philosophical; give it a rest."

"We know what we are, but know not what we may be."

"If you say so," she replied, and took another bite. "I never understood two words out of ten."

But Acton, apparently, wanted to steer the conversation back on-topic. "Did Father Clarence happen to speak of his Foundation?"

She lifted her brows, as she wiped Edward's fork—he'd dropped it on the floor, but luckily no servants were about, to observe this breach. "He did not. What's this, now?"

Slowly, Acton related, "He has lately filed the paperwork

to create a 'Trestles Foundation'. It is of interest, because this was accomplished without first securing my permission."

Confused, Doyle glanced his way, as she deftly parried her son's attempt to dip an apple-slice into his water glass. "Tell me what this means, Michael—I haven't a clue."

Acton explained, "A Foundation is rather like a Corporation, and ostensibly used for charitable purposes— although oftentimes the great bulk of the proceeds are used to support those who are running the Foundation." He paused, and then added, "My mother is listed as the Foundation's sole trustee."

Doyle paused in minding Edward, and stared at him in astonishment. "Faith, Michael; that's a bit ominous, isn't it? D'you think Father Clarence is lookin' to weasel money out of your mother? He does seem to be her pet, lately."

He tilted his head. "Do you have the sense?"

Frowning, she thought about it. "No—but I wasn't lookin'. And anyways, if that's his plan, it's not a very good one; I thought she was forced to hang on your sleeve, because she doesn't have any money."

Acton nodded thoughtfully. "He may be presuming she does, though. Originally, she did have some money in her own name—the settlements from her marriage to my father. Unfortunately, my father spent most of it—unlawfully, of course."

"Of course," Doyle agreed. "Your wretched father was a crackin' blackheart."

"*A little more than kin, a little less than kind.*"

"Not kind a'tall, to my way of thinkin'. Everyone in this tale is thoroughly disagreeable. Save you," she added, a bit belatedly.

This, however, was not necessarily true; Acton had proved

rather ruthless in protecting what was his, and she had to admit that—from his point of view—such ruthlessness seemed to have been entirely necessary. With so much at stake, it was as though there was a constant knife-fight going on to come out on top, and with no holds barred. Which—when you thought about it—only went to show that not much had changed, in the past ten centuries, or so.

Thinking over this unlooked-for development, Doyle ventured, "Mayhap there's an innocent explanation, Michael. If Father Clarence means to sell this stupid history-book he's writin'—and he probably thinks it will be a *huge* bestseller—then mayhap he's set-up this Foundation so as to donate all the proceeds. He's a priest, after all, and he's taken a vow of poverty."

"Very possible," Acton agreed. "If you have the opportunity, I would appreciate it if you could sound him out."

Doyle made a face. "Aye, then; even though I'll have to listen to more tales of your heroic ancestors, even though they weren't as much heroic, as they were happy to seize the main chance."

But Acton only pointed out, "You may as well be loyal to the cause that is most likely to enrich your coffers."

Doyle made a face. "Aye—trust you, to see it their way. And speaking of loyal to the cause, now poor Reynolds is in your black book, and he was already moped, because Edward broke that stupid Chinese bowl on his watch. D'you think we could ease his mind, and replace it?"

In a neutral tone, her husband advised, "I'm afraid it would be very difficult to find a replacement."

Staring at him, Doyle blew a tendril of hair off her face. "Faith, Michael; there's somethin' completely wrong with that—and not just because it's Edward, who broke the thing. It's naught but a lump of clay, after all, and people are miles more important than things." Much struck, she added, "That was the main point of that Parable, I think—that people are more important than things. I wish I'd said it, at my class; I'll try to work it in, next time."

"Tomorrow is the next one?" This, asked in a mild tone.

"Aye," she replied rather firmly. "Prepare to skulk about in the parkin' lot, again."

But he made no protest, and instead said, "Perhaps I will arrange for a visit with the Warden, instead."

"She'll only fawn all over you," Doyle warned.

"No—I meant the Men's Warden. I should meet with him."

This was of interest, and Doyle ventured, "Are you goin' to talk about the DCS?"

"Indeed," he replied.

The former Detective Chief Superintendent of Scotland Yard was currently serving a lengthy sentence at Wexton Prison, courtesy of Acton, who'd exposed a network of corruption at the Met. However, the man had since found religion, and had turned a new leaf, with the result that he'd started a successful Prison Ministry. His Ministry had become so popular, in fact, that his sermons were now broadcast throughout the Commonwealth, and the donations were such that it was now supporting other Evangelical ministries, and outreach projects.

Leave it to the Evangelicals, to turn a prison sentence into a fundraiser, thought Doyle, a bit cynically. But she shouldn't speak ill, because the former DCS had rather heroically saved the fair Doyle, once upon a prison riot, which meant that Acton had worked quietly behind the scenes, ever since, to have the man's sentence commuted. An amazing turn of events, all things considered, and one which gave her hope that her husband wasn't nearly as ruthless as he seemed.

Thinking on this, she said, "You know Acton, you're very loyal, in a strange sort of way, even though anyone who knows you probably wouldn't think it. It's that 'noble's oblige' thing they talk about, where you never forget a favor."

"If you say," he replied in a neutral tone, and offered Edward a grape.

Stubbornly, she persisted, "Don't try to deny it; the DCS is a prime case-in-point. And there's Tim McGonigal, too— you're always willin' to come to his rescue, since he's come to yours, and more than once."

Acton glanced up. "Speaking of which, McGonigal tells me he's met someone."

She blinked in surprise, because Acton's friend was rather shy, and unlikely to put himself forward. "He has? I thought you were throwin' Callie his way, like a lure on a fishin' line."

"McGonigal invited Father John over for Christmas dinner, and he brought with him an Irishwoman, who works at the Embassy in London. Apparently, she was at loose ends, for the holiday."

"And?" asked Doyle, agog.

"And she and McGonigal have started dating, which was no doubt Father John's object in bringing her along."

"Everyone's windin' up with the Irish," Doyle pronounced in wonder. "We may have lost all the battles, but we're winnin' the war, by infiltration and stealth."

"I believe you won my battle," he teased.

She gave him a look. "You're the one who won it, my friend. And it wasn't much of a battle, in the first place— more like trussin' up a goose in a sack."

"My finest hour," he observed. *"There is a divinity that shapes our ends."*

"Well, you definitely shaped my end."

He chuckled, and leaned over to kiss her. "McGonigal would like us to meet the woman."

"Wants to parade me about, to help his cause," she guessed. "For once, you're not the one who's the main draw."

"I will happily take a secondary role."

"As if that would *ever* happen, Michael—you wouldn't know how to take a secondary role. And speakin' of such, please try to lighten-up on poor Reynolds, who's only doin' his best, and hates it when you rap his knuckles."

But her husband held firm. "A reprimand was called for, certainly."

She sighed. "Let's not start in, again; I'm in no shape for fisticuffs."

Edward threw up his arms. "Titty-cups," he said brightly, and they both laughed.

CHAPTER 7

*A*fter they put Edward down for his nap, Doyle decided to take a walk out to the stables, whilst Acton worked on his caseload—a DCI didn't have the luxury of taking a true holiday, especially someone like him, who was often placed front-and-center on high-profile cases. The public loved the idea of the aristocrat-turned-detective—probably because they'd read too many fictional accounts of such a creature; if the public-at-large knew some of the things that Doyle knew about the man, they'd be miles less adoring. Or mayhap not; people seemed to love their pirates, too, and basically Acton and his ancestors were nothing more than state-sanctioned pirates.

So, she took this opportunity to have a bit of a walk-about —not to mention she should give Grady, the stableman, a head's up about Savoie's bringing Emile to ride the horses.

It remained rather cold outside, although weak sunlight was breaking through the clouds, and Doyle gratefully lifted her face to it. Usually, Acton liked to walk with her—he was always wanting her to take a walk-about, during pregnancy —but she was happy to be alone for a few minutes, because there was something bothering her—something she couldn't quite put a finger on.

For the past several months—after her altercation with the perp—her thoughts had been a bit scattered, but now she felt more or less back to her old self—although her thoughts had always been a bit scattered, truth to tell, as anyone who'd read one of her police reports could tell you.

But it did seem as though lately, her trusty instinct was prodding her to pay attention—although nothing in particular stood out; instead, it was a jumble of minor things, that all seemed to be trying to claim her focus.

First, there was the situation at her prison-class, with Harrison, the brash prisoner, and Charbonneau, the Confidential Informant. Charbonneau was hiding her annoyance with the woman—who was an annoying one, to be fair—but there was something else, too; Charbonneau was wary, and Doyle had obtained the rather strange impression that the prisoner was wary of her fair self.

It could easily be that she knew Doyle was a police officer —it only made sense; if she was a CI, she was probably familiar with Scotland Yard personnel. But for whatever reason, Doyle had a certain conviction that the woman was trouble, and that she should be wary, in turn—although how the prisoner could cause trouble was unclear, since she was currently stuck in prison. Nevertheless, the fair Doyle should probably take a look into her file-jacket, and see what there was to see—although Acton obviously knew all that there was to know, and seemed rather resigned that there was little to be done. After all, even if Doyle somehow managed to winkle-up evidence that the woman had got away with murder, double jeopardy would provide immunity.

So; there was truly no point in getting herself worked-up over it—the justice system did the best it could, and sometimes the villains managed to slip through the cracks. You learned this sad truth, literally, your first day on the job; there was no point in trying to chase the unchasable.

Doyle took a long breath, and lifted her gaze so that it rested on the top branches of the chestnut trees for a moment, before reluctantly admitting to herself that the main reason this Charbonneau subject kept biting at her was because Acton knew more than he was telling her. Her wedded husband knew something about the prisoner that he didn't want her to find out, but—interestingly enough—it wasn't something that meant he didn't want the woman in Doyle's class.

He'd said Charbonneau had a connection to Savoie, Doyle remembered; mayhap Acton didn't want her to discover something distasteful about Savoie. This actually made sense, and was in keeping; Savoie was another person who'd come to Doyle's rescue, once upon a time, and so in Acton's mind, he was another person to be protected—there it was again, that 'nobles oblige' thing. In Acton's mind, a loyal alliance was miles more important than the rule of law, or the occasional murder most foul.

And—come to think of it—she'd got a funny little vibe, when she was speaking to him about his loyalty to people who'd done him a favor, and he'd changed the subject, quick as a cat. So; perhaps Acton was protecting her from discovering something gafty about Savoie, which seemed a little strange, since Savoie had an occurrence-sheet as long as your arm, and there was little she could learn that would shock her about the man.

I can't sound-out Charbonneau, since she's a CI, and I don't want to put my foot in it; instead, I'll sound-out Harrison, she decided—I've a feeling it's important.

Feeling relieved—now that she'd come to a decision—she continued with her walk until the stables came into view, dawdling a bit, because she was thoroughly relishing the fact that she was unattended, for once. She'd never really adjusted to having servants constantly underfoot, and she marveled that the nobs managed to stand it; she'd always been a solitary soul, and—between the ghosts and the servants—Trestles was no place for solitude.

Which brought up another little oddity, niggling away at the back of her mind; she'd realized it was very strange that Trenton wasn't here. Trenton acted as their private security-man in London, and usually, he traveled with them when they came to Trestles. She'd been reminded of his absence, when Melinda had confessed that she'd been spying on Edward and Callie, at the pond. In the usual course of things, Trenton would be the one to put a stop to all spyings-upon, and he would have also been the one to bar the door to Melinda, so as to enforce Acton's instructions—not poor Reynolds. It was passing strange, that Trenton hadn't come with them this trip, and it was even more passing strange that Acton had never mentioned why this was.

And then, there was Acton's playing the piano.

She paused, rather surprised that she'd included this, in her list of unsettling things. Acton played the piano as a hobby, and he seemed to enjoy it very much. He didn't have a piano at home, and so it stood to reason that he'd play quite a bit when he was here. It was only—it was only that she'd the sense he played so as to think deep thoughts—which in itself, wasn't necessarily a bad thing; she wasn't a deep thinker, but to each, his own—and when Acton went into deep-thinking-mode, Katy bar the door.

Could her husband be up to something? With a small frown, she pondered this possibility, as she approached the stables. Not much to be up to, locked away here at Trestles. Still and all, she'd the persistent sense there was something afoot, and she'd best look lively, if she was going to be called upon to appeal to the man's better angel, yet again. And trust Trestles to have this effect on him—the place was a standing testament to generations of schemers, cooking up their scheming schemes so as to confound their enemies. The fair Doyle and her Parables were no match for the generations of ruthless ambition that positively permeated this place.

Her thoughts were distracted when she caught a glimpse of the little African boy's ghost, peering at her shyly from around the corner of the stables.

"Hallo," she offered softly, but he ducked away.

"I'm over here, Lady Acton," Grady called out from the interior.

"Oh—yes. How are you, Grady?"

"Fair to middlin'," the stableman replied, in his taciturn way. Grady was a fellow Irishman, but he hailed from the Ulster region, which meant he didn't necessarily see eye to eye with the lady of the manor. Nevertheless, they rubbed on well enough, as long as the subject of comparative religions wasn't raised, which was of course not very likely, here in the confines of the stables.

However, in this she was proved wrong almost immediately, because Grady hurried over to a shelf, so as to switch off his radio device, which had been playing the Prison Ministry podcast.

"Oh—do you listen?" Doyle asked with great interest. "I know the people at the prison, who put it out."

"D'you?" he asked, in the manner of one who is surprised by this glimpse of redeemability. "I like him—he's a good speaker."

"A good man," Doyle agreed. "A prison convert, of all things."

Grady lifted his brows. "Oh? Is that so?"

Doyle made a wry mouth. "He's got a conversion story that rivals St. Paul's, my friend. He visited here, once upon a time." Best not to mention that he'd come, on that occasion, to arrest the master of the house.

"Did he? Well, isn't that somethin'?"

"Aye, that," said Doyle. "But I don't want to interrupt; I only wanted to tell you that we are goin' to have visitors, day after tomorrow. A Frenchman named Savoie is comin' with his son, Emile. Emile is horse-mad, and would very much like to ride."

Grady nodded. "Has the lad ridden before?"

"I don't know," Doyle admitted.

"How old?"

"Seven or eight?" Doyle guessed. "Faith, he just had a birthday, and I should keep better track."

"No worries, ma'am; we'll work it out."

"I won't be ridin'," she added.

"No, ma'am," he agreed.

A bit stung, she defended herself, "People have been

killed, you know. The Slough Field was a hazard, back in the day."

"I could see that," he replied. "Mayhap that was why they put in the drainage system."

"They'd troubles with the sheep, gettin' stuck in the bogs," Doyle explained.

"Sheep are that stupid," he agreed. And then, with an innocent air, he observed, "There was a priest, roamin' about there, yesterday."

Doyle could only admire the subtleness of the insult, as she explained, "Father Clarence. The Dowager has him workin' on some borin' history-book, and best avoid him—a word to the wise."

The stableman lifted a brow. "Heavy-set fella, to be walkin' about, out there."

"You are welcome to tell him that gluttony is a mortal sin."

He unbent enough to smile, slightly. "The Dowager is convertin', then?"

Doyle had to chuckle. "Now, wouldn't that make Paul himself goggle? I don't think so. I think she just craves company, and he's happy to be fed for it."

"Aye, then. I won't set the dog on 'im."

Doyle raised her brows. "There's a dog?"

A bit nonplussed, her companion admitted, "Aye, ma'am. I've a collie-dog, but Lord Acton asked that I keep him well-away when you are in residence, bein' as you'd a bad experience."

"Oh—oh, I didn't know. I suppose that's just as well."

The truth of the matter wasn't that Doyle didn't like dogs —instead, it was that dogs didn't much like Doyle, and tended to bark their fool heads off when confronted with her.

It was a bit embarrassing, truly—other animals didn't seem to object, it was only dogs, who were made uneasy by her fair presence. And trust Acton, to quietly see to it that such a confrontation would never take place. A fine husband, he was, those times when he wasn't masterminding at the piano.

CHAPTER 8

"Is there any place, here, that's not under surveillance?" Doyle asked Acton thoughtfully, as they drove through the prison's entry gates.

Understandably surprised, he glanced over at her. "Very few places," he offered cautiously.

"Thanks, Michael. You're a great help."

"Tell me first why you wish to know."

"It's not about Charbonneau-the-CI, don't worry; instead I want to sound-out Harrison about some of the remarks she made. It is beyond my powers to figure out how to do so in the course of a Bible lesson, though."

He was not happy with such a plan, of course, but only pointed out in a mild tone, "Even if you discover something of interest, remember that they are all post-conviction."

"Aye—can't dig up old bones," she reluctantly agreed. "It doesn't seem right, to me; you should never be immune from criminal charges."

"I think the idea is more that you should be immune from endless persecution by the Crown."

Reluctantly, she nodded, seeing the wisdom of this. "I suppose that's true. And there will always be justice, in this world or the next—even though it's mighty frustratin', sometimes, to see the villains skate."

"We have to pick our battles, I'm afraid."

"You, more than most," she noted, and waited.

He didn't respond, and so she decided to try a different tack. "Where's our Trenton, by-the-by? It's past Christmas, and time he was back to work—he's the one who should be bearin' your scoldings, in Reynolds' place."

He smiled slightly. "Trenton remains in London."

As he offered nothing more, she prompted, "Is he lyin on our sofa, watchin' the telly, and eatin' us out of house and home?"

"No; instead, I've asked him to perform another assignment for me—an off-the-books surveillance."

She lifted her brows. "There's a wrinkle; what's the case?"

"I'm afraid I'd rather not say."

She quirked her mouth. "Of course, you'd rather not, if there's secret surveillance, afoot. And speakin' of such, I'd be very much surprised if you didn't have a jammin' device, close at hand."

"You will have guessed correctly," he replied, as he pulled the Range Rover into the parking lot.

It only stood to reason; Acton was inveigling a release for the DCS, and probably wouldn't want his conversation with the Men's Warden to be on the record—heaven only knew how he would apply the pressure to achieve his ends.

"Can I have it?" she asked.

"I need it," he protested.

"Have you a spare?"

"The security personnel will think it very strange, Kathleen, if you are jamming transmissions."

With a scornful lip, she replied, "No, they won't; they're a bunch a' bureaucrats, with little motivation to think about anythin'—not unless they're worried it might hurt their paychecks."

He smiled, as he shifted the gear to park the car. *"The insolence of office.* I am shocked by your cynicism, DS Doyle."

"I'm just bein' a good detective, DCI Acton, and puttin' two and two together. If you're using such a device, it only stands to reason."

"Touché," he admitted, and reached into his suit breast pocket to pull out what appeared to be an ordinary button.

"Wow," she said inspecting it closely. "D'you have one to match every suit?"

"Press if firmly, like this," he explained, indicating with a finger and thumb. "A personal jamming device only has a perimeter of three feet surrounding, so have a care."

"Aye, sir." Carefully, Doyle transferred the button to her coat pocket.

He was silent for a moment, as he gazed upon the dreary grey building that rose up before them, framed by equally grey clouds, and razor-wire fencing. "If you would, try not to instigate another riot."

A bit hotly, she defended, "I didn't instigate the last riot, Michael; that was Savoie, back when he was servin' his time, so go and jawbone at Savoie, instead." The accusation stung a bit, mainly because on that memorable occasion, the fair Doyle had blundered into the prison without a good plan, and had paid a mighty price.

"I suppose that is true," he soothed, and ran a hand along her arm. "I didn't mean to jawbone."

Fairly, she added, "And no amount of jawbonin' at Savoie is goin' to matter, anyways, since it seemed clear that he ran this place, back when he was bein' held here. The guards were smokin' cigarettes with him, and larkin' about like everyone was on holiday. For the love o' Mike, they were playin' football in the halls."

"I cannot say I am surprised."

With some disgust, she shook her head. "It's a sad testament to the minders who worked here—although good luck, if you're a dopey bureaucrat, tryin' to rein-in someone like Savoie; he eats those types for breakfast."

"Again, I cannot disagree."

"Enough, with the backwards-speak," she chided in exasperation. "I get enough of that at Trestles." It had come to her attention that Acton tended to go all House-of-Lords in his speech when he stayed at his ancestral estate; talking like a nob—or, more accurately, talking more like a nob than was his usual.

"I do beg your pardon," he teased, in his public-school voice. *"But break my heart, for I must hold my tongue."*

"Snabble yer gob, else I'll give you the back o' me hand," she warned, in her broadest accent.

He chuckled, and leaned to kiss her. "It will be interesting to see how Edward turns out."

"He'll be able to rub elbows in the House of Lords and at the Sailortown Docks," she declared. "A very useful skill set."

They walked through the entry doors, and were immediately greeted by an escort who was hovering at the security desk—a woman in a business suit, who'd clearly been tasked with handling their important visitor. "Right this way, Lord Acton. The Warden is quite looking forward to your meeting."

"Allow me to wait with my wife," Acton demurred.

"Of course," the escort assured him, a bit flustered. "I believe Dr. Okafor is on her way, Lady Acton. May I offer tea?"

"No, thank you," said Acton with all politeness, although Doyle was aware that this heavy dose of fawning was setting his teeth on edge. "Although I imagine my wife would like coffee."

"Always," Doyle agreed, pleasantly surprised by this unexpected boon.

"Oh—oh, of course," the woman said; "I will fetch a cup."

I stand corrected, thought Doyle, as she accepted her coffee from the escort with an inward smile; Savoie doesn't run this place, Acton does.

CHAPTER 9

*D*r. Okafor was buzzed-in from the hallway, and the Nigerian woman greeted Doyle with a warm smile, her headscarf a spot of bright color against the bland and sterile surroundings. "Hallo, Kathleen. Hallo, Lord Acton."

Doyle had first made the doctor's acquaintance when the woman had acted as a key witness in an illegal pharmaceuticals case, and—because that clinic had been forced to close—she was now working here as the prison doctor, a position that had been put forward by Acton's friend Tim McGonigal, who was also a doctor, and had been rather sweet on Dr. Okafor.

At her greeting, Acton offered his hand. "Michael; please."

Doyle intercepted a jolt of surprise from the escort, who was standing beside them. She's that surprised that Dr. Okafor and Acton are on a first-name basis, Doyle thought, and small blame to the woman; I'm barely on a first-name basis, myself.

"Come to my office, Kathleen, and I will give you the class materials," Dr. Okafor said, as she gestured her forward. "And, Martina Betancourt has asked to assist with your class —as long as you do not mind."

"Not a'tall," Doyle replied, and hid a smile, because Dr. Okafor must have decided that the fair Doyle was in need of reinforcements—which, in truth, would be welcome, and in no way resented. Not to mention that Doyle wouldn't mind seeing how Martina was getting along; the young woman was currently serving a soft sentence, here, because—with some regret—she'd decided to murder her husband. Nevertheless, she and Doyle were friends-of-sorts—although, when you thought about it, between Martina and Savoie, it did seem that the fair Doyle tended to have friends who dabbled in major crimes.

Doyle bade her husband goodbye, and then accompanied Dr. Okafor to the administrative floor, where the Prison Ministry had its office. She'd visited the dingy, cramped office once before, on a best-be-forgot occasion, and she wasn't overly-surprised to see that the bullet holes in the walls hadn't yet been patched.

Dr. Okafor indicated the class materials, which were neatly stacked on a desk. "Your lesson today will center on the Parable of the Prodigal Son."

"We're back to the evils of greed," Doyle noted, and tried to remember if there was anything in the Parable to make a sex-joke out of.

"Yes," Dr. Okafor agreed. "As well as the evils of self-righteousness."

"Of course," said Doyle, who hadn't read the lesson plan,

like she was supposed to.

Dr. Okafor continued, "It is a good story, for these women, because it illustrates how generous the offer of salvation is, and how it is applies equally, to all."

Reminded, Doyle asked, "Speakin' of such, is the DCS about? I wanted to tell him about a new fan he's made—one of the people who works at Trestles."

"Oh—I will tell him you have said, Kathleen. He was called-in to a meeting this morning, but perhaps you can visit with him later, after class is over."

Oh, Doyle thought, as she followed Dr. Okafor out the door; no doubt he's in that meeting with Acton and the Men's Warden. Here's hoping it all goes well; fingers crossed.

At the cafeteria, Martina Betancourt stood at the front table, ready to assist, and the young woman greeted Doyle with a warm smile. "Kathleen. How good it is to see you."

"I hope you are doin' well, Martina." This seemed the diplomatic thing to say, since she was serving time here, courtesy of the House of Acton. Martina Betancourt belonged to an ancient and shadowy Church Order out of Spain, and before she'd wound up in Wexton Prison, she'd traveled around the world doing questionable deeds, for the supposed betterment of the RC Church—although Doyle could not necessarily approve of her methods, since they seemed rather ruthless.

Unfortunately, Martina had lost her bearings, somewhat—mainly because her husband wasn't doing right by her—and so she'd killed him, after she'd managed to convince herself that she wasn't killing him out of anger, but out of concern for his immortal soul.

Because Martina and Doyle had struck up an unlikely friendship, Doyle had been secretly relieved that Sir Vikili, her solicitor, had managed to avoid murder-one, so that instead Martina was here on a voluntary manslaughter charge, with a soft sentence of two years—which only went to show that Sir Vikili was a miracle-worker of the first order.

And in turn, it wasn't much of a surprise that Martina had volunteered to help Dr. Okafor with the Prison Ministry; Martina was religious to a fault—if such a thing was possible —and even though she was staunch RC, she surely could appreciate the efforts the Evangelicals were making, for the salvation of lost souls.

They had no further chance to speak, because the prisoners began to file in, and as Martina distributed the class materials, Doyle noted that the raucous Harrison was not present, today. This was a disappointment, because— although the woman was a crackin' annoyance—Doyle would not get the chance to do any probing about her remark about the Warden, or her animosity toward Charbonneau; there was no need for Acton's jammer, after all.

Although, mayhap all was not lost—Martina may know what the woman had meant, when she'd made the remark. Martina had a long history of ferreting-out shadowy schemes, and was the type of person who always kept one ear to the ground, and so, instead, Doyle would take the opportunity to sound-out Martina, and see if she had any idea what Harrison had meant.

Charbonneau seated herself toward the back, this time around—next to Marcelin—and once again, Doyle had the impression that the refined young woman was wary, as though she half-expected Doyle to do something alarming.

Although, now that Doyle was aware that Charbonneau was a CI, that would explain it; she may be worried that Doyle was going to expose her, inadvertently. Which would be a valid concern, after all; the last place a CI would want to be exposed was in a prison, where one could readily assume that more than a few inmates were there, courtesy of her fine self.

In any event, Charbonneau didn't address Doyle, but instead said in a taunting voice to Martina, "I see you've found a new way to kiss-up, Betancourt."

"You will mind your manners," Martina replied, with a hint of steel.

"Or else, what?" asked Charbonneau, lifting her well-tended brows. "You'll report me?"

"Let's get started, shall we?" Doyle interrupted, as she processed the interesting fact that the animosity displayed between the two wasn't, in fact, genuine—although why they were pretending to be at odds wasn't at all clear. Did it have something to do with Charbonneau's role as a CI? Could Martina be helping her stay undercover, for some reason?

Before she could think about this strange development, Marcelin raised her hand. "If you please," she said; "What is 'prodigal'? I could not understand this word."

"Oh," said Doyle, in confusion. "That's a very good question."

"It means the same as 'wasteful', Martina explained. "He was a wasteful son, who spent money on wasteful things."

"Like prostitutes," Charbonneau offered in an innocent tone, as her gaze slid to Marcelin.

"No call for that," Doyle admonished, who noted with some exasperation that her wretched students had managed to find a sex-angle, after all.

"What? It's true—he spent his money on prostitutes," Charbonneau defended herself, spreading her hands, and feigning sincerity. "It says so, right here in the story."

Smythe chimed in, "And, let's face it; that's the first thing a man would do, if he came into money."

Naturally, this remark prompted everyone to laugh in agreement, save for Marcelin.

"In the story, he had to be shown to be a sinner," Doyle explained. "That's the whole point; he was a sinner who repented, and was forgiven." And then, reminded of what Dr. Okafor had said, Doyle added, "There's another point to the story that's just as important; the 'non-sinners' mustn't look down on the sinners. It's part of the lesson, in fact; the older son gets in trouble, too, for bein' self-righteous, and thinkin' he was so much better than the younger son." She paused, struggling to explain. "We shouldn't judge, because we're all in the same boat."

"All right then; I'm sorry, Marcelin, I shouldn't judge you," said Charbonneau, who sounded as though she didn't mean it in the slightest.

"You mustn't pick on her," scolded Martina. "You're such a bully."

"I'm not the one who's a bully," Charbonneau retorted with a glare.

"Let's just read the Parable," Doyle hurriedly suggested. "If everyone would take a verse, please, and we'll go around the room."

"I'll help Marcelin," Martina offered, as she settled-in next to the young Haitian woman, on the side opposite Charbonneau. "She can't read very well, as yet."

"She's never needed to," Charbonneau noted slyly, in an undertone.

"You're to be quiet, Ms. Charbonneau," Doyle said sternly. "Else you'll be out of the class."

"Sorry," the woman replied, without a shred of sincerity.

CHAPTER 10

*A*fter the class had concluded, Martina stayed behind to assist Doyle in gathering-up the materials, and Doyle tried to decide what she should broach with the woman, mainly because the playacting that she'd done with Charbonneau—about being at odds, and sniping at each other—had given her pause.

Thinking it over, Doyle decided that whatever the reason Martina was pretending to be annoyed with Charbonneau, it wouldn't preclude asking about Harrison's remark, and so she said to Martina in an undertone, "Go slow; I need to ask you somethin'. I've a jammin' device, so let me engage it." Casually, she dipped into her pocket for Acton's button.

Martina made a sound of impatience, and indicated her own security pass, hanging on a lanyard around her neck. "No need; I've got one. If you turn your own jammer on, there will be traceable feedback."

Doyle blinked. "Holy Mother; it's like a James Bond film, in here."

But her companion didn't seem to be in a joking mood, and asked, "What is it, Kathleen? Quickly."

"What's happened to Harrison?" Doyle whispered, as she put the pencils back in their box. "I wanted to ask her about a remark she made, last week."

"What sort of remark?" asked Martina doubtfully. "Harrison's someone who will make-up things, just to cause trouble."

Doyle made a wry mouth. "Don't worry, I know the type —we see it every day, at the Met. But it was somethin' about the Warden's bein' greedy, and so I thought I should follow up. It seemed a strange thing to say." Not to mention that when the prisoner had made the remark, Doyle had known it to be true, but this was not something she could tell Martina.

Martina glanced around to ensure there was no one within earshot, and replied quietly, "Yes. Well, there is a skimming operation going on, with respect to the Prison Ministry's donations. I imagine the Warden is in on it."

Doyle stared at her in surprise. "Faith, that's *terrible*."

"Shhh," Martina warned. "Better not to speak of it."

Doyle bent her head, and busied her hands. "Right, then; thanks for the head's up, I'll have Acton look into it."

But Martina's next words brought her up short, as the young woman glanced sidelong at Doyle. "I am not sure that is a wise course, Kathleen. It looks to be a sophisticated enterprise." She paused, and added meaningfully. "It may be best that you not mention it to anyone."

Very much shocked by this implication, Doyle paused, recalled to the unfortunate fact that Martina-of-the-shadowy-religious-Order knew a great deal about Acton-of-the-shadowy-doings; in fact, that was how they'd first met— Martina had been hip-deep in investigating an Acton-scheme.

But after thinking this over for a few dismayed moments, Doyle slowly shook her head. "I honestly don't think Acton's behind it, Martina—if for no other reason than he knows that if I found out, I'd skin him alive."

Martina nodded. "If you say. But, either way, you needn't worry—I'll handle it."

"Are you able to handle it?" asked Doyle, a bit surprised by the woman's confident attitude. "Don't risk yourself, Martina."

"I won't, don't worry; I'm counting the days until I'm out of this place, and back where I belong. *Blessed are those who have been persecuted for the sake of righteousness, for theirs is the kingdom of heaven.*"

Doyle decided not to mention that being persecuted for killing one's husband may not actually qualify, and instead asked, "Is Harrison involved in the skimmin' rig? She did make that remark."

But Martina shook her head, slightly. "No—I don't think so. And besides, she's in the Infirmary, because she came down with a fever—that's why she wasn't at the class."

In a neutral tone, Doyle continued, "How about Charbonneau—could she be involved? You don't like each other much, I think."

"I wouldn't be at all surprised," Martina replied in a quiet tone. "Charbonneau is very slippery."

But before any further insights could be gleaned, they were interrupted by the Women's Warden, herself, who entered the cafeteria to greet Doyle warmly. "I hear your husband also visits us today, Lady Acton." She was the type of person who very much enjoyed saying "Lady Acton."

"He does, indeed, ma'am," said Doyle. "Here's hopin' he

minds himself, so you don't have to lock 'im up, alongside the DCS."

The Warden laughed a little too loudly at this witticism, and Doyle noted that Martina laughed a little too loudly, right along with her. She's playing her up, Doyle decided; and leave it to Martina—this particular Warden is a ripe target, for playing-up.

And Martina's currying-of-favor seemed to have made a dent, because the Warden turned to the prisoner with a benign eye. "Thank you so much, Ms. Betancourt, for your help with the kitchen supplies situation." She then turned to Doyle to explain, "Betancourt volunteered to help improve our ordering system."

"I was very happy to help, ma'am," Martina said in a humble voice, but met Doyle's gaze significantly, behind the woman's back.

Oh, thought Doyle; this must be how Martina is handling the skimming rig; she's infiltrated the operation, so as to throw a mighty wrench in the works—after all, she's well-used to infiltrating. And since Charbonneau is an infiltrator, too, mayhap their feigned animosity is a mutual cover, so they can gain trust in the right places.

And it was a sad testament that Doyle was not exactly shocked, to discover that the prison personnel were skimming with sticky fingers, left and right. Places like this were always an easy target for blacklegs, and it was the same story for nearly any large bureaucratic institution; the people in charge weren't much motivated to take more than a cursory look at the books, because it wasn't their own money that was being spent. Indeed, it was the very reason there was a Public Accounts Commission—a watchdog committee run by Parliament—who worked with the Met to put a stop to institutional embezzling. It all boiled down to the age-old problem; people were aware of what was right and wrong, but temptation was so very, very tempting, when it came to material gain, and even more so when it seemed likely that no one would ever find out.

Smiling and nodding at whatever the Warden was saying —the woman was going on-and-on, in her self-important way—Doyle entertained a sudden qualm; during the previous sex-trafficking scandal, here at the prison, those who'd tried to grass on the enterprise were promptly murdered, for their sins. Martina had best have a care, because she was at a disadvantage in here, with her wings clipped. Which—come to think of it—was probably the very reason she was currying favor with the Warden.

Doyle declined the Warden's offer of tea, and took a pretend-glance at her mobile, to make the excuse that she was due to meet-up with Acton. Before the woman had the chance to include Acton in her invitation, Doyle hurriedly thanked Martina for her assistance, and then beat a hasty retreat.

CHAPTER 11

*A*cton was waiting for Doyle at the Security Desk, and —after he bade farewell to his escort—they left together through the entry doors.

"I didn't need the jammer," Doyle reported. "Harrison wasn't there, and when I followed-up with Martina, it turned out that she had her own."

"Did she indeed?" He opened the car door for her, and then came around. "How went your class?"

She blew out a breath. "Well, I've a million things to tell you, and I'm not sure that I can sort them in order of importance, and so I'll just start with the fact that Martina thinks you might be skimmin' money from the Prison Ministry."

"I am not," he assured her, as he turned his head to back the car out. "Quite the opposite, in fact."

"There's a relief—not that I thought it was true," she hastily assured him. "And not to mention you'd be hauled into divorce court, quick as the cat can lick his ear."

"Is that what would do it?" he teased.

"Don't test it out," she warned. "And I'm that uneasy, because the main reason I borrowed your jammer was to ask a few questions of Harrison, but Harrison didn't come to class, this time—it turns out she's sick, and in the Infirmary. Not to mention Charbonneau seemed all on-end, for some reason, and Martina was pretendin' to be at odds with her, but she wasn't—not truly."

He raised his brows, as he drove the car out of the lot. "That is impressive, DS Doyle."

But Doyle shook her head. "I can't make heads nor tails of any of it, though." She frowned, slightly, as they navigated down the entry road toward the gates. "I know it sounds like a bunch of trivial things, Michael, but I don't think they're trivial, for some reason."

"Your instincts are very good," he agreed. "What do you think it all means?"

Slowly, she tried to sort out her thoughts, and voice them out loud. "I'd be very much surprised if Charbonneau's not hip-deep in this skimmin' rig, somehow—although if she's a CI, she may be settin' up a sting, or somethin'." She glanced at him, because if such were the case, it stood to reason that a DCI would be aware of it. "Does the Met have a sting operation, underway? Would you know?"

"I am not aware of one."

Nodding thoughtfully, Doyle returned her gaze to the front windscreen. "Well, then I shouldn't be surprised if Charbonneau is up to no good. And half the reason I think so, is because the Women's Warden doesn't seem smart enough to mastermind a skimmin' operation, but Charbonneau does."

"I would agree with that assessment." Her husband

placed a reassuring hand over hers. "I will look into the situation, Kathleen. Please do not worry."

Turning over her hand so that it clasped his, she teased, "And—now that I know what's afoot, here—I have to say I'm that proud of you, Michael, for resistin' this mighty temptation. It must be like catnip, for you, to see a bunch of dopey bureaucrats in charge of massive bundles of cash."

"You malign me unfairly," he protested.

She smiled, slightly. "No need for aristo-speak, Michael; it's only me. You sound like you do when you've been drinkin', although that can't possibly be the case."

"My time would have been better spent, believe me."

She laughed at his tone. "Well, next time, bring a bottle o' scotch, and go back to lurkin' about in the car."

"Will there be a next time?" Presumably, he was sincerely hoping not.

"There will, my friend," she replied in a firm tone. "I'm tryin' to do good works—although I can't say it seems to be takin', very well—not to mention that there's people embezzlin' the dickens out of everythin', which is somethin' we should probably try to put a stop to."

"I thought we were on holiday," he protested.

"No rest for the weary," she advised. "We need to swoop in, and save the day—by which I mean you need to swoop in, since you're the one with the authority to set-up a sting."

"As you wish," he replied in a mild tone.

She eyed him. "No aristo-speak, please. *Have* you been drinkin?"

"No—upon my honor," he teased.

Slightly annoyed, she blew a tendril of hair from her forehead. "It's not a laughin' matter, Michael; recall that the last time there was an unholy mess at Wexton Prison, people were gettin' themselves killed, over it. Martina's not one to temper her actions—"

"As we well-know," he noted.

"—and if Charbonneau's involved in the skimmin' rig, that's a bit ominous, because I think she's killed someone, and got clean away with it."

"Charbonneau or Martina?" he asked, in a mild tone.

Annoyed by this reminder, Doyle retorted in exasperation, "The point is this: the people on the side of the angels are bein' robbed, and we should put a stop to it."

"I am sorry, Kathleen," he soothed, and squeezed her hand. "Of course, I will look into it. Please don't worry."

She took a deep breath, and dropped her head back with a thud against the headrest. "No—I'm the one who's sorry for snappin' at you; it's only that the place gives me the willies. And you'd think all the villains who were workin' there would have been weeded out, courtesy of the last scandal, and yet here we are, all over again, with yet another murky scheme up and runnin'. Faith, there seems to be no end to smoky prison personnel, but I suppose that's because the higher-quality bureaucrats are goin' over to skim money from the Home Office, where the pickings are better."

"Now, there's catnip," he agreed.

"Anyways, I've gone off-track, and I have to tell you that I'm a bit worried about this Harrison-prisoner, who's suddenly sick. She was makin' sly remarks about the Women's Warden's bein' greedy, last time, and Charbonneau was tryin' mighty hard to get her to be quiet about it."

Acton glanced over. "What do you think of the Women's Warden?"

Doyle made a face. "Not much. Full of herself. Martina's curryin' favor, in between sniffin' out embezzlement

MURDER IN MATERIAL GAIN

schemes." Reminded, she asked, "And speakin' of curryin' favor, how did your meetin' with the Men's Warden go—are you allowed to say?"

He glanced at her, amused. "Allowed by whom?"

She laughed. "Oh, I'm that sorry, aristo-person; I'd forgot that no one tells the likes of you what to do. So, what happened?"

But his thoughtful answer surprised her. "I have the sense that the DCS is likely to decline a commutation."

With some surprise, Doyle asked, "What—he doesn't want to get out? Faith, there's where he's falls out with St. Paul; even Paul was happy to get sprung out of prison."

Slowly, Acton answered, "I imagine he feels his Ministry work is all-important, and it serves his work better if he is a repentant prisoner, rather than a former prisoner."

"Saints," said Doyle, much struck. "I suppose that only makes sense, from his point of view."

"Indeed."

She turned to smile at him, and gently shake the hand she held in hers. "Someone more powerful than you is pullin' his strings; how that must rankle."

He smiled in return. "I will gladly defer, in this case."

Turning her head to watch the road ahead, she suddenly knit her brow. "You know, Michael, I'd be very much surprised if the DCS doesn't know about this skimmin' rig. If money's bein' embezzled from the Ministry, he must have spotted it—he's nobody's fool."

Acton considered this for a moment. "What would you have him do?"

With a small sigh, she conceded, "I suppose that's a good point. Although he could try to raise the subject with you—was the Warden always present, at your meeting?

Mayhap he couldn't say, because the Men's Warden is in on it, too."

"It is possible, certainly."

At these careful words, she straightened up in her seat, and turned to gape at him in astonishment. "Holy *Mother*, Michael; you—you already *knew* about this—about this skimmin' rig—you heard about it from the DCS, didn't you?"

The penny dropped, and suddenly, it all made sense; the reason Acton didn't mind the fair Doyle coming over to the prison to teach this class was because it gave him cover to come over himself, and nose around. He hadn't mentioned it to her, of course, because he'd not wanted to distress her—these people were her friends, and he wouldn't want her to worry.

Her suspicions were confirmed by his next words. "I promise I will see to it. Please don't worry Kathleen, and I would ask that you delve no further."

She drew down the corner of her mouth, as she viewed the passing scenery. "I wouldn't, if I knew what 'delve' meant. You *have* been drinkin'," she declared. "Or mayhap it's just Trestles, seepin' into your bones."

Teasing her, he replied in his public-school voice, "*Hang out our banners on the outward walls.*"

She rolled her eyes at him. "Well, if your ancestors are hangin' out their banners, you'll have to steel yourself to stand firm; no one has sticky fingers like they do, my friend."

"I suppose that is true," he conceded. "*Thy ambition; thou scarlet sin.*"

"Stop it, Michael; you're makin' my hair stand on end. And speakin' of which, I understand that your mother is comin' over for dinner."

All teasing aside, he glanced her way. "We can cancel, if you'd like."

This was said in a hopeful tone, but she replied, "No—she's Edward's gran. And she's been behavin' herself, more or less—not that we see her as much, what with Father Clarence, takin' up her time."

"An unexpected boon," he agreed.

She teased, "Next, you'll be tempted to grant him access to the archives, just to keep him about."

"Very unlikely."

"No—more likely you'd throw him down the well, with no one the wiser." Since the archives room was in the original keep, it had an ancient well, beneath the floorboards.

He glanced over at her in amusement. "*So sweet was never so fatal*, Lady Acton."

With mock-contrition, she replied, "Sorry; Trestles must be seepin' into my bones, too."

CHAPTER 12

*A*lmost immediately, Doyle regretted her decision to allow the Dowager over for dinner, because the woman rendered an exaggerated show of surprise upon beholding little Edward, seated at the majestic dining table. "Oh," she said, and sighed rather dramatically. "I did wonder why we were dining so early."

With a mighty effort, Doyle held on to her temper. "I thought you might enjoy a visit with Edward, ma'am."

"It will be quite like a picnic," the Dowager agreed, with an attempt at enthusiasm. "I should have worn my patents."

"May I seat you, madam?" Reynolds asked with all deference.

As she accepted his offer, she teased in an arch manner, "Thank you, Reynolds—we do have footmen, you know."

"Quite," the servant replied, in a tone that relayed his opinion of a household that would allow mere footmen to wait upon her.

"I ran into Father Clarence, two days since," Doyle began,

thinking this might be a pleasing subject. "He was very busy, chartin' out his map."

"An excellent man," the Dowager agreed. "So very kind." This, said with the implication that others who surrounded her were not as much so.

Doggedly, Doyle continued, "He seems very grateful for the project—how lucky, that you hit upon the idea."

"It was a fine idea," the Dowager agreed graciously. "And he was only too happy to participate; he is very interested in the history, here." She sighed, rather dramatically. "I imagine Acton's ancestors would be most surprised, if they could see the changes my son has wrought."

Since the only change that could be laid at Acton's door was the bringing-in of a low-born Irish Countess, Doyle quickly turned the subject. "Has Father Clarence any relatives, in the area, ma'am? I remember he spoke of his mother, once."

"No; they are all up north," the Dowager replied, and then nodded her appreciation to Reynolds, as he personally served-out her bisque.

Doyle caught a nuance, behind her tone, and thought— why, she's rather pleased about his family being at a distance; mayhap she likes the idea that she has no competition for the priest's attention—not to mention there were very few RCs in this area, to otherwise take up his time. It was a far cry from her hometown of Dublin, where there was no such thing as an idle priest—or a fat one, for that matter.

Hard on this thought, the Dowager continued, "And, in a rather shocking development, Melinda is now taking instruction from Father Clarence. You remember Melinda, Acton?" This, said with a hint of innuendo.

"I do, indeed," he replied.

The Dowager sighed with sad regret. "It is only a passing fancy, of course, but I suppose we must support her, in this." And then, with an exaggerated show of having a sudden idea, she turned to her son. "Perhaps you can counsel Melinda, and speak about your own conversion, Acton—you will have much in common, after all."

Hatchet-faced harridan, Doyle thought, barely hanging on to her temper.

"Gran," little Edward piped up. "You're pretty."

Astonished, the older woman turned her attention to the small boy for the first time. "Oh—oh, why thank you, young man." Very pleased, she turned to the others. "Did you hear that?"

"I did, ma'am," Doyle laughed. Since this declaration was very unlike her son, she could only conclude that Reynolds had been coaching the boyo, and had given him a signal. God bless Reynolds, she thought, and not for the first time.

"You are a very clever little fellow," Edward's grandmother offered, in a condescending tone.

"Edward does love it here," Doyle offered, knowing what would best please. "He especially loves bangin' on the piano with his da."

"With 'Acton'," the Dowager corrected gently. "We mustn't allow the boy to be too familiar, my dear; it is not fitting."

With a mighty effort, Doyle managed to suppress her impulse to describe how much Acton liked to pig-a-back Edward down the long gallery, and instead replied, "I will keep it to mind, ma'am."

The Dowager turned to her son, her thin brows arched in surprise. "You've a piano, Acton?"

Oh-oh, Doyle thought with some dismay; I've put my foot

in it, now—not a good subject to raise. Acton's horrible father had been a brilliant pianist, when he wasn't wreaking havoc on everyone around him. Acton had also played in his youth, but after his father's death, he'd ceased altogether, and it was only recently that he'd acquired his fancy piano, and had begun playing again.

But her husband did not seem discomfited by the topic, and only replied, "I do, mother. I keep it upstairs, in the library."

He's very pleased about his piano, Doyle duly noted. So much so, that he doesn't even mind his mother's needling. To forestall any further such needling, she offered, "Edward likes to play at it—don't you, Edward?"

To demonstrate, Edward began to pound his hands on the table, which had the unfortunate effect of spilling his water glass, but since the Dowager had been softened up with compliments, she only regarded him with a benign eye, as Reynolds hurried forward to mop up the spillage.

The Dowager began to converse with Acton about other aristocrats of their acquaintance—the topic undoubtedly chosen to exclude Doyle—but Doyle didn't mind at all, and was content to help Edward with his newly-replenished glass, since she was made nervous by the fact they'd given him crystal—the household was still reeling about the stupid Chinese bowl.

As she was thus occupied, she contemplated the wall opposite her, where they'd switched-out the dead-animals still-life painting, and now had a much less gruesome painting in its place—one of an impressive sailing ship. It was the olden-days type—with all the sails puffed-out in the wind, and the waves breaking alongside the hull, as it sped along.

The subject-matter truly wasn't much better, however, since Doyle knew that the Lord Acton who'd owned this particular ship had been knee-deep in the opium trade, and thus had made a fortune off the misery of others. Which was a common theme, when you thought about Acton's ancestors —they all seemed to think the ends justified the means, and so they were all rather ruthless, in their pursuits.

And by contrast, the Prison Ministry was making a fortune from the salvation of souls, which made them ripe for the plucking, since the opium people wouldn't have hesitated to slay anyone who tried to interfere with their ill-gotten gains. It was the old, old story of good versus evil, with "good" at a huge disadvantage, because they were less inclined to be as ruthless as "evil."

She paused, a bit surprised, because her instinct was prodding her to pay attention; that there was something there —something important. But what? It wasn't a news-flash, that people tended to believe the ends justified the means, especially when the goal was material gain. A lot of murders were motivated by the mortal sin of greed—they saw it often enough, in their detective work.

She frowned, slightly, her gaze resting on the painting. To be fair, though, oftentimes those who supposedly pursued "good" did the exact same thing, with Martina Betancourt serving as a prime example. The young woman worked toward "good" with just as much ruthlessness as the evildoers worked toward "evil," and so you could say that— in her own mind—she just as certain that the ends justified the means. In fact, a person could also argue that Acton felt the same way—after all, no one more ruthless than Acton, when he wanted to achieve his ends.

Oh, she suddenly realized, as her brow cleared; I asked

about Harrison's illness, and Acton diverted the subject—sent me off, like a dog sent to fetch a bone. But—but what did Harrison's illness have to do with her husband's tendency to be ruthless, in achieving his ends? After all, he was not the one who was embezzling from the Ministry—he was telling the truth, when he'd said it wasn't him. And he was also telling the truth, when he said he was putting a stop to it. Which was all well and good, save that there was something that he didn't want her to know—she was not to 'delve' into the Prison Ministry's problems.

"Do you need to lie down, Kathleen?" Acton interrupted his mother mid-sentence, no doubt due to the fact that his bride had spent the past few minutes frowning at the wall.

"Not a'tall," she replied, and turned to smile at the others. "I was just lookin' at the boat paintin'."

"It is not a 'boat', my dear, it is a 'ship'," the Dowager corrected, with an indulgent smile. "It belonged to the nineteenth-century Baron; a very clever man, who amassed a fortune with the East India Company."

"Well done by him, then." Doyle decided not to mention that he'd died of the pox, from visiting prostitutes with his ill-gained riches. Which seemed rather fitting, to her.

Acton must have caught the nuance in her voice, because he assured her, "Not slave-trading."

"Certainly not," the Dowager pronounced with full disapproval. "We did not condone such a distasteful activity; I do not know what would have put such a thought into your head, my dear."

"More wine?" asked Reynolds, as he replenished the Dowager's glass. "And may I say it is quite an impressive painting; is it a Benedict?"

The Dowager rapped his hand playfully. "Now, Reynolds;

you've made me confess that indeed it is. It is rather an embarrassment, what with his history."

"Ah, well; *ars artis gratia*, madam," Reynolds noted with a small smile. "Much can be forgiven."

"The artist was something of a n'er-do-well, who died in debtor's prison," the Dowager explained to Doyle, in the tone of someone explaining to a child. "The Fleet."

"Oh," said Doyle, in some confusion. "I didn't know they had fleets for debtors."

"Your *coq au vin*, madam," Reynolds offered smoothly.

CHAPTER 13

*D*oyle and Callie were upstairs in the nursery, monitoring Edward's bath, when Reynolds tapped on the door jamb and entered to bring Doyle a small silver serving-tray, laden with a coffee pot and delicate porcelain cup. Since her husband was always trying to limit her coffee intake whilst she was pregnant, Doyle rightly interpreted this gesture as her husband's apology for letting loose his stupid mother on his poor beleaguered wife.

Reynolds set the tray down. "Lord Acton asked me to relate that he must first meet with Hudson about tomorrow's schedule, and then he will join you to put Edward to bed."

With all gratitude, Doyle left Callie to her wet and splashing work, and retreated into the boy's nursery, so as to lower herself into a chair and savor her rare reward. "You're a trump, Reynolds, and I don't know how you do it. If I were you, I'd have taken a garrote to the woman, long before now."

"Surely not," the servant soothed, as he poured out her

coffee. "And we must be sympathetic to the fact that the Dowager Lady Acton has been supplanted, here, which must be difficult, for a lady of her personality."

"Well, if she keeps needlin' me, Acton will take a garrote to her, himself."

And—since this was well-within the realm of possibility—she decided to move away from that particular topic. "Faith, it's lucky, we are, that she needs to hang onto his sleeve, to keep body and soul together. Or mayhap it's not so very lucky—if she'd a fortune, she could go live a thankless live of riches and ease, elsewhere, and offer her advice to other people, for a change."

Reynolds raised her brows in surprise. "Surely, the Dowager has adequate settlements to maintain her lifestyle, madam?"

Doyle shook her head. "No—apparently not, and so she has to come ask Acton for money, which he is reluctant to give her, because she needles me for sport. So 'round and 'round we go."

Philosophically, Reynolds offered, "Difficult relatives are a cross we must bear, I suppose."

Doyle smiled at him, as she savored her coffee. "I never had any, so's I wouldn't know, my friend."

It seemed clear that this had been an item of curiosity to him, and he ventured, "There is no one back in Ireland, madam?"

"Not that I know of—there was only my mum and me. She never spoke of anyone, leastways, but I always had the impression her family washed their hands of her, which means I'm perfectly happy to wash my own hands of them."

The butler closed the silver coffeepot with a small,

satisfied click. "With hindsight, we can be assured that they regret their actions."

"Mayhap," she shrugged. "I don't even care enough to rub it in their faces."

They were interrupted when Callie exclaimed, and then Edward came racing, naked and wet, through the bathroom door.

"Careful," warned Reynolds in alarm, but Doyle only lifted her cup out of the boy's way with practiced ease, as he ran across the room to evade Callie.

"Sorry," Callie offered, as she hurried after him with a towel. "He's a slippery little rascal."

"He's a rollin' ball of mischief," Doyle agreed, and watched fondly as between them, Reynolds and Callie corralled the giggling Edward. She would have offered to help, but she'd earned a well-deserved cup of coffee, and wasn't going to set it aside for love or money.

"Sorry, madam," Callie said again, as she bundled him back into the bathroom.

"No worries, Callie; the boyo's an escape artist."

With a small sigh, Reynolds shut the door behind them. "As I learned to my regret; I thought there would be no harm in bringing him into the Great Hall, to spend his energy."

"Whist, Reynolds," Doyle said crossly. "I'll hear no more; 'twas naught but a stupid bowl."

But the servant would not be consoled. "You may not be aware, madam, that it dated from the Ming Dynasty—only think of the history it has seen." With deep sadness, he shook his head. "And to my shame, it was destroyed on my watch; I should have been more vigilant."

But Doyle thought it all nonsense, and offered, "Not your

fault, for heaven's sake; you're not supposed to have a 'watch' to begin with. "Where was our Callie, at the time?"

"Miss Callie was meeting with Lord Acton, madam."

There was the barest hint of disapproval in his tone, and, with a gleam, Doyle teased, "Not to worry, Reynolds; she's not his type."

Aghast, he disclaimed, "Oh—I would never imply such a thing, madam. I only note that Miss Callie often does not seem as respectful, as perhaps she ought."

"She's young, Reynolds, and I'm not sure that she's cut out to be a servant," Doyle offered diplomatically. "Let's give her some time to find her feet—I imagine we'll not have her for long, anyways, if she's a mind to be married, and start her own family." In fact, Doyle was half-hopeful that Tim McGonigal would fulfill this role; he was somewhat older than Callie, but Acton was somewhat older than Doyle, and things had worked out well. Fingers crossed, of course; Acton was talking like a nob again, which always made her uneasy.

Hard on this thought, her husband appeared in the doorway, and she bestowed a grateful smile upon him. "Thanks for the coffee, Michael; Reynolds is talkin' me down from the ledge."

But Acton was a high-born sort of person, and not about to discuss family affairs in front of a servant. "Thank you," he said politely to the butler, who recognized a dismissal when he heard one, and promptly retreated out the door.

"Your mum's a treat," Doyle observed. "I thought mayhap she'd mended her ways a bit, but I was sadly mistaken."

"Then she will learn to mend them again," he said, and bent down to kiss her. "I am sorry, Kathleen."

"My own fault, and you've naught to be sorry about; I feel

that I can't just ignore her, Michael—we haven't many relatives between us, to begin with."

"You are very generous."

She sighed. "No—not truly; I was harborin' some unholy thoughts, I promise you. Although I thank you for puttin' Reynolds on the watch; he did a fine job of steerin' her away from the rocks."

"I did not put Reynolds on the watch," he offered mildly.

She caught a faint hint of disapproval in his tone, and straightened up in her chair. "Oh—oh, you didn't? Never say you're annoyed about it?"

Acton tilted his head. "It is not his place, to intrude into such matters."

It was on the tip of her tongue to admonish him—to make a remark about how Reynolds felt more like a good friend, to her, and how uncomfortable she was with the idea of having servants in the first place—but she resisted the impulse. Whilst it was true that she considered Reynolds a good friend, it also seemed clear that Reynolds was always careful to keep their relationship on what he considered the correct track. Acton did the same thing with the man, of course, and she supposed it would be like whistling in the wind, to try and undo that particular thousand-years mindset, on either side. Reynolds was proud of his affiliation with the House of Acton—prouder than she was, truth to tell—and she should probably try to respect that, and respect the man's wishes, despite the fact she thought it all a pack of nonsense.

And so, she changed the subject. "Savoie's still comin' tomorrow?"

"He is. They should arrive mid-morning."

She warned, "If Emile is going to ride, Edward will want to ride, too. Best tell Grady to gird his loins."

Acton smiled. "He is standing-by for a Code Nine," which was police code for a lockdown.

"Edward! Come back here!" Callie could be heard calling, from the next room.

"Be advised," Doyle said to Acton. "The suspect's slippery and dangerous."

CHAPTER 14

*T*hat night, Doyle had one of her dreams.

As part-and-parcel of her perceptive abilities, she would have strange and vivid dreams, on occasion. The dreams usually featured someone who was dead, and who'd shown up—ghost-like—to issue warnings, or to give advice. It was a bit strange, in a way, because she didn't need to be asleep to see the ghosts who haunted Trestles—faith, there were heaps and heaps of them, which only made sense, in a house that was this old. But the dreams were a different sort of thing, and experience had taught her that she should listen to the message carefully, since the ghosts seemed slated to deliver a warning—a head's up—about something she needed to pay attention to.

As was usual, she found herself standing on a rocky outcropping, with the wind blowing about her in the darkness, even though she couldn't feel it on her skin. A man stood before her, much the same age as herself, and dressed in old-fashioned clothes—although Doyle wasn't very good at guessing the era. It seemed clear he wasn't medieval, like the Trestles knight was, but was from a more modern time.

This fellow was thin, with hair that fell to his shoulders, and was a bit disheveled. He wore a kerchief, knotted around his neck, with his shirt rather casually unbuttoned beneath it, and his general air was of someone who'd lived a bit frivolously. A "night bird," Doyle's mother would have called his type, and given Doyle a lecture about avoiding such men as potential husbands, no matter the incentive.

The ghost smiled at her a bit vaguely. "Hallo," he said.

"Hallo," she replied. And then, when he seemed disinclined to offer anything further, she asked, "Are you a Trestles-person?" He didn't seem to be as well-dressed as all the previous Lord Actons who haunted the place, but he didn't strike her as a servant, either.

With a negligent gesture, he shrugged. "I suppose I am. I used to come stay here, quite often—had a frightening good time, with Bertie." He smiled slightly, thinking about it. "Too good a time, as it turned out."

She nodded, thinking that he had the look she'd seen many a time, amongst the petty-crime suspects in London. Drug-addled, and living hand-to-mouth in a rough existence, but not motivated enough to take the few, simple steps that would make their lives miles better.

He continued, "Your husband thought you'd like *The Empress* better than the last one. You have to give him points for trying."

Frowning, Doyle asked, "Who's 'the Empress'?"

"*The Empress* is the ship. Tell him that there's a Rousseau in storage—flooded with flowers. You'd like it much better, I think."

The penny dropped, and Doyle ventured, "So—you're the boat-artist?"

"I am." His mouth twisted, as he gazed off into the darkness for a moment. "Bertie asked for a rendering—the man dearly loved that ship."

Since she could not approve of the ship's purpose, Doyle offered diplomatically, "It is a very nice paintin'. And it must be worth a lot, else they'd not have it hangin', here."

He nodded in casual agreement. "Oh, it is—it is. I was good at it, and there aren't very many of them."

"That's a shame," Doyle ventured, having a good guess as to why this was.

"Couldn't stay off the pipe." He shrugged. "Didn't much want to."

"I see," said Doyle.

"I was a by-blow." He leaned forward, and added, "Say what you will about these nobs, they take care of their by-blows. But then, Bertie died, and the heir could hardly wait to move in, and throw me out. I'd hid one of Bertie's treasures away—to sell, if I needed to, but the new regime had me arrested straightaway, before I'd the chance to retrieve it." He paused, remembering. "They held a meeting in Leadenhall, and led me to think it was to hash-out my inheritance. Instead, I walked straight into an ambush; they had me arrested, and thrown into The Fleet."

"I'm sorry to hear it," Doyle ventured, "but you mustn't steal things in the first place—it's wrong."

"If you say so," he replied with a vague smile. "Nothing much mattered, save the pipe."

Suddenly struck, Doyle ventured, "Did Bertie bring back a little African boy on *The Empress*? About five years old, or so?"

Chuckling, the man replied, "Oh, no—you've got it by the wrong leg, there. He's just waiting for his mum—he wants to see his mum. He's too shy to tell you." He smiled. "That, and he's never seen anyone with red hair."

With an unfocused expression, he gazed off into the darkness again, whilst Doyle tried to decide why she was hearing the tale of the doped-up artist, who'd died before his time. "Were you murdered?"

"Oh, no," he disclaimed. "Just caught a whiff of cholera, and off I went. Not a nice place, The Fleet."

"I'm that sorry," Doyle offered.

"I'm sorry in turn; the knight, here, is unhappy that I hid the jade axe, and he doesn't let me forget it."

"Oh. Well, I'd hate to be on his bad side."

The artist-ghost lifted his brows. "Exactly."

Suddenly, Doyle was awake, and staring out at the dimly lit room. She and Acton liked to leave the velvet curtains open at night, and the diamond-paned windows were illuminated by the glimmering moon.

Aye, then, she thought, as her husband slept beside her; I was never one to turn down a treasure-hunt.

CHAPTER 15

The next morning, Doyle struck out with Edward and Callie to take a their usual stroll-about, before Savoie and Emile arrived; they'd decided it was doubly-important today—to wear down the boyo for a bit—before placing him atop an unsuspecting horse. Acton was working in his office, and would join them as soon as the guests arrived. This was just as well, since Doyle had a few questions for Reynolds all lined up, and it gave her an opportunity to pose them.

As she followed the others out the door, she casually asked the butler if he'd mind fetching her a go-cup, and then crossed her fingers that he'd have the sense to fill it with coffee, instead of tea, for the merciful love o' Mike. Although the poor man was already walking a thin line with Acton, and so mayhap he wouldn't be so bold as to thwart his standing orders, in such a way.

She needn't have worried; Reynolds had fashioned a compromise, so that when he caught up with her to deliver the cup, it was indeed filled with coffee, but only one-third full.

Grateful for any boon, she savored a sip, and before he could turn to return to the house, she asked, "Remember when you were flirtin' with the Dowager, about that boat paintin'?"

With some disapproval, Reynolds replied, "I would not describe our conversation as 'flirting', madam."

"Don't be so prickly—I'm all admiration, and better you than me. I wanted to ask you about the artist."

"Benedict," the servant readily replied. "And an unusual subject, for him. He was instead known for his architectural themes, and his sensitivity to light and contrast."

"Well, that's grand," said Doyle, who hadn't a clue.

"*The Empress* is a very valuable painting," Reynolds added, and then unbent enough to disclose, "Hudson will be quite happy, madam; Lord Acton suggested that he change-out the still-life for a more pleasing piece."

"I hear there's a Rousseau in storage, somewhere," Doyle ventured.

With a mighty effort, Reynolds managed to hide his extreme surprise. "Is there? I had no idea you admired his work, madam."

Doyle frowned, slightly. "Where is 'storage', by the by? I know there's a dungeon, somewhere beneath."

"A strong-room, instead, madam," Reynolds corrected, with a tinge of disapproval.

Doyle let it go, since the butler hadn't the benefit of the various ghosts who'd been guests in the "strong-room," and were not at all happy about their experience. "Do they use it for storage, nowadays?"

"It is still used as a strong-room, I believe. Very few have access."

"I doubt that's it, then," Doyle mused. "If he was hiding it from Bertie, it had to have been hidden somewhere where Bertie wouldn't think to look."

Reynolds was understandably at sea. "Who is 'Bertie', madam?"

"Never you mind, my friend. And now, tell me—what's a 'by-blow'?"

Reynolds paused, ably hiding his flare of alarm. "Where did you hear this, madam?"

"Just answer the question, please."

"It is a—a slang term, for a child born out of wedlock," Reynolds explained carefully. "Usually applied to a nobleman's bastard child."

"Oh," she said thoughtfully, lifting her brows. "I suppose that's in keepin', after all; the man fancied himself quite the jack-the-lad, back in the day, and he was throwin' all that opium money about, like seed for the birds."

"Which man is this, madam?" asked Reynolds, unable to completely hide his dismay.

She laughed aloud at his expression. "Not Acton, you knocker—for heaven's *sake*, Reynolds."

But the servant only explained, very much upon his dignity, "Lord Acton was a bachelor for quite some time, madam."

"That's fair enough, I suppose."

They were interrupted when Edward insisted—as only a small boy can do—that she hold a muddy and abandoned bird's nest for him, to which she willingly agreed, before he scampered off to find his own version of hidden treasure.

Thus prompted to move on to her next question, Doyle

asked, "D'you know anythin' about a 'jade axe'? Is it what it sounds like?"

Again, Reynolds managed to maintain his expression only with an effort. "Indeed, madam. In fact, one was found at the burial site in Canterbury, not very long ago—although several have been found on the Continent, also. They are quite ancient; a symbolic hand-axe, and not meant for any practical purpose. Scholars are puzzled about their significance, and believe they must have served as valued prizes, of some sort, since the graves where they have been found do not appear to belong to nobility."

Frowning slightly, she asked, "So; they aren't very big— not like a regular axe?"

"No, madam. Six or seven inches, only. They were fashioned in the shape of a hand-axe."

Doyle thought it amusing that he thought she had the slightest idea what a hand-axe was shaped like, but made no comment, since she was contemplating the rather daunting fact that the axe could be easily hidden, just about anywhere.

She allowed her gaze to wander over the branches of the ancient trees overhead, and the expansive lawns that surrounded them, and thought, I imagine the artist hid the axe outdoors, somewhere. He couldn't take the chance that a servant might find it if he hid it indoors, and besides, he had to leave it where he could sneak in and retrieve it, after Bertie was no longer in charge. But there's miles of outdoors, here, and I haven't the first idea where to start—it would be impractical, to begin pulling up random turf, here and there. More information is needful.

"Good morning."

She looked up to see that Acton approached them, bearing two go-cups. He lifted one, as he came close. "I brought you a new variety of decaf, that Hudson hopes you might find acceptable."

Since decaf was never, ever, going to be remotely acceptable, Doyle offered up a semi-grateful smile. "I'll try it, then, and many thanks to him."

"I will return your old one, madam." With a deft gesture, Reynolds quickly lifted the go-cup he'd brought, and departed with all speed.

"Caught him out," Doyle remarked to Acton, as she took a tentative sip of the new offering. "Poor man."

In a mild tone, her husband replied, "He shouldn't be acting against orders, Kathleen."

She glanced up at him, genuinely curious. "And what happens if my orders are opposite your orders?"

He smiled slightly, as they began to walk along together. "You'll not want to hear this, but my orders win."

But she only shrugged, philosophically. "I'm used to that, sir; that's just how it is at the CID, except that I'm usually not carryin' a bird's nest."

"Exactly," he agreed, and put a fond arm around her.

She added, "I understand, Michael; the hierarchy has to be respected, else it all falls to chaos."

The words she spoke to him were only semi-sincere, however, because in truth of fact, there'd been more than one occasion—both at the Met and at home—when Doyle had not respected the hierarchy, in her determined quest to save Acton from himself. And there were several memorable times when she'd managed to convince Reynolds to assist her in this aim, but this would remain their little secret; no need to rock poor Acton's hierarchy-world.

And speaking of such, she was reminded to ask, "D'you have any by-blows, Michael?"

He smiled, surprised by the question. "I do not."

"That you know of," she added fairly.

"A good point. May I ask why you raise the subject?"

She smiled into her cup, as she pretended to take a sip. "Reynolds was wonderin'."

"*Reynolds* was?"

She laughed aloud at his reaction. "It sounds worse than it was, and please don't blister Reynolds any more than he's already been blistered, between the stupid Chinese bowl, and the stupid Dowager. The poor man is my only support—he's the Barnabas to my St. Paul."

Acton offered, "He did suggest to Hudson that the strawberry jam here was inadequate, as you were not partaking with the same enthusiasm as at home."

"There you go—he tries to smooth my way, since I'd never have the wherewithal to ask such a thing of Hudson, myself. I'm a stranger in a strange land."

In mock-chagrin, he pulled her against his side. "It is your land, too," he protested.

She lifted her face for his kiss. "I know, Michael. But I'm a dandelion in the flowerbed, and no amount of 'madams' is goin' to change that fact. I don't think I'd even want to change it, in the first place—I'm tasked with keepin' you grounded, so that you resist your medieval impulses."

"There is that," he agreed, in a mild tone, and bent to kiss her again.

Oh-oh, she thought; Katy bar the door, indeed—he was up to something medieval, which only seemed to confirm the vague sense of unease she'd entertained, ever since they'd taken-up residence here. Absently, she took a sip of the horrid decaf, and then immediately regretted it.

Edward ran up with a small white pebble, to place in the

bird's nest, and as she bent to accommodate him, her attention was caught by the little black boy, who was hiding behind a tree, and peeking out so as to watch Edward. She smiled at him, and he met her gaze with his own shy smile, before he backed away, and vanished.

Reminded, she asked Acton, "Were there no redheads in England, way back when?"

Willingly, Acton tilted his head to answer this seeming non-sequitur. "I imagine there have always been redheads in England. In fact, there is credible evidence that the Baron who fought at Agincourt was married to a redhead."

With some surprise, Doyle glanced up at him. "The knight's wife? The woman who first owned my tiara?"

He nodded. "The very same. She was described by a chronicler as 'raede' and it is believed the term refers to red hair."

Doyle thought of the stern and faintly contemptuous Trestles knight, who'd nevertheless come to her rescue, a few times. "Fancy that; now, there's irony. Although she was a hero, you know—she agreed to marry the wretched man so as to hold the truce, even though he'd killed a bunch of her people."

"I believe it was a common enough occurrence, at the time. The dynastic houses tended to arrange marriages to form alliances, and to protect themselves."

"Or to bring in riches, like King Solomon's wives."

"That, too," he agreed.

With a small sigh, she noted, "I didn't bring you any riches a'tall, to my shame. And with your looks, you could have had the pick of the crop, I would think."

He ran a fond hand down her opposite arm. "No one remotely interested me, save you."

She teased, "I'm not sure that's true, Michael. There was Melinda, and Fiona."

But he only replied, "Nowhere near the same."

This, of course, was as true as true could be; no doubt Acton himself had been utterly taken aback by the fact that he'd fallen like a ton of bricks for a junior officer—one he'd never met, but had simply spotted from his window, one fine morning.

They walked a few more steps, before he asked, "What is this about, if I may ask? Are you angling for information?"

She made a face. "No—not really. I'm tryin' to find out why someone said somethin' to me."

He glanced her way. "Shall I ask who?"

Lightly, she replied, "No, you shall not, lest you cast me off, and marry someone miles more worthy."

She knew that it made him uncomfortable, when she spoke of the ghosts she saw, so she tried to avoid telling him about them. Which was just as well, since the ghosts tended to issue vague warnings, most of them having to do with the present-day Lord Acton.

Curious, she lifted her face to ask, "Would you have married someone to save Trestles, if it came down to it? Like your grandfather was forced to do?"

But his answer was classic Acton. "I would have arranged matters so that it was not necessary."

"A'course," she agreed, as she took another pretend-sip of the stupid decaf. "Goes without sayin'."

CHAPTER 16

Savoie and his son Emile arrived at Trestles, and as Acton politely shook Savoie's hand in the foyer, Doyle was suddenly struck by the odd fact that Acton had allowed this visit, in the first place. After all, her husband was trying to keep her wrapped in cotton-wool, and was vigilantly guarding against any and all incursions onto the premises.

Although, she supposed, if there were to be an exception, it would be for Savoie. The Frenchman had saved the fair Doyle's life, once upon a time, and she suspected that his actions on that best-be-forgot occasion were what made Acton tolerate Savoie to the extent that he did. In a strange way, it was another thousand-years mindset; Acton owed Savoie a debt of honor, and that debt would take precedence over anything else the man ever did, going forward. By virtue of his actions, that long-ago evening, Savoie had managed to gain immunity from any and all Acton-consequences.

And so now, an underworld kingpin could count on a

Scotland Yard DCI as a staunch ally, and Doyle knew that the two men were involved in business ventures together—ventures that could not withstand close scrutiny, since they seemed to involve the smuggling of illegal weapons. Acton kept Doyle well-away from any knowledge of their doings, and it was rare, indeed, when the two men were even in the same place at the same time, as they were today; usually Acton was very careful to keep his distance from Savoie, at least publicly.

Of course, on this occasion Doyle had invited Savoie to bring Emile to ride the horses, and so Acton couldn't very well bar the door. Although, on second thought, Acton wouldn't hesitate to bar the door, so mayhap he was softening-up a bit.

Savoie, himself, seemed to be softening-up a bit, too, and, all in all, it was an amazing testament to the power of love. Not many people knew it, but Emile was actually the son of one of Savoie's sworn enemies—a rival Russian kingpin, who'd been killed in Wexton Prison, of all places. It was like something out of a Greek tragedy, that Savoie had taken-in the son of his rival, and was now a doting father to the boy.

And—as was always the case when younger boys were put in the presence of older boys—Edward was beyond excited to see Emile, who willingly let the toddler chase him about, whilst the party headed outside to walk over to the stables.

They arrived to find the horses already saddled and dozing at the railing, with Grady waiting beside them. Doyle had to admire their determination; how any creature could sleep whilst the two boys were making such a racket was a marvel.

"Come over, now; mind Mr. Grady, please," Callie said, as

she steered the ecstatic boys a safe distance away from the horses' hindquarters.

"I think Grady's the only soul Edward *does* mind, Callie," Doyle replied with some amusement. "Although I suppose I should add Cook, too—"

But her words were interrupted when they were treated to a sudden cacophony of barking, coming from the stable loft's window above, where Grady had his living quarters.

"Whist, Laddie," Grady shouted up in annoyance, as he lifted Emile onto his saddle.

The dog, however, had heard Doyle's voice, and continued barking like a mad thing, through the half-opened window.

"Laddie, quit," Grady called up more firmly, but to no avail.

"If you would," Acton said in a clipped tone to the stableman, and—with an embarrassed tug at his cap—Grady hurried off to try and constrain the dog, somehow. Good luck to him, thought Doyle; that dog sounds like a stubborn boyo, and I think he wants nothing more than to come downstairs and harass me to pieces.

In Grady's absence, Acton took it upon himself to hoist Edward atop the old grey horse, and as he was adjusting both boys' stirrups, Savoie took the opportunity to walk over to speak to Doyle.

Abruptly, the Frenchman asked, "You have heard from Marie, yes? She is well?"

Savoie referred to Mary, Doyle's nanny, who was not here because she was expecting a baby at any moment. It was rather sweet, that Savoie would show an interest in Mary— although to be sure, the nanny was a fixture in Emile's life, since Mary's daughter and Emile played together nearly every day, at the park or at school, and oftentimes little Edward would join them. They hadn't seen one another lately, of course, because Doyle and Acton were here at Trestles.

With a small pang, Doyle tried not to think about how much she missed her old routine, and said, "Yes, I spoke to Mary yesterday, in fact. She's overdue, poor thing, so she's climbin' the walls, with nothin' to do but wait for this baby to make its appearance. Faith, I'm near climbin' the walls, myself, even though I've nowhere near as good an excuse."

She paused, surprised that the words had come out of her mouth. On reflection, though, it was true; she was someone who didn't like to be idle—another strike against her, as aristo-material—and she was sick to the gills, of doing nothing all day.

"And Mademoiselle Gemma? Her adoption—it is complete?"

"Oh; I forgot to ask, but Mary didn't say anythin' about it, so I don't think it's gone through, yet. I'll ask her what's happenin' on that front, when I go visit tomorrow." Doyle smiled at him. "We'll need to throw her an adoption party, after all."

Savoie had—very kindly—asked to be informed as soon as Gemma was officially adopted by Mary and her husband, because he wanted to throw a party for the little girl. It was not what one would expect, from the likes of him, and it only went to show how much the Frenchman had turned over a new leaf, from his questionable past. Acton had hinted more than once that Savoie's history did not bear close scrutiny, and so it was a shrine-worthy miracle that the man was bound and determined to throw a party—of all things—for Doyle's nanny's little girl.

Of course, little Gemma stood as a sister-figure to his own Emile, and there was no question that Savoie doted on Emile. Which—when you thought about it—was the most extraordinary thing of all; it was almost as though the notorious Frenchman had been given an unlooked-for chance to create his own family, and he'd seized it with both hands— he was probably just as surprised as anyone else. Doyle had gained the impression that Savoie had weathered a hard childhood—he'd grown-up poor, just as she had—and so mayhap there'd been a desire to make up for it, hidden within the man all the while. If Dr. Harding were here, he'd know what she meant—it was probably some psychological thing-or-other.

"Sorry, sir," Grady apologized, as he returned to the stable yard. "I don't know what's got into the dog."

"No matter," said Acton, as he unwound Edward's lead rope. "Let's be off, shall we?"

"You won't ride?" Doyle asked Savoie, and then carefully ignored the faint, muffled barking sounds that her voice had inspired.

"*Non*," he replied. "Me, I did not learn the horses."

"Me, neither," Doyle confessed.

"Me, for a third," laughed Callie. "We'll just be left to watch."

Grady gave the boys some brief instruction, and then the two men mounted, and led the two boys into the paddock to see how things went, before they'd attempt a meadow ride. Doyle watched the process—a bit anxiously, since Acton wouldn't coddle her son as much as his mother would like— and then she caught a movement, from the corner of her eye; near one of the trees that lined the pathway.

Thinking that it was the little African boy, again, she

turned to see that it was instead Melinda, pausing to watch them, as she walked the pathway from the Dower House.

As Melinda seemed inclined to tarry, Doyle decided she'd kill two birds with one stone by keeping the woman well-away from Acton, and at the same time withdrawing herself from the stupid dog's orbit, so that mayhap he'd be quiet, for two seconds at a time.

"Edward, mind your da," Doyle called out to her son, and then casually walked over toward the other woman.

CHAPTER 17

As Doyle approached, Melinda stood with her arms wrapped around her coat, unperturbed by being caught-out, spying. "What's to-do? I was coming in from the Dower House, and I saw that the horses were out."

"We've some visitors. Don't invite yourself to lunch," Doyle warned. "It makes Acton cross."

"Well, that's to be avoided," Melinda said absently, as she watched the riding party depart through the paddock gate.

Since it might be a good idea to give warning that Melinda shouldn't be quite so much underfoot as she'd been, Doyle ventured delicately, "How's the religious instruction goin'? Will it be windin' up soon, d'you think?"

"I hope so," the woman replied, not at all discomfited by this hint. "Although Father Clarence wasn't in, today. I believe I'm just about finished, and so I'll not be so much in evidence, going forward."

A bit ashamed that she'd been so heavy-handed, Doyle asked, "When's your Confirmation ceremony?" This inquiry was made with a hint of trepidation; Acton's Confirmation ceremony wound-up having a body count, and so Doyle was a bit gun-shy.

Melinda looked at her blankly. "Oh. Is that what usually happens?"

Surprised in turn, Doyle explained, "Well, yes. The local Bishop would be involved."

"Oh, right; I will ask about it," Melinda replied, in her vague manner. "But first, you must tell me who *that* is."

Doyle followed her gaze, and saw she referred to Savoie, who was leaning with his arms thrown over the paddock fence, watching Emile chattering away, as the group took a circuit around the paddock.

"That's trouble," warned Doyle immediately. "And an even more direct route to making Acton cross, I promise you."

But Melinda only laughed lightly. "Oh, my; even more intriguing. But first things first; has he any money?"

"It doesn't matter, Melinda," Doyle said firmly. "Besides, he's got that little boyo—the one on the brown horse—and he's a ragin' handful. You'd be run ragged."

Melinda's eyes narrowed, as her gaze rested on Savoie for a thoughtful moment. "It might be worth it, depending on how well-off he is."

Suddenly struck, Doyle held a horrifying thought—it couldn't be Savoie, that Melinda was after, could it? He was RC, and it would explain her cream-pot conversion—not to mention the reason that she kept the mystery man's identity shrouded in mystery.

After an anxious moment, however, she quickly discarded the idea; it seemed clear that Melinda hadn't yet met Savoie, and even Melinda was unlikely to convert her religion for someone she'd never met. Although Melinda didn't even know that a Confirmation ceremony was in the offing, so obviously she wasn't paying much attention to the instruction lessons. She was a hard person for Doyle to read, being as she never seemed to think or behave in a logical manner. For a moment, Doyle wondered what Melinda's own childhood had been like.

Recalled to the conversation, Doyle summed up, "Best to stay well-away from that one, Melinda; a word to the wise."

But the other woman turned to regard Doyle with unadulterated surprise, her thin brows raised. "Heavens; whoever told you I was wise?"

Doyle had to laugh. "Now, there's a very good point."

Melinda turned her attention back to Savoie, and rendered a heartfelt sigh of regret. "He'd be just my type, you know; attractive in a *dangerous* sort of way."

Doyle decided that the last needful thing would be to mention that dangerously-attractive Savoie was also a Frenchman, and so instead she warned, "Dangerous is not necessarily a good trait in a husband." Doyle knew of which she spoke, of course.

"Spoilsport," the other teased. "You're the dog in the manger."

As these were potentially rough waters, Doyle avoided them, and instead reminded her companion, "I thought you'd someone on the string, already. It would be a shame if all your fine conversion-work was for naught."

With an exaggerated gesture, Melinda squared her shoulders. "Agreed. I should stay the course."

There was a nuance to her tone that made Doyle's antennae quiver, and a bit suspiciously, she took a cast. "D'you ever run across Sir Stephen, when you're over at the

Dower House?" Hopefully, Melinda had not been enlisted in whatever schemes they were weaving.

"I do see Sir Stephen there, every once in a while," the other woman answered vaguely, and made an equally vague gesture with a languid hand.

Doyle decided to take the bull by the horns. "There's yet another trigger that would make Acton cross, Melinda. If Sir Stephen is doin' any schemin', stay well-away."

But Melinda only turned down her mouth. "It's *so* unfair; why am *I* not allowed to scheme? Everyone else gets to."

"Everyone else is schemin' for all the wrong reasons," Doyle retorted in a firm tone. "It never works out, and I'll warn you again, don't cross Acton, because there's another thing that never works out."

"You know him best," Melinda deferred, with all good will. "But I'll bet a ha'-pence that if I pleaded for mercy, at least he'd listen."

Oh, thought Doyle, rather shocked and much dismayed by the sudden glimpse she could sense behind the light words; poor Melinda has pled for mercy before, it seems, but her pleas had fallen on deaf ears. She realized, suddenly, that she didn't know much about Melinda, or the various husbands she'd had, and felt a pang of shame, because she truly didn't want to get involved—she'd enough on her plate, as it was.

Melinda lifted her fingers in farewell. "I'll go. Cheers."

Made uneasy by the glimpse of bleakness she'd seen, Doyle offered, "I'm sorry if I was short with you, Melinda."

"Not at all," the other woman replied, as she re-wrapped her scarf around her neck. "You're never cowed, do you know that? You're an inspiration to us all."

CHAPTER 18

*I*t seemed an opportune time, and so she decided she should seize it, while they were alone for a few minutes. "I wanted to speak with you, if you don't mind. It's important."

He brought his gaze around to her, and raised his brows politely. "Yes?"

"I know about—about your plan, I guess you'd say."

He smiled slightly, in an indulgent fashion. "Yes? Which plan?"

"About Mary. And her husband."

Suddenly, his gaze was sharp upon her, and all trace of indulgence disappeared.

She continued in a practical manner, "You must see that it's not going to be as easy as you think. I wonder if perhaps you are not thinking very clearly."

The pale gaze did not falter. "Who told you this?"

"No one," she assured him. "But you don't hide your feelings very well."

He'd recovered his poise, and now offered in a chiding voice, "You speak nonsense, Mademoiselle Callie."

She always liked it when he said her name, because he emphasized the second syllable, and it made her sound much more mysterious, and worldly.

Ignoring his words, she continued in a sincere tone, "I hope you will consider an—an alternative plan, so to speak. I like you—I like you very much. Perhaps you would consider having me, instead."

She paused, and then had to smile, because he was staring at her in utter disbelief. "It's true; I do like you," she insisted. "And Emile likes me. I know it wouldn't be the same for you, but you should think about how devasted she'd be. It's only your bad luck, that you came around too late, but you are too late, and you should face facts."

There was a long, silent pause. "You are the very strange girl," he said slowly.

She turned to grasp the fence-rail, and gaze out, toward the riders in the distance. "I like living in the city—I can't imagine going back to live in Meryton, now. I wouldn't mind having plenty of money, for a change, and I think I'd be good for you. I understand you—or at least, I think I do. And I definitely understand Emile." She paused, and then added in a more somber tone, "And you mustn't do away with Mary's poor husband. It wouldn't turn out the way you think—instead, it would destroy her."

Of course, he was not going to admit to any of this, and so shook his head slightly, as though bemused. "Why do you say such terrible things?"

She shrugged, slightly. "I put two and two together. You're in love with Mary—I could tell, by how you behaved, when Lady Abby was being so hateful. And you want to know when Gemma's adoption is completed, because you don't throw it off the rails by—by completing your plan too early."

With all seriousness, she met his eyes with hers. "It's not a good plan, Philippe—may I call you Philippe? She loves him, and besides that, she'd have the new baby—she'd be a wreck, if you killed him. I'm sorry it didn't work out the way you wanted, but I think my plan is a good second-best, and all I'm asking is that you think about it. I've started on-line French lessons, and I'm learning French cooking—the Cook, here, is helping me with it."

He continued to stare at her silently, and so she said in a practical tone, "You're looking to build a family around Emile, and so you might as well choose someone who doesn't have one, already. And it's not as though we wouldn't stay in close contact with Mary and Gemma, anyway—I like them very much, myself. We'd see them every day, just as we do, now."

Slowly, he turned his head to watch Emile again, and she dared not plead her case any further, since she could see that Lady Acton was returning from her visit.

CHAPTER 19

*D*oyle was lying in bed that night, gazing out at the diamond-paned windows, and thinking about things. "Are you awake?" she whispered softly.

"I am," he whispered back.

"Well, if you're not busy, I can think of somethin' for you to do."

He chuckled, and shifted onto his side, so as to draw her close. "Is that so?"

"It's the horse ridin', and the boots," she explained. "Faith, but you're a lusty sight."

"And you waited until now?"

"Nothin' for it, unless I want the servants to join in—and don't think that hasn't happened, back in the day."

He murmured into her neck, "You shock me, Lady Acton."

"Well shock yourself into action. Less chit-chat, please."

Willingly, he drew his hands down her body. "Are we doing the short version, or the long version?"

"Short," she decided. "Time's a-wastin'."

And so, after a brief and vigorous session of love-making, Doyle lay in a contented haze with her head on her equally contented husband's shoulder, gently pulling at the hairs on his chest. After trying to come up with a subtle way of discovering what it was that he was lying awake about, she decided to simply ask the man; Acton could run rings around her in the subtlety department, but sometimes when she surprised him, she managed to get a quick glimpse of his emotions. "Are you goin' to tell me what was keepin' you awake?"

"I'm afraid not," he said apologetically.

So much for the ambush theory; ah well—it was worth a try. She decided she'd best start with her major concerns, and then work backwards toward the minor ones. "So; you never did say what's happened to Harrison, and I've a feelin' it's not good."

"She was transferred to hospital, and has died of her illness," Acton admitted.

"Why didn't you want me to know?"

She could feel his chest rise and fall. "Matters are complicated."

She lifted her head to eye him in suspicious disbelief. "You will tell me, husband, here and now, that you are not coverin' up for the blacklegs who are skimmin' money from the Prison Ministry."

He met her gaze and assured her, "I am not skimming the money, and I am putting a stop to the skimming rig. My word of honor, Kathleen."

As she lowered her head again, she frowned slightly, because he'd changed her words 'round, for some reason. It didn't seem to matter, though—he was telling the truth, about putting a stop to the rig. Which truly wasn't much of a victory; Acton may be mightily tempted to lay hands on all the money that was washin' about, but he knew that if the wife of his bosom found out about it, she'd be most unhappy with him, and making her unhappy was the one single thing he avoided.

Her scalp prickled, and—a bit surprised—she wondered why it would. It wasn't a news-flash; she'd discovered early-on that she was at the center of her husband's universe, and his outsized devotion to her made him do things that were not his natural inclination—his natural inclination being to take no prisoners, and sort things out exactly as he wished.

Wishing she knew why her perceptive ability was acting up, she frowned slightly into the darkness, and reminded him, "Recall that you can't go about killin' people, husband—I've told you a *million* times."

"I did not kill her, Kathleen."

"But I think you know who did, and it sure feels like you're coverin' up for 'im."

He was silent, and she blew out a breath in exasperation, "Just because you've a title, and you've bushels of money, that doesn't mean you can arrange things to suit your fancy—you have to follow the law, Michael."

"I have two titles," he corrected, in an apologetic tone.

"Even worse. And don't try to throw me off the subject, husband—it's very important that you listen to me, for a change."

"I have listened to every word you've ever said to me."

The sincere words had the effect of calming her down a bit, and so she offered in a milder tone, "Just because you're rich, and famous, and everyone always does your biddin', it doesn't mean you have some kind of—of immunity, Michael.

There's no point to gatherin' up riches and power, because in the end, it doesn't matter two pins—it doesn't protect you from a reckonin'. In fact, you only make the reckonin' that much worse. That's why those Parable people are such an excellent example."

"As is the DCS."

Surprised, she lifted herself up on an elbow, and brushed back the hair that fell across her face. "Oh—oh, why, yes—that's an *excellent* case-in-point, Michael. He doesn't want you springin' him out of prison, because he's no longer interested in worldly things—not with heaven, in his sights."

He lifted a hand to finger a strand of her hair. "A very surprising turnabout."

"Aye." She leaned to kiss him, and then lay back down again, settling-in beside him again. "The point is this, my friend; we *are* rich, but only because we have each other."

"I cannot disagree."

Charitably, she decided not to protest the backwards-speak, since they were having such a fine discussion, and she mustn't keep jumping on him over every little thing. His own turnabout may not be as biblical as the DCS's turnabout, but it was a turnabout just the same, and so she mustn't discourage him by railing at him like an archwife. She'd had an outsized influence on the man, and she should take what victories she may.

Although—although whilst it was true that she'd an outsized influence on him—and he definitely cared about not making her unhappy—she'd learned that the 'nobles oblige' thing was very important to him, too. It was bred into his bones, and never more apparent than when he was here, at Trestles—what with ancient notions about what was expected of him, with his debts of honor, and such. It was a glimpse into a completely different mindset that was oftentimes a bit incomprehensible, to a simple soul like herself.

He thinks I'm naïve, she thought; with my Parables, and my right-is-right, and wrong-is-wrong. But its miles easier than the complicated and burdensome rules he lives by—it would be exhausting, for someone like me. Small wonder the Trestles knight thinks me a dimwit.

She began to drift off into sleep, and then he gently squeezed her against him. "Are you still awake?"

"I am," she said sleepily, and gathered-up her wits for another go-round, which was exactly what she deserved for jumping the man's bones, all unexpected.

"I wanted to say that you are recovering nicely, I think."

"I am," she agreed. "I feel much like my old self."

"Would you like to return to London, soon?"

With some surprise, she readily answered, "Aye, that."

Amused, he dropped a kiss on her temple. "Did you think I was going to lock you away here, forever?"

"I shouldn't have been surprised," she answered honestly. "You go all medieval, when you're here."

"Two weeks," he decided.

She pondered whether two weeks would be sufficient time to find the stupid jade axe, and decided that it may be necessary to seek-out a bit of help. "Remember how we found some old treasure, hidden in that well that's under the archives floor?"

"I do."

"Is there anything similar, out-of-doors? Any abandoned wells, or such?"

"If there are, I do not know of them."

As this was not welcome news, she frowned. "It only

stands to reason," she insisted. "There must be wells—they didn't have any pipes, and they needed to have water."

"The well in the keep was only to be used in the event of a siege, Kathleen. Otherwise, water is plentiful; a stream runs along eastern border of the Slough Field. In fact, there was an overabundance of water there, which was why a drainage system was installed. A very expensive operation, for its time."

Doyle lifted her brows. "Oh? I'm amazed he put some of that money to good use."

"Which money is this?"

"The wrong kind of material gain, my friend. Are you busy?"

"Again?" he asked.

"It's my hormones, runnin' amok. You can do the long version, if you need a bit more time."

"Challenge accepted," he replied, and drew her to him.

CHAPTER 20

*D*oyle was not much surprised when the artist made another appearance in her dream that night. "I'm workin' on it," she assured him. "But it's a massive place for a treasure hunt, and so a hint or two may be needful."

But the ghost only shrugged his shoulders in a vague apology. "I am not certain I could describe the place, now."

Doyle stared at him in exasperation. "Well, you should at least make the attempt, for heaven's sake, else I've little chance of findin' it. It's you, who wants it found, not me."

"It's the knight, who wants it found," he corrected. "It doesn't much matter, to me."

"Nothin' much ever did, I think," Doyle chided. "Save for the pipe."

He was silent, and she was immediately ashamed. "Sorry —I shouldn't judge."

"Judge not, lest ye be judged," he agreed.

There was a pause, whilst Doyle ventured, "That's it—it's

that Parable, isn't it? The lesson about bein' too self-righteous. It's important, for some reason, but I don't understand why."

Helpfully, he added, "And you've a Foolish Farmer, too."

She raised her brows. "I do? Is it Acton?" She frowned, thinking this over. "I don't think he's the Foolish Farmer— he's rather generous with his money, actually."

"Just like Bertie," the artist reminisced. "A shame, that he died too soon; he was great fun. Loved his dogs, loved the hunt."

"Well, there's only one dog here, now," Doyle informed him. "And he doesn't like me, much."

The ghost explained, "He's not the kind of dog who worries about being friendly. Bertie had a marvelous pack of hunting dogs—you can't think of them as pets, they've a job to do."

"Well, this one's job is to bark at me." She then paused; her brow knit. "Acton doesn't like it—he doesn't like it when he's reminded that I'm—that I'm fey, or whatever you'd call it. He's always worried that other people might see it."

"He'd a close call, once, and doesn't want to repeat the experience."

She glanced up at him. "Did he? Poor man; I upend his carefully-ordered life."

With a faint smile, the ghost agreed, "Exactly—you're the wild card. He's trying to play piquet, while you're playing lottery tickets. You keep disrupting the play of his game."

With an answering smile, she offered, "More like I overturn the card table, and throw everything down on the floor."

"Yes," he agreed. "It's great fun, actually—who would have thought?"

"Well, it's not much fun for him, poor man—I keep

throwin' a spanner in his wheel of many works. He likes to feel he can control things."

The ghost shook his head slightly, as though amused. "What makes you think he is not 'controlling things' now? He's moving the chess pieces, as we speak—he's only got to move them around you."

Her brow knit, Doyle thought about this for a moment. "Aye. It's the same old song; he doesn't want me to delve-out somethin', but I've a feelin' it's important that I do some delvin'."

"You won't forget the axe, will you? I'm in enough trouble, as it is."

Doyle could well-imagine how the Trestles knight would be treating this no-account fellow, and offered with sympathy, "I'm sorry, if I was unkind. And your paintin' is lovely."

"So's the Rousseau," he said, a bit slyly.

Astonished, she stared at him, open-mouthed. "You *forged* it? *Shame* on you."

But he only shrugged, unrepentant. "His style was close enough to mine—it was easy enough. And I needed some money—I was a by-blow, don't forget, and I had to look out for myself."

"That's no excuse," she scolded. "Plenty of people are born illegitimate, and they manage just fine." Doyle knew of which she spoke, of course, and so she added, "I think you just wanted to be able to get more opium, if Bertie were to cut you off. The drug addicts I've met don't much care about anythin' else but their drugs."

"Are you judging me, again?" he asked in a mild tone.

Honestly, she admitted, "It's hard not to judge, when you're in the business I'm in."

"That's fair, I suppose."

With a sigh, she climbed down off her high horse. "No, it's not," she admitted. We're not in charge of decidin' what's fair, and what's not fair. None of us has a clear picture of the whole."

"Very true."

Reminded, Doyle told him, "You were mistaken about the little African boy. Acton says there've been redheads in England for a long, long time."

But the ghost only chuckled in gentle amusement. "You've got it by the wrong leg, again. That little lad never lived in England."

CHAPTER 21

he next morning, Doyle was driving with her husband from Trestles back to London, so that she could make her monthly visit to the obstetrician.

A bit anxiously, she asked, "He's not goin' to draw blood, this time, is he? D'you promise me, Michael?" Doyle hated needles. She hated doctors, too, but mainly because they were often the people who were wielding the needles.

"If he even makes the attempt, I will draw my weapon."

She smiled out her window. "You can't shoot him, Michael—he needs to deliver Tommy. Although he didn't deliver Edward, so I'm not sure why we bother payin' him all those buckets of money."

"That was not his fault, surely?"

"No—the fault was mine, alone. I'm the wild card, in your ordered game of piquet."

Very much amused, he asked, "Did Reynolds tell you this?"

"No; Reynolds would never presume to say such a thing, Michael. I'm just very well-read, I'll have you know."

He chuckled, at this out-and-out falsehood "Please don't ever change—not one iota. I will have your promise."

"I won't then; all my iotas will stand steadfast. And I won't be doin' any delvin', either; not for a tinker's minute."

He reached to clasp her hand. "I love you."

She smiled out the window. "You don't have to say; not to me."

They drove in contented silence for a few minutes, and she thought, I should try to use this opportunity to winkle some information out of the man, but I wish I'd a better idea about what it is I'm supposed to be winkling—the ghost doesn't make himself very clear. By-blows seem to keep coming up in the conversation—although Acton says he hasn't any. Mayhap he's mistaken? And then there was that reference to the Parables. Was someone wasting money? Unlikely it was Acton—Acton was not a money-waster. Was someone being self-righteous, and judging things, where they shouldn't be? Again, it seemed unlikely it was Acton; almost surprisingly, Acton never seemed very judge-y, probably because his own moral principles could best be described as extremely flexible.

And then, there'd been that comment about the jade axe—about how the ghost said he couldn't help her find it, since he'd not recognize the hiding place. As this seemed a likely topic for a bit of winkling, she ventured, "Trestles hasn't changed much for a long time, right? Everythin' seems so old."

"Very true," he agreed.

"When's the last time they changed somethin' around?"

"It has been quite some time."

"Give me some dates, please," she asked, a bit impatiently.

He considered this. "The drainage system in the Slough Field, was perhaps the most recent major improvement."

"But that didn't really *change* anythin' around," she mused. "When did the pond get put in?"

"Capability Brown. The eighteenth century."

She frowned. "That means the seventeen-hundreds, right?"

"It does."

She blew out an exasperated breath. "It's always so confusing—why do they say 'the eighteenth century' when they should just say 'the seventeen-hundreds'?"

"That is an excellent question."

"It's not *funny*, Michael," she said crossly.

"I beg your pardon," he said, and lifted her hand to kiss its back.

She subsided into silence, and thought it over, as she watched the scenery pass by. This jade-axe business seemed to be a dead end, but there was also the remark about the little African boy—about how he'd never lived in England. So; he was from somewhere where there weren't many redheads, which would indicate Africa, as most likely, but there hadn't been any slave-trading at Trestles, and Doyle was at a loss as to why he'd been brought to her attention.

The ghost had said the boy was waiting to see his mother, which made no sense, since presumably his mother was long dead. Although—although mayhap she was making an assumption that she shouldn't; the ghost had said she'd got it by the wrong leg, and so mayhap the boy wasn't from the olden days, at all. He was never inside the house, but always outdoors, which would lend some credibility to the idea that he was different from the others who were wandering about, and haunting the wretched place. Mayhap he was just visiting, for some reason.

But this breakthrough seemed to bring her no closer to the solution—she didn't know any ghostly African boys, past or present.

"How's Jean-Luc?" she turned to ask her husband. "He's not dead, is he?" Jean-Luc was the son of a Rwandan cab driver she'd known, and—last she'd heard—the boy was living with relatives in Africa.

Surprised, he glanced at her. "I had not heard such a report. I understand that he is doing well."

She nodded, since it didn't seem to fit, in the first place—Jean-Luc had lived most of his life in England.

After deciding she was pig-sick of trying to decipher the ghost's ramblings, she moved on to more practical topics. "How's it comin' along, with the shuttin' down of the skimmin' rig?"

"As well as can be expected."

As this seemed to be one of his patented non-answers, she eyed him sidelong with a full measure of suspicion. "Meanin' what?"

He tilted his head. "It is a delicate matter, and should probably be resolved with as little public scrutiny as possible. After all, it would be a simple thing for the perpetrators to cast blame on the DCS, or even Dr. Okafor."

"Oh—oh; you're right, of course." Struck with an unwelcome thought, she asked a bit anxiously. "Neither one of them is involved in the wrongdoin', are they? I'd be that shocked."

"As would I. No, I can find no indication they are involved."

Reassured, she turned again to review the scenery. "You're right, though; it's probably best to roll-up that rig with as little fanfare as possible. Even if the DCS wasn't involved, it's not the kind of PR he needs, for the Ministry."

As she gazed out her window, she thought again about how it was rather surprising that the DCS hadn't nosed-out this rig, himself. But trust Martina to have twigged it—she was not about to allow the unrighteous to steal from the righteous, after all; and putting a stop to such things used to be her stock-in-trade, before she'd gone off the rails, a bit.

Her scalp pickled, and she frowned, trying to decide why it would. Mayhap it was because Martina tended to be a bit reckless, in her righteous ways, which meant that she'd best have a care. "Are we worried that anyone's in danger?" she asked slowly. "If we think that Harrison may have been murdered, that might be a warnin' for the others."

Acton tilted his head. "Again, since the Ministry is involved, it must be handled carefully."

"Aye," Doyle agreed. "And Charbonneau's a CI, to boot, so, it's doubly-delicate. But if she's goin' about, killin' people, Michael, the CI Unit needs to kick her out of the ranks, and make her do hard time in a hard place."

"I would agree."

Doyle nodded thoughtfully. "Aye; I truly think that Charbonneau's a bad 'un. And Martina has to remember that her wings have been clipped, and so she mustn't ruffle the wrong feathers. She tends to be headstrong."

He made no response, and—making a wry mouth—she took a good guess as to why this was. "I know you're not inclined to rescue Martina in the first place, Michael, and small blame to you. But recall that she did you a massive favor, once, by not rollin' you up for your many misdeeds, when she could have done." She paused, and added fairly, "But then I suppose she put paid to any and all goodwill, when she served me such a nasty trick, and let her wretched husband into our flat."

"All very true," he agreed.

Doyle then reasoned, "Although you served her a nasty trick in return, and framed her up for multiple murder-one."

"It is all very confusing, to try to sort it out," he agreed.

"Well, I think everyone's even, now," Doyle decided, as she cleared her brow. "And I suppose it doesn't much matter, because she's in prison for the nonce, and well-out of your hair."

"And you are fond of her," he added.

Blowing out a breath, she admitted, "I suppose I am, despite everythin'. At least, I like her enough to have spoiled all the come-uppance plans that you'd made for her."

He smiled. "It was well-done, I must say."

She laughed aloud. "I like how you're so proud of me, for sortin' you out, Michael."

"I don't know why I underestimate you," he admitted, still smiling at the memory. "You are so very clever."

She accepted this accolade without demur, because he didn't like it when she started talking about the stupid ghosts, even though the stupid ghosts could not stop talking about him. What had the artist said? He'd said Acton was moving the chess pieces, as he always did; only this time, he was moving them around her. Which sounded a bit ominous, when you thought about it.

Wishing she hadn't held the thought, she ventured, "Well, don't forget I'm the wild card in your picket-game, and that

I'm tasked with savin' you from yourself. It's steady work, my friend, but I will pitch my tent in the land of hope, because we both learned a hard lesson, after all that went down last year. We can only be stronger, goin' forward."

"My ministering angel," he agreed, and again, kissed the back of her hand.

CHAPTER 22

*A*fter her doctor's appointment, Acton dropped-off Doyle at Mary-the-nanny's for a visit, whilst he went into the office to catch-up on things. Mary lived with her husband, an up-and-coming MP, in a posh little flat in the Royal Borough of Kensington and Chelsea, just around the corner from Doyle's own flat.

Doyle had first met Mary when the young woman was a witness in a homicide case, and Doyle had known immediately—in the way that she knew things—that their lives were fated to be intertwined. In a strange way, Mary's life-story was somewhat similar to Doyle's, in that they'd both been vaulted from a scratching existence into a life of luxury, thanks to their unexpected marriages.

And—again, in a similar fashion—the happily-ever-after had featured a few bumps in the road, here and there. Once the target of corrupt people, Mary's husband had gone into politics with an aim to reform the aforesaid corruption. Unfortunately, he'd run up against the natural inertia of government, and had been forced to make some compromises, out of practical necessity. Doyle knew that Mary was uneasy about the nature of those compromises, even though Doyle didn't know the specifics—politics had never much interested her, as it all seemed rather purposefully complicated, and she was someone who liked to keep things simple. And at the simplest level, when it came to politics, things were very similar to that thousand-years mindset at Trestles; everyone was trying to raid everyone else's sheep, and get clean away with it.

Since it was just the two of them, Doyle prepared a cup of hot water with cinnamon sticks for Mary—since Mary's neighbor had told her this was guaranteed to induce labor—and Doyle took the opportunity to brew herself a cup of coffee, since she was the one manning the kitchen, and no one would be the wiser.

"Thank you," said Mary gratefully, as Doyle carefully handed over the hot cup. "Although you shouldn't be waiting on me, Lady Acton."

"Such a pack of nonsense, Mary; you must put your feet up, when you've a chance, because there will be precious few opportunities to do so, goin' forward."

Mary smiled, as she waited for her cinnamon concoction to cool. "It's a bit easier, with Gemma going back to school in the mornings. And, of course, Lizzie's been so very helpful."

Doyle paused, mid-sip. "Lizzie? Lizzie Williams?"

"Yes—ever since she's been helping Nigel on his project, she's been so sweet, when she comes over; she helps me cook, and runs the odd errand, even though she's got her own baby at home to mind."

Doyle blinked, as this was unexpected, and in no small part alarming. Lizzie Mathis—now Lizzie Williams—worked in the Scotland Yard forensics lab, but even more to the point, she was one of Acton's henchmen—or henchwomen, more properly—and Doyle had long since learned that the young woman's unexpected presence was a sure and certain indicator that Acton was in the midst of masterminding some scheme. And there could be little doubt that such a scheme was afoot; not only was Lizzie Mathis a busy new mother, as Mary had pointed out, but Lizzie was the last person anyone would describe as "sweet."

A bit dismayed by this revelation, Doyle teetered on the edge of asking a few pointed questions, but hesitated, because it seemed evident that Mary assumed Doyle was already aware of whatever-it-was she was talking about.

Her thoughts were interrupted when Mary tentatively took a sip, and confided, "I'm not sure whether I want the cinnamon to work. I suppose I'm a bit nervous, now that the time is finally upon me."

"I know the feelin'," Doyle agreed. "It's as though you've been happily building a boat in your basement, and then it suddenly occurs to you that you've got to get it out the door, somehow."

Mary laughed. "Yes—please tell me all will be well, Lady Acton."

"A cake-walk," Doyle advised stoutly, and decided to change the subject, as her own birth-story was not for the faint of heart. "We saw Savoie and Emile, come to visit Trestles, yesterday."

Mary smiled. "Yes, Mr. Savoie mentioned it, and Emile couldn't stop telling Gemma about his horse. They were at the park yesterday, after Gemma got out from school; Gemma was so happy to see everyone, again—although she misses Edward, of course. And she loved to see Miss Callie."

Once again, Doyle blinked. "*Callie* was there? Yesterday?"

"Yes—she came along with Mr. Savoie and Emile. And it was just as well she was there, since Mr. Savoie insisted that I sit on the bench, and rest."

Doyle frowned slightly. "Oh; well, since she has afternoons off, mayhap she went to help-out with Emile, and earn a bit of money, on the side."

"Very likely," Mary agreed. "She's wonderful with Emile, who can be a bit—a bit energetic."

"He's a hazard," Doyle offered bluntly, "As headstrong as the day is long, but at least he minds his Papa. And Callie, too —she's a brick, with our own boyo. Poor Reynolds, on the other hand, is not a brick, and is worn to a thread; Trestles is not child-safe, and neither is Reynolds."

Mary laughed, and then added, "Your friend came by, too —she stopped by to say hallo to Mr. Savoie." In an apologetic tone, Mary admitted, "I can't remember her name—the one who came to your dinner-party, and who wears the lovely cross-necklace."

"Oh, yes," said Doyle slowly. "Martina Betancourt, you mean." After a moment's hesitation, she decided not to mention that Mary was mistaken, since Martina Betancourt was currently locked up, and serving time. In fact, best not open that subject a'tall; Mary was the type who'd be very distressed to learn that Doyle was friends with people in prison, let alone husband-killers.

"How does Mr. Reynolds?" Mary asked. "Please give him my warmest regards."

Doyle made a wry mouth. "He's in his glory at Trestles, because he's a throw-back, when all is said and done. And so is Acton, I suppose."

Thus prompted, Mary leaned forward a bit. "I wanted to

tell you that Nigel so appreciates Lord Acton's help on the project, Lady Acton—I know he's not supposed to talk about it, but I do know that he's very grateful. I don't think I'm speaking out of turn when I tell you he was very worried."

Thoroughly at sea, Doyle decided it would probably behoove her to find out what they were talking about, in the event that she needed to swing a joint stool at her husband in the car on the way home. Tentatively, she probed, "Actually, he hasn't said much about it, bein' as it's such a delicate matter."

Distressed, Mary lowered her cup. "Oh—I hope I haven't said more than I should."

"Not a'tall, Mary; I know your husband's been burdened lately, poor man." This was a sensible guess, being as the man's former amour had been fished out of the river as a suicide—although Mary didn't know that his former amour was not so very former, and so Doyle had best have a care about what she said.

"Yes; he'd been dealing with a very nasty lady—she was such a thorn in his side—but now she's in prison, and he seems like a new man."

Charbonneau? guessed Doyle, lowering her gaze. I'd not be a'tall surprised to hear that she's in the thick of whatever this "project" is, and now it seems as though the dots are finally getting themselves connected. Now, I've only to figure out what the ghost is nattering on about—it doesn't help matters that the man's a drug addict, and can't seem to keep a straight thought in his head.

Mary confided, "Nigel's been speaking about getting out of politics." She shook her head, slightly, her expression grave. "It hasn't gone at all how he thought it would—he feels he could do more, if he was in an advocacy group."

"You'll be that relieved," Doyle observed. Mary was not one to enjoy going to political dinner parties, and she was especially not one who could be careful about what was said to who, which had been ably demonstrated by the tidbits she'd let drop, today. Although in her defense, she'd assumed Acton would tell the wife of his bosom whatever it was that was going forward—a fond hope, but good on her, for thinking such a kindly thought.

They could hear a key card in the slot, and Mary quickly cautioned, "Here he is—don't say anything."

Nigel Howard came in to greet Doyle in a friendly fashion, but she was a bit shocked to see the change in the man—he'd aged ten years, since last she'd seen him, and there was an aura of concern, hidden beneath his smile. "I'm so glad you've come to visit; my poor Mary has been climbing the walls."

"Not much longer," Doyle offered. "And it will all be well-worth it."

"Has Mr. Trenton came up?" Mary asked her husband, and then turned to Doyle with a smile. "I thought you might want to say hallo."

Howard called out from the kitchen, "No—he stayed downstairs, Mary."

For the third time, Doyle hid her surprise, and as Howard was rummaging around in the fridge, she lowered her voice, and ventured, "So; is Trenton working on the project with Lizzie?"

"Oh—oh no, instead Lord Acton has loaned Mr. Trenton to Nigel, because our PPO is on holiday." At Doyle's blank look, she explained, "Nigel has a protection officer—a PPO."

"Oh; oh, well—I suppose that explains where Trenton's been," said Doyle. The words were said slowly, though, because she was fast-coming to some very disturbing conclusions.

"Yes; it was very kind of Lord Acton to loan him out, while you are staying at Trestles. Nigel get threats of course—they all do, and I try not to think about it too much. Nigel's on the Public Accounts Commission—the one that watches over how the public's money is spent—and I think they get more threats than most. They've already had a scare this year, when a member was beaten, and sent to hospital."

"That is alarmin'," Doyle offered slowly, which was only the truth, knowing what she knew. "Mayhap he can step down—or at least, take some time off, when the baby comes."

"He may not be able to," Mary replied in a regretful tone. "He says it depends on how the project is going. Poor Nigel—and we're so very frustrated about Gemma's adoption, of course."

Doyle raised her brows. "Oh—I was goin' to ask. Gemma's adoption hasn't come through, yet?"

Mary shook her head slightly. "No. It is so frustrating, Lady Acton, but there's yet another hurdle—one of the forms from the Russian agency wasn't in English, and so we're got to get it translated." She sighed, hugely. "It seems to be one silly thing, after another."

"Bureaucrats," Doyle pronounced. "They always have a hard time, seein' the forest for the trees."

Mary continued, "It's nothing important, I'm told. But the delays seem so pointless."

"Very pointless," Doyle agreed absently, and immediately texted to let Acton know she was ready to be picked up. She considered issuing a warning, to tell him that he should check-out a helmet from the riot-gear locker, but then remembered, with great regret, that she hadn't a nightstick.

Acton's moving the chess pieces, all right, she thought a bit grimly; but I haven't a clue what he's doing, or why the ghost thinks it's important that I pay attention. And this is exactly what I deserve, for complaining that I've been too idle, and in need of a project—suddenly, the projects are raining themselves down on my poor head.

CHAPTER 23

Once he had Doyle settled in the car, Acton got behind the wheel and pulled away into traffic, "How was your visit?"

"It was harrowin'," Doyle informed him bluntly. "And now I'm thoroughly alarmed, thanks to you, which is no state for a pregnant lady to be in. What's afoot? It looks to me as though you've built a hedge of protection around Mary, and it makes me very uneasy that you haven't told me why—not to mention that Lizzie and Trenton were playing least-in-sight during my visit, so that I wouldn't find out that they were part of the hedge."

He was quiet, for a moment, and she eyed him, prompting, "You've forgot that Mary's even more of a gabbler than I am, which is truly sayin' somethin'. Unsnabble, if you please."

Slowly, he replied, "The hedge of protection has been built around Howard, instead."

She blinked. "Oh. All right, and I do feel slightly better.

Something to do with his Public Accounts Commission, and threats being made?"

"I am afraid he is at risk," her husband agreed. "And so, I am taking every precaution."

"What's the mysterious project, that you're helpin' him with?"

Again, he was silent, and so she declared, "I'm countin' to ten, Michael."

Choosing his words carefully, he disclosed, "A CI is bringing him information to expose a major embezzlement scheme." He paused. "There are far-reaching implications."

But Doyle only frowned at him, as she thought this over. "But isn't that an everyday occurrence, for the Public Accounts people? That's their bread-and-butter, after all, to nose out people who've got their hand in the government till. Why's the poor man at risk, all of a sudden?"

He was silent, and the penny dropped, as she stared at him in astonishment. "Unless there are members of the Commission who are in on it."

There are a few corrupt members, it seems," Acton disclosed in an even tone, which was how he always disclosed cataclysmic things.

"Holy *Mother*," she breathed; "Is no one honest, anymore?"

"Howard is, as near as I can tell."

"Aye," she said, remembering that day when she'd first met the man, and informed Acton that—despite all appearances to the contrary—he was true-blue, and was being framed. "So—is he bein' framed-up, again?"

"I'm afraid I am not at liberty to say."

Her brow knit, Doyle stared out the windscreen, thinking over what he's said. "It's a bit disheartenin', to think that the people who are supposed to be the watchdogs are throwin' in with the wolves, Michael."

"It would not be the first time," he reminded her, and—with a reassuring gesture—took her hand. "Please don't worry; I am confident the matter will be resolved shortly." He paused, "I hope I don't have to remind you that you mustn't say anything to anyone about this."

"Right," she said. "I'm to button my lip."

"We are at a crucial juncture, and then we should be able to move forward in all safety."

Doyle made a wry mouth. "I hope so, Michael—poor Mary is a bit bewildered by it all, but thank God fastin' that she's a simple soul, and thinks Lizzie and Trenton are just hangin' around to be helpful. Not to mention she's past ready to have this baby, and there's been another hold-up with poor Gemma's adoption."

"So, I've heard. Only a temporary set-back, it seems."

"I hope so," she replied, but she said the words absently, as she gazed out the window and processed the rather alarming fact that—unless her wires were crossed, for some reason—she had the sudden feeling that it was Acton, himself, who was delaying the adoption. That made no sense a'tall, though—why would he do such a thing? Did Howard's troubles on the Commission impact the little girl's adoption, for some reason? It seemed unlikely—what would be the harm, if Gemma's adoption came through?

She thought this over, but came up empty—if Acton was indeed holding up the adoption, he'd have good reason, since he knew that it would put Mary's mind at ease about the little girl's future—and that his fair wife would be celebrating right alongside her. Mayhap some shirt-tail Russian relatives were making claims, and trying to extort some money out of him—

good luck to them, if this was the case; Acton was not one to be manipulated by anyone. Save herself, of course.

Her scalp prickled, and—tired of trying to figure it all out —Doyle decided to embark on a new topic. "Mary said Callie was watchin' Emile, yesterday. We'd best look lively; Savoie will jump through hoops for that little boyo, and if Emile decides he wants Callie at his house, Savoie will shovel massive amounts of money at her, and steal her away."

"She'd only benefit, from a bidding war," Acton pointed out.

Doyle teased, "Who has more money, you or Savoie?"

"I thought that money was not as important as people," Acton reminded her. "*A man's life does not consist in the abundance of his possessions.*"

"Faith; the devil's citin' scripture, again," Doyle declared. "All right, then; keep your secrets—not that it ever seems to work out, for you."

"Sometimes, it does," he defended himself, and Doyle duly noted that this was true.

They arrived home to participate in their usual ritual with the footman, Hudson and Reynolds, but before it could be enacted, Grady's dog skittered around the corner of the main building, going full tilt, and carrying a large bone in his mouth.

Upon sighting them, the dog slid to a halt on the gravel driveway, dropped his bone, and began barking at Doyle with wild abandon, crouching down on his haunches with his front legs straight out before him.

Acton immediately stepped between the dog and Doyle. "Down," he commanded, as he made a gesture with his hand, but the collie paid little attention, and kept barking furiously, apparently unimpressed with Acton's authority.

Quickly, Hudson ordered the footman to go over and secure the animal, but this turned out to be no easy task, as the dog easily eluded the man, barking madly as he ran in circles.

Into this chaotic scene, Grady came in at a full run. "Laddie! That'll do!"

The dog immediately flattened to the ground, and was silent.

Panting from exertion, Grady hurried over to grasp the dog's collar. "I'm that sorry, sir—I don't know what's got into him."

But Doyle was no longer thinking about the stupid dog, because she was peering around her husband at the bone that he'd dropped on the driveway. "Holy Mother, Michael," she breathed, "Isn't that—"

"A femur," he agreed.

CHAPTER 24

"Well, here's a wrinkle," Doyle remarked to Reynolds. They were looking through a window on the second story of the main house, watching as the local Coroner's team loaded the remains of Father Clarence into the waiting van. The body—or what was left of it—had been discovered in the Slough Field, after Grady had sent Laddie off to show them where he'd found the bone.

"It is so very distressing, madam," Reynolds observed with some consternation. "To think that no one realized he was dead, so that his remains were left as carrion for the animals." He shuddered delicately.

But Doyle only shrugged. "Not so unusual—a lot of times that's how we find a body on the Heath; the local dogs start draggin' the bones in. It will be interestin' to see what the Coroner says—although I suppose it's not much of a mystery. Grady himself was sayin' that a man of Father Clarence's heft shouldn't be trompin' about in the far field, so I imagine it was a heart attack, that did him in."

"His poor family," remarked Reynolds. "Perhaps they will be spared the particulars."

"Acton will handle it, I imagine. Father Clarence's family's not in the area, so we'll have to track them down, where ever they are. I know he's got a mother, livin' somewhere up north."

As she watched Acton and the Coroner speak together for a moment, Doyle's eye was caught by a slight movement amongst the trees. "There's Melinda," she remarked. "Come to see what the fuss is about." The woman was standing on the pathway to the Dower House, her hands in her pockets, as she watched the proceedings from a small distance. "Mayhap she was supposed to have a lesson, today."

"How very distressing, for all concerned."

Doyle decided not to mention that Melinda didn't seem half as distressed as Reynolds, and so instead, she watched as Melinda lowered her head, and then continued on her way toward the front gates.

"Do we know how long he—he's been deceased, madam?"

Doyle offered, "From the looks of it, he's been dead a few days. Last I spoke to him, he was makin' ready to map-out the Slough Field, and it must have happened shortly after. A shame, but it's one of those happenstance things—no one would be lookin' for him to return at any particular time, and so no one would realize he hadn't come back."

The Coroner's van drove away, and as Doyle watched Melinda step aside so as to allow the vehicle to pass, she thought; Melinda reminds me of someone—the way she walks—but I can't think of who. Lizzie Mathis, mayhap? Funny, that I've never noticed, before.

"In light of these events, madam, do you still plan to travel to Wexton Prison tomorrow?"

With a small smile, she glanced over at him. "I do indeed, my friend. You're forgettin' that decayin' bodies are a penny a pound, to people like Acton and me."

The servant nodded briskly. "Lord Acton has asked that I accompany you into your classroom, madam."

"Why's that?" she asked in surprise. "Won't he be comin', tomorrow?"

"I believe he plans to accompany you, madam. But I imagine he wishes to take extra precautions, since Trenton is not available."

"Aye, then—the more, the merrier," said Doyle, and kept her thoughts to herself since Reynolds—one would think—would be the last person her husband would assign to bodyguard duties. I wonder what my wily husband is up to, she thought; I imagine I will find out, and hopefully sooner, rather than later.

Thinking on this, she advised, "You can't tell the prisoners that you're my butler—they'd have a field day. We'll say you're my assistant, or somethin'. Or mayhap you're comin' in to observe, so as to set up your own program, in another prison."

"Very well. I will be as unobtrusive as possible, madam."

Below, Acton turned to re-enter the house, and Doyle said, "Let's go down to see what's what; I'm dyin' to find out."

"As you wish, madam."

Doyle found her husband giving Hudson an update, and, after seeing her entry, he readily broke off the conversation to walk over to join her.

"What do we know?" she asked, all agog.

"Very little, as yet. No sign of trauma. Two days, is the guess."

Doyle nodded. "Aye—As a matter of fact, I think I was the last to speak with him, just before he went out there."

"Is that so? Any observations?"

Doyle cast her mind back. "He was sweatin' up a storm, even though it was cold, but I put it down to his weight, and the fact he was trompin' about the property like a cow in a cornfield—very happy to be doin' it, I might add. Didn't seem distressed in any way."

"Short of breath?"

Slowly, she shook her head. "No. He was talkin' and talkin', the way he does."

Acton nodded. "I've requested a tox screen, just to be thorough, but it does look to be death by natural causes."

She teased, "A shame, that no one will ever see his report on those Lambcaster people who lived here. I'm sure it would have been spellbindin'."

"I would have read it," he protested.

"Well if you need to know anythin', I could probably tell you, although much of it would make your hair curl. A slateful of ruthless people, with a long history of bein' ruthless." She paused, much struck. "Never mind—you'd all be peas in a pod, and so it wouldn't make your hair curl, in the least."

Understandably, Acton turned the subject, since he didn't much like talking about the ghosts who consorted with his mad wife. "I understand you have requested that the Rousseau be installed in the dining room."

"Well yes; I'll have you know I'm a huge admirer of his," she teased.

With a tilt of his head, he offered, "I must warn you that it was placed in storage, because there is some question as to its authenticity."

"Oh, it's not authentic, my friend, but it's more to my taste, which is the only thing that's important, here."

He frowned slightly. "I wasn't aware you'd seen it," he admitted.

"It has fields of flowers," she pronounced, sidestepping a direct answer. "Much more my speed."

He gave her a look, because he knew that he wasn't hearing the full story, and he was also aware that this was probably just as well. "By all means, then."

With a fond smile, she twined her arm around his, even though the servants could easily observe this unseemly display of affection. "Don't tell your mother it's a fake, though. And while you're at it, give her the boat one, with my compliments."

CHAPTER 25

That night, the ghost made another appearance, which was something of a relief to Doyle, since she felt as though she were floating along in a confused sea of protection-hedges and dead priests.

"You were right," she said immediately. "He's movin' the chess pieces with a vengeance, although he doesn't want me to know the true reason."

"Oh—oh, yes," the ghost agreed, as he tried to focus his attention on her. "Keep at it."

"You told me about goin' to Leadenhall," she reminded him. "Is that important? Who lives in Leadenhall?"

He twisted his mouth. "No one. That's rather the point."

Puzzled, Doyle regarded him a bit impatiently. "I don't understand, and it would be mighty helpful if you'd pull yourself together, and try to focus for two seconds at a time."

"His hands are tied. He made a promise, once."

Incredulous, Doyle stared at him. "Are we speakin' of *Acton's* hands bein' tied?"

He chuckled, at her reaction. "You are amazed."

Completely bewildered, she asked, "But—but what did he promise, and to who?"

"Whom," the ghost corrected.

"What*ever*," she retorted crossly. "Was it a promise to me?"

The ghost shook his head. "Oh; oh, no—you are in no need of any promises. He's dedicated to you."

"I suppose that's a good point," she agreed. "Is it Melinda?"

The ghost shook his head. "Oh no—he's annoyed with her; she can't help intruding."

Doyle frowned. "Aye—he wants her to stay away."

As the ghost seemed disinclined to offer anything more—honestly, sending an opium-addicted ne'er-do-well seemed a strategic mistake—Doyle thought about it for a moment, and then made another guess. "Did Acton make a promise to Howard? Is that why he's buildin' his hedge of protection around him?"

This ghost didn't seem to be paying attention, and—after a moment's reflection—Doyle decided, "No—I don't think that's it. I've never had the impression that Acton was tight-as-a-tick with Howard, so as to be makin' him promises. Although if Howard's got a whistleblower who's blowin' the whistle on some high-level corruption, that's always a dicey situation; mayhap Acton promised his protection, as long as Howard came forward."

Again, she paused, since this also seemed unlikely. Acton was not about to put his honor on the line to help ferret-out political corruption; instead, it was much more likely that he'd seize the chance to divert a portion of the corruption-money into his own coffers, and think it a job well done. The

House of Acton wasn't going to align with any particular political power, unless and until it suited their own ends; it had been that way for centuries, and wasn't going to change anytime soon. But for some reason, Acton was helping Howard with his project, and that project seemed to be about ferreting-out the corrupt members on the Public Accounts Commission.

In fact, this might raise another possibility, so as to make some sense from these seemingly random occurrences, and she lifted her gaze to the ghost's. "Is Acton tryin' to protect the whistleblower?"

With a small chuckle, the ghost smiled. "No. You are the one who is protecting the whistleblower."

She stared at him in abject surprise. "*I* am? You're hittin' the pipe again, I think—I don't know anythin' about anythin'."

The ghost nodded. "Exactly. And he's hoping to keep it that way."

A bit crossly, Doyle retorted, "Well, so are you, I might mention. A bit more information would be very helpful."

He shrugged. "It can't come from me, though."

Reluctantly, Doyle had to acknowledge the truth of this. "Aye. He doesn't like it, when I know the things I know from the ghosts—it made him that uneasy, when I told him about your fake painting. I suppose it's all a bit too barkin' mad, even for him—and since he's a bit barkin' mad, himself, that's truly sayin' somethin'." She paused, and then noted in wonder, "It truly is like that play, with the ghosts, and everyone drivin' each other mad."

"Very true. But there is always a method, to his madness."

She thought this over. "It's me, isn't it? I'm the method."

"Exactly. You're his lodestar; in this, and in everything."

Since Doyle wasn't certain what was meant, she made no response.

The ghost sighed, and gazed rather petulantly out into the distance. "I wish I'd been someone's lodestar. It's not easy, being a by-blow—it all seems so unfair. You tend to rebel, which is why I pilfered the axe." He glanced up. "Don't forget about it."

She groused, "Mother a' Mercy, but that seems like the last thing I should be worryin' about. It's not like it's somethin' I'd have much use for."

But she was suddenly awake, and staring at the canopy that stretched out over the bed.

CHAPTER 26

The next morning, they were assembled in the front foyer, waiting for the car to be brought 'round so as to make the drive to Wexton Prison. Acton motioned to Hudson, and informed him that the Coroner would make a visit later that day, but in the meantime, no one else should be allowed on the premises, and no information should be shared until the Coroner made his report.

Doyle took this opportunity to ask Reynolds in an aside, "What's a 'lodestar', Reynolds?"

The butler raised his brows. "Polaris, madam."

"Not a clue. Speak English, please."

He amended, "Polaris is considered a lodestar, because it is very close to the north celestial pole."

Reading her silence aright, he hastily added, "A lodestar is a star that helped ships navigate, madam—before modern electronics. At night, sailors charted their course by observing certain stars in the sky."

She frowned slightly, as she thought this over. "A lodestar is a guiding star, then."

"Yes, madam."

Skeptical, she mused, "I'm not sure I'm doin' much guidin', though. More like I'm hangin' on to his coattails, and the devil take the hindmost."

Reynolds raised his brows. "I beg your pardon, madam?"

"Never you mind, my friend. Just thinkin' aloud."

Callie came forward to take Edward, and it was on the tip of Doyle's tongue to mention the girl's visit to London, but at the last minute, she refrained. The last needful thing was to make poor Callie feel that she had no privacy, and—after all —she may not want it known that she was helping Savoie with Emile, so as to earn some extra dosh on the side.

"Have we found the 'object' yet?" Doyle asked the girl, in an undertone. They'd experienced a Code-One emergency, yesterday, when Edward's favorite dinosaur toy went missing. Attempts to give him a substitute at bedtime were only semi-successful, and so the servants had been directed to scour the house for it.

Callie smiled. "You're going to laugh, Lady Acton, but Mr. Grady said that his dog brought it in. Edward must have dropped it outside."

"That *is* funny, and quite a change from the last thing the wretched dog fetched-in. Was our poor dinosaur the worse for wear?"

"No—he's in the wash, now, and should be good as new."

Acton signaled that he was ready to leave, and as they drove to the prison with Reynolds in the back seat, there wasn't much conversation in the car, because Acton didn't like to have personal conversations in front of the servants— it was one of those "nob" things. But Doyle didn't mind the silence, because she needed to think over what the ghost had said, and to try to make some sense of it.

She wasn't making any progress on the jade axe, but she hadn't a clue where to start—and the ghost wasn't being very helpful, because he'd said that he would have a hard time finding it, now. But Acton said that not much had changed at Trestles, since the ghost had been living there with Bertie, and so this all made little sense. The stupid ghost kept bringing it up, though, and so mayhap later today, she should walk the grounds with Edward, and try to come up with ideas— mental note.

It was ironic, truly; the poor ghost died in prison, because he wasn't given the opportunity to retrieve the valuable treasure that he'd hidden to prevent just such a fate. Of course, he shouldn't have stolen it, to begin with—not to mention that if he'd sold it, he probably would have used the proceeds to buy more opium. It was all very complicated, to determine who was the villain in his tale, and so Doyle decided she'd best stick with what the Parable taught, and not even try to make the attempt.

And then there was the promise. Acton had made a promise to someone other than his fair wife, and that promise was making things difficult for him. Melinda seemed to be the obvious candidate, but the ghost said it wasn't Melinda— Acton was annoyed with Melinda. Since Acton was not about to make any promises to his mother or Sir Stephen, she was therefore stymied—who would have such a hold over him, so that he couldn't hale off and do whatever he wished, which was his standard operating procedure?

After deciding that—yet again—she needed more information, she moved to ghost-topic number three, which was that—apparently—the fair Doyle was protecting

Howard's Public Accounts Commission whistleblower. This seemed a bit fantastic; she wasn't protecting anyone, just now —they were on holiday, and locked away in the seventeenth —eighteenth?—century. Her only charge was Edward, but since Edward was not yet aware of what money was, in the first place, she could probably rule him out as a whistleblower.

Frowning out the window, she was wondering whether a ghost could still be suffering from the effects of opium, when Acton glanced into the rear-view mirror to address Reynolds. "We should offer to hold a funeral for Father Clarence, once we have the family's contact information. I imagine they will want the remains transported to his home town, but please make the offer, nonetheless."

"Very good, sir."

"If you would arrange for a Rosary, at the appropriate church, and send a wreath, along with a letter of condolence."

"Yes, sir."

"Don't mention the dog's chewin' his bones," Doyle warned.

"Certainly not, madam." There was a pause. "Have we any personal anecdotes, that I might include?"

There was a small silence, as Doyle struggled to come up with something complimentary. "Well, he liked to talk about history—very dedicated, he was." She quirked her mouth. "I suppose we can't really say that he was equally dedicated to never missin' a meal."

As Reynolds could not approve of disrespecting the dead, he smoothly offered, "Perhaps we could say he was a good man, and dedicated to his calling."

"Yes," Acton agreed, but Doyle didn't say anything, because she'd gained the impression that Father Clarence wasn't necessarily dedicated to his calling—he seemed a weak reed, to her, and not at all cut from the same cloth as Father John, or the other stouthearted clergy she'd known. Faith, he couldn't hold a candle even to a layperson like Martina Betancourt, who was the opposite of a weak reed—whatever that was. A mighty oak, mayhap.

Her scalp prickled, and she frowned, wondering why it would. Martina was indeed a mighty oak, but—like the Prophet had said—it only took a clap of thunder and a bolt of lightning, to leave her a shattered wreck. Her husband had wronged her, and she'd come undone from her grounding tethers, as a result.

Oh, she thought; suddenly stilling. Oh—wait a minute—wait just a blessed minute; could Martina be the whistleblower? That would make perfect sense, of course, and Doyle wondered why it hadn't occurred to her before now, since it would be very much in keeping with the young woman's past record—after all, she used to roam the earth, taking down the enemies of the Church. And if she'd discovered that the prison people were skimming money from the Ministry, it only stood to reason that she'd step up, and blow the whistle on them. Faith, it would explain why she carried a jammer—it would explain everything. And mayhap Mary wasn't mistaken, when she'd said she'd seen Martina walking about at the park—mayhap she'd been smuggled-out, so as to speak to the authorities.

I'm a crackin' knocker, not to have put two and two together, Doyle thought, a bit disgusted with herself. And it just goes to show how rusty my detective-brain has got, what with all the stupid peacefulness at Trestles.

It was on the tip of her tongue to say something to Acton about it, but she decided he'd not appreciate her broaching the subject in front of Reynolds. And I have to have a care, she reminded herself; I can't say the wrong thing to Martina, and put her in even more jeopardy than she already is.

This, of course, was a valid concern, in that Doyle had a lengthy history of acting on impulse—often with disastrous results. Or, not really *disastrous* results; more like dangerous results that tended to turn her poor husband's hair grey. In point of fact, her impulsive acts tended to save the day, more often than not, but this time, it seemed that heroics wouldn't be necessary, and that—between Acton and Martina—all was well in hand.

Smiling to herself, she continued to gaze out the window during the silent car ride. One less thing to worry about, then.

CHAPTER 27

They'd arrived at the prison, and Doyle only nodded in understanding when yet again, Acton expressed his preference to stay in the car, and take the opportunity to work on his caseload. Now that she'd had her epiphany about Martina, Doyle surmised that he was probably monitoring the woman through surveillance, as she interacted with the various blacklegs that infested the prison. Or he was monitoring either one of the Wardens—take your pick—and he needed to be within a certain perimeter, for the surveillance to be picked up.

Struck with the thought, she realized that yet another mystery was solved; Acton had—uncharacteristically, for him —agreed that she should sally forth into the bowels of Wexton Prison to teach this class, despite the fact he wanted her to recuperate at Trestles. Now she knew why he'd done so—he was in need of an excuse to lurk in the parking lot, and monitor his surveillance. Faith, he'd probably asked Martina to throw out Doyle's name to Dr. Okafor, so as to set the whole scheme in motion—she'd been dim indeed, not to have realized it, before.

The only odd thing, really, was why he didn't want the wife of his bosom to know what was afoot; none of this was much of a surprise, truly, and it wasn't like he didn't trust her to team-up with him on a take-down. Of course, this one was different—she doubted that an official case-file would ever be opened, if Acton was worried about repercussions. Instead, he'd do his usual sleight-of-hand to keep it well-away from public consumption, if he felt the bad publicity might wind up hurting the Ministry.

Although—although, in point of fact, he wasn't doing his usual sleight-of-hand. This was definitely not his usual style, what with coming in through the gates in his fancy Range Rover, so as to skulk about in the parking lot, with the guard at the guard-gate fully aware that he was here. Usually, Acton was smooth-as-silk, and this set-up seemed a bit clumsy— almost like an over-the-top James Bond movie, in truth. Hopefully, her husband wasn't losing his usual deft touch.

As Reynolds accompanied her to the entry, Doyle decided to help Acton's cause by airily explaining, "Acton doesn't like to come inside, when I come to teach. Everyone fusses, and he doesn't abide fussin' very well."

"Yes, madam," said Reynolds, in the tone of one who was well-aware of this fact.

"The prisoners tend to be a bit bawdy," Doyle warned. "Be ready to plug your ears."

"I will sit at the back, madam, and observe quietly," Reynolds assured her.

They were escorted to the Ministry Office, and Doyle saw that both the DCS and Dr. Okafor were within, on this occasion.

"DS Doyle," her former commanding officer greeted her, as he offered his hand with a smile. "I must say you bring back memories, and not necessarily tranquil ones."

This was true; when last they'd met, they'd been ducking flash-bangs in the prison stairwell—not a tranquil memory, at all.

"Not to worry, sir; I'm goin' to stay well-away from this place, when my due-date approaches—I don't want to be temptin' fate."

Despite her teasing words, she was privately a bit alarmed; the DCS looked haggard, and worn to a thread. It seemed to be a trend—who else had done? Oh—Howard, too; another man who seemed to have aged mightily, in a short space of time.

Dr. Okafor, on the other hand, exuded the same tranquil good nature she always did. "Hallo Kathleen; your lesson today will be the Parable of the Good Samaritan."

"Well, there's a relief; I was tellin' Reynolds, here, that the prisoners tend to be a bit bawdy, but they'll be hard-pressed to find a sex-joke, in that one."

"Don't underestimate them," the DCS joked with a smile, but Doyle could see that his heart wasn't in it, and that he was distracted.

Dr. Okafor said, "Martina would like to assist you again, Kathleen, if that is all right."

Doyle nodded, fully expecting this, now that she'd realized Martina was the whistleblower. Mayhap the young woman would try to give some hint of her role to Doyle, or try to pass along a message for Acton—although she hadn't made such an attempt last time, so mayhap not. Operational security was paramount, when a whistleblower was gathering evidence, because oftentimes they risked their lives. And in this case, they'd already seen how ruthless the players were; Harrison had gabbled too much, and then had been dispatched without a moment's hesitation.

Dr. Okafor added, "I will probably not be available, after your class; I have a meeting with the prison's Personnel Board." She glanced toward the DCS. "If you would hear Kathleen's report, please."

"I would rather attend the meeting," the DCS said, in an even tone.

"No," she replied, and did not look at him.

What's this? thought Doyle in surprise. How strange to see these two at odds—although they were very polite-odds, to be sure. And the DCS was emanating some sort of strong emotion, beneath his politeness.

Perhaps realizing that she'd been a bit brusque, Dr. Okafor turned to the DCS, as she and Doyle headed out the door. "Thank you," she said softly.

He met her eyes, but did not respond, and as the security door swung shut behind them, Doyle made a mighty effort to hide her astonishment; they were in love, these two—the very air between them nearly resonated with it. How perfect, and how wonderful—and what an unbelievable road they'd each taken, to wind up here, in this dingy little bullet-strafed office, so as to find the other.

Humbled yet again by the amazing power of love—that always found its own way, and always would—Doyle followed Dr. Okafor in bemusement, and decided that this turn of events served as an excellent reminder that perhaps the universe was unfolding according to plan, despite how it seemed, sometimes.

They arrived at the cafeteria, and found that Martina was already waiting, and ready for Doyle. With a show of surprise, she said, "Why, Mr. Reynolds; how nice to see you again."

Since the last time the two had met was at a thoroughly forgettable dinner party—not to mention there'd been a lot of rough water under the bridge, since then—Doyle could only admire Reynolds' polite mask, as he returned the woman's greeting; it was something they must teach in butler-school, and Doyle could stand a few lessons, herself, being as she'd never got the hang of the polite-mask. And it also made her hastily revise the tale she'd would give for his presence, here, since Martina was well-aware Reynolds was no volunteer from another ministry.

And so, as the prisoners began to file in, Doyle gestured toward her companion and simply explained, "Mr. Reynolds is here to take notes—"

But she paused, because Charbonneau had halted, and was standing stock-still, staring with an expressionless face at the butler, as she emanated waves of extreme alarm.

"We meet again," Reynolds said, with a polite little nod. "How are you, Ms. Charbonneau?"

CHAPTER 28

*N*aturally, Doyle was now so distracted that she'd a hard time concentrating on the lesson. It didn't take a genius, to figure out that Reynolds must have been sent along into the classroom for just this reason—to shake-up Charbonneau—but yet again, Doyle was at a loss to understand why. Her wily husband seemed to be moving the chess pieces, yet again, but for some reason he didn't want to give the wife of his bosom any kind of hint, about what was unfolding.

It seemed clear that this was some sort of a shot across the bow—especially since Doyle had expressed her concerns about the CI's questionable loyalties—but Doyle had no idea what it meant. And how would Reynolds—of all people— know Charbonneau? And why would the woman be so thoroughly alarmed by his presence, here?

"I believe the lesson today is about The Parable of the Good Samaritan," Martina prompted.

"Yes," said Doyle, thus recalled to her duties. "It's a story about how we're supposed to help each other—all of us, without worryin' about whether we're too important, or not from the same background."

Smythe offered thoughtfully, "So; it's a lot like the older son—in that Parable about the two brothers."

Doyle managed to hide her surprise that Smythe had come up with this insight. "Why, yes; that's a good point. A lot of the Parables seem to have similar themes."

Tentatively, Marcelin raised her hand. "If you please, what is an 'ass'?"

"My ex-husband," a woman loudly announced. "Born and bred."

After everyone had laughed, Doyle explained, "An ass like a donkey, I think."

Smythe riposted, "Let's hope so; otherwise to say he 'loaded him up on his ass' would be a bit too saucy, for a Bible story."

And here we go, thought Doyle, with resignation.

The other prisoners howled in appreciation, and then another added, "Well, the robbers had already stripped 'im, so he was primed, and ready."

Trying to make her voice heard above the din, Doyle called out, "I think we need to get back on track."

"You mustn't make light of the Parables; it is sacrilegious," Martina scolded.

"Stuff it, Betancourt," Charbonneau retorted. "Who put you in charge?"

Oh, thought Doyle; oh—she's playacting, again; pretending that she's angry with Martina. And now it makes sense, in a way; it must mean that Charbonneau is assisting

Martina in the whistleblowing, in which case I have to revise my opinion of the miserable woman—she must not be such a bad 'un, after all.

"Miss High-and-Mighty," sniffed Smythe in agreement, as she gave Martina the side-eye.

"Everyone needs to settle down," Doyle announced, in her best police-officer voice. "We're not learnin' much from this lesson, if we're so rude to each other."

"Right, then; sorry," said Charbonneau to Martina, with a barely-concealed smirk.

"Yeah—sorry," Smythe agreed, grudgingly. "I'm not supposed to judge, I guess."

Holy Mother; some of this is sinking in, thought Doyle in amazement. She then instructed briskly, "Let's go about the room, then, and take turns readin' the verses."

This had the desired effect of quieting everyone down, and the rest of the class went without disruption—which was just as well, since Doyle was itching to buttonhole Reynolds, and extract some answers from him.

Therefore, as soon as the class was over, Doyle quickly thanked Martina for her help, and then turned to walk down the hallway with Reynolds, glancing around to make certain no one was within earshot.

"How do you know Charbonneau?" she asked, in an undertone.

"A chance acquaintance, madam," the servant explained carefully. "I cannot recall, precisely."

As this was not true, Doyle grimly warned, "I'm countin' to ten, my friend."

Reynolds pressed his lips together for a moment, and then admitted, "I have been asked not to say, madam."

"I'll bet." She remembered what Acton had said, about how she was second in the pecking-order, in terms of who Reynolds obeyed, but she decided to persevere, nonetheless. "Unsnabble, if you will, Reynolds; I've a feelin' it may be important—somethin's afoot, and it seems passin' strange that I've been left out of the loop."

"I assure you, madam, there is no need for concern. I am afraid I can say no more."

Doyle lowered her voice yet further. "Is Charbonneau another whistleblower, then? Are we tryin' to protect her, somehow?" This was a bit hard to reconcile, though, because —whilst the ghost had said that the fair Doyle was protecting the whistleblower—there was no question that Charbonneau had been mighty unhappy to behold Reynolds, standing before her. It all made little sense—mayhap the woman was worried that Reynolds' presence would blow her cover as a CI, for some reason.

But her thoughts were interrupted when Reynolds surreptitiously touched her hand. This was unexpected, as Reynolds would rather be tortured than presume to touch her hand, and—surprised—she glanced down to see that he'd a note, cupped within his own hand, and he turned over, briefly, so that she could read it. The note said, *There is a listening device sewn into my cuff.*

Only momentarily taken aback, Doyle pulled herself together, and continued in a scolding tone, "Don't think I'm not goin' to get to the bottom of this, my friend. If you don't tell me, I'll presume the worst, and suspect that you're havin' a jailhouse affair with the wretched woman."

Thoroughly disapproving, Reynolds replied in frosty tones, "I can assure you, madam, that such is not the case—"

"Spare me your disapproval; I'm the one who's been kept in the dark, who's been sent like a lamb into a den of thieves—"

"I believe you mean a lamb amongst wolves, madam—"

"And you're the head vulture, in the nest."

"I believe you mean viper, madam—"

She paused, mid-stride, and pressed her palms to her eyes. "Reynolds," she warned in an ominous tone; "Stop it."

"Very well, madam." This, however, was said in the tone of one who did not truly feel that he had transgressed.

After turning-in the class materials to an empty office—the DCS had apparently forgot he was supposed to hear her report—they left by way of the Security Desk, and stepped out the front doors.

As Doyle watched Acton come 'round to pick them up—all calm, and innocent-like—Doyle decided that she was plenty ready to give him what-for, and find out why he'd set Reynolds to spying on her. Although, to be fair, it was unlikely that Reynolds was spying on *her*, of course; instead he was acting as a surveillance post for her husband. Not to mention that she probably shouldn't let on that Reynolds had come clean about the listening device; Acton lived and breathed his stupid hierarchy-world, and he'd probably fire poor Reynolds on the spot. Or slay him; either-or.

Nevertheless, she was itching to read her husband the riot act, and let him know she didn't appreciate being blindsided, but unfortunately, they'd Reynolds as a witness, and no doubt Acton would be aghast, if she went after him, hammer and tongs, in front of a servant. Small wonder all these aristocrat-types were so neurotic, when they were constantly surrounded by witnesses, and couldn't just stomp about and throw things, when the occasion warranted—another point to the Irish, when all was said and done.

Therefore, as they drove along the main highway, she remarked in a deceptively light tone, "You know, Michael, we don't ever take nice, long, walk-abouts, like we used to."

Her husband was understandably surprised, since Doyle avoided long walk-abouts like the plague. "Oh?"

"Aye; remember when we took such a nice walk together, along the Embankment? It was during the park-murders case."

"I do," Doyle's husband replied, as well he should, since that particular walk-about featured Doyle giving him a righteous bear-garden jawing, for keeping important information from her.

In the same fond, nostalgic tone, she continued, "And that other time—remember? When we were takin' a walk-about at the Art Museum. Such a lovely memory, it was."

"Quite," Acton replied, now hiding his amusement, because at the time, she'd been a hair's-breadth away from crashing a chair down over his head.

As though suddenly struck with the thought, she turned her head to him. "You know, mayhap we can take a nice walk-about today, soon as we get home."

"Can Edward come?" he asked, hoping for a reprieve.

"No." She turned to Reynolds, and said in her best Countess-voice, "If you would mind Edward for us, Reynolds?"

"Certainly, madam," said Reynolds, in a wooden tone.

So that the butler would know he wasn't off the hook, either, she added, "Have we any more Ming-bowls? Or have they all been broken?"

"There are several pieces in storage," Acton admitted. "Under lock and key."

"Good. Best keep them away from me."

Her husband returned no reply, and the remainder of the drive was made in silence.

CHAPTER 29

To Hudson's great surprise, rather than follow their usual ceremony of coat-taking before being formally escorted into the dining room for lunch, Acton expressed his desire to postpone the meal, so that he could take a walk around the grounds with Lady Acton.

The estimable Steward was not one to question his betters, and so he merely bowed his head, and asked the footman to relinquish his umbrella, since it was starting to rain with a vengeance.

"You don't have your wellies," Acton noted, as he and Doyle took off together down the pathway. He put his arm around her to draw her close, under the umbrella. "How far will we be going?"

"The Slough Field," she replied, with a great deal of meaning.

"You'll never get away with it," he warned. "Reynolds will testify we were quarreling in the car."

She made a wry mouth. "So; you think Reynolds would grass on me?"

"I'm sure he would regret it, but grass he would."

She decided that she wouldn't press the point any further —poor Acton didn't know how many times Reynolds had already upset the hierarchy apple-cart—and so she turned to the subject at hand. "I'm not one of your chess pieces, my friend. You will tell me what's goin' on, and immediately."

He tilted his head in apology. "It is a personal matter, I'm afraid."

She glanced up at him in surprise. "So personal that you can't tell *me*, Michael?"

"Yes," he said, and it was the truth.

Frowning, she ventured, "Is Charbonneau a former light o' love, or somethin'?"

He was amused by the very idea. "No, she is not."

"Are you protectin' her? Are you protectin' Martina?"

Interestingly enough, he didn't answer immediately. "In a way, I suppose I am."

Crossly, she said, "I don't fancy playin' twenty-questions with you, Michael."

He pulled her to him, so as to kiss her temple. "I am sorry, Kathleen. I can say no more."

"Tell me this, then; is this a sanctioned case?"

"No," he readily admitted. "It is off-the-books."

This was not a surprise; the fact that he'd sent his wife into the prison—and his butler, too—was a fairly obvious indication that this operation was not something the Met knew anything about. And if it had to do with the embezzling rig at the Prison Ministry—which it surely must do—he'd already indicated that he wanted to spare the DCS the bad publicity. But, why couldn't he just tell her, what was going forward? He well-knew that his wife was exasperated about being kept in the dark—what was so important, that he risked her righteous ire? It was as the ghost had said; Acton was moving the chess pieces with a vengeance, but he was necessarily moving them around his wife, for some reason.

He's sparing me, she decided, as they trudged along in silence, with the rain sluicing from the edges of the umbrella. Because that's what he always does—especially now, when I'm supposed to be recuperating. But this seems a very strange method of "sparing" me—to herd me into the prison like a clueless sheep, sent in amongst the wolves.

Suddenly, her brow cleared. "I'd a listenin' device on me, didn't I? When I taught that first class. And you were in the parkin' lot, monitorin' it."

"Yes," he admitted.

She quirked her mouth. "So, the button you gave me was just a plain old button, and not a jammer at all."

"Yes."

Frowning again, she thought about it, as the pond came into view. "But then, Martina threw a wrench, because she'd a jammer, and so you had to create another listening post, in the form of Reynolds."

"Yes," he agreed. "I am sorry I could not tell you, Kathleen."

She found she couldn't be angry at him, and instead she slowly shook her head in wonderment. "Mother a' Mercy, but you didn't do this lightly, my friend."

"No."

Utterly perplexed, she contemplated the ground ahead of them, as a rumble of thunder could be heard, and the wind made the water ripple on the surface of the pond. He'd made a promise, the ghost had said. And apparently, that promise was something she couldn't know—and not only could she not know of it, but it took priority even over his beloved wife, who served as the center of his universe.

Abruptly, she decided that this made no sense a'tall, and that obviously, she was missing an important piece to this puzzle. There was no possible way that Acton would promise anything to anyone on earth, at the expense of his wife's safety.

On the other hand, she'd the sure sense—courtesy of the fact that a ghost was haunting her dreams—that there was something here that she needed to pay attention to. It was all so very complicated—although it was Acton, so when was it ever *not* complicated?—but she'd the feeling that she'd best figure it out, and soon.

Slowly, she ventured, "I trust you, Michael—truly, I do—but I'm wonderin' if there's somethin' here that you're missin'."

Since Acton greatly respected her intuition, this gave him pause, as he bent his head to hers. "How so, Kathleen?"

She made a sound of frustration. "I don't know—I wish I did. I only know that I am mighty uneasy, about all of this."

"I will roll it up, very soon," he assured her.

She nodded, relieved. "Just be careful."

His mobile pinged, and—since it had to be important, to interrupt the lord and lady's walk-about—Acton glanced at the message. "Hudson says the Coroner is here, to turn over the autopsy report on Father Clarence. There's no hurry to return—Hudson will see to it that he is made comfortable."

"No—we can turn back. I'm glad you've been semi-honest with me, Michael."

He squeezed her to his side in apology. "I'm sorry that semi-honest is the best I can do."

The storm, and the close presence of her handsome husband was stirring-up Doyle's hair-trigger hormones, and so she asked with some irritation, "Why's the Coroner here? Can't the man use the phone?

Acton tilted his head. "An invitation to Trestles is always appreciated."

She made a face. "Well, that's all kinds of cringey. Next, he'll be tuggin' at his cap, like Grady does."

But Acton only said mildly, "It never hurts, to cultivate the local authorities."

They headed back, and as Doyle contemplated the manor house, framed by the blowing trees, she remarked, "Shame on you, for spyin' on me; what if I'd made a run at the DCS, or somethin'? It would have served you right." Suddenly reminded, she lifted her face to his. "Oh—oh; here's a wrinkle; I think the DCS loves Dr. Okafor, and that the feeling is mutual."

"Is that so?" asked Acton in surprise. "I suppose that would explain a few things."

"Well, it makes it stranger still, that he doesn't want you to spring him out of prison. He can't pursue much of a relationship with her, whilst he's incarcerated, and she's staff."

"Very true," he agreed.

As they trudged along the sodden garden path, she made a wry mouth. "Poor Tim McGonigal—a step too slow, yet again—although his new Irishwoman sounds promisin'. And there's always our Callie, to bind up his wounded heart—although with his luck, I don't have high hopes."

"Nor do I," he agreed in a mild tone, and it was true.

CHAPTER 30

The Coroner rose to greet them, from his seat at the massive mahogany table, where he'd been partaking of tea and biscuits, courtesy of the ornate silver tea service.

"I am so sorry to have kept you waiting; may I offer more tea?" Acton asked, signaling to the servant.

"Oh, no—thank you very much. And I must say, these are lovely biscuits."

"Our cook makes excellent pastries," Acton admitted with a small smile, as he seated Doyle. "I confess I must pace myself."

The man laughed heartily. "Yes; I'd best not have any more, or I might propose marriage to your cook, sight unseen."

"You mustn't steal her away," Acton cautioned, with an amused glance at Doyle.

Will you look at this? Doyle thought, as she dutifully

smiled in return. It shames me, to see that everyone's got an inner bootlicker, when it comes to the wretched aristocracy.

Acton then sobered. "A sad unpleasantness," he offered, in a discreet prompt.

"Yes, sir." Recalled to business, the Coroner placed a hand on the manilla envelope that sat on the table. "The preliminary report is consistent with accidental death—heart seizure. We ran a tox screen, and nothing very unusual—I've brought you a copy."

"Thank you," said Acton, as he accepted the envelope. "I truly appreciate it."

"We contacted the fellow's Bishop—who was most distressed, of course—and he gave me his mother's information—Mrs. Madeline Clarence, a widow living in Yorkshire. They will rely on her local priest, to handle the notification."

Slowly, Acton raised his head, and Doyle could sense his sudden leap of interest. "May I have her contact information, also? My wife and I would like to express our deepest condolences."

"Certainly; quite right, of course." The man pulled up the information, and came around to share it with Acton.

Something's up, Doyle thought with some surprise, as she watched them. My husband's wheels are turning with a vengeance, and he doesn't like where they're leading him.

The Coroner thanked them profusely for the tea, and then renewed his thanks, when Acton asked the footman to see to it that any extra biscuits were packed, to send along home with him.

The door closed behind him, and Doyle was left in the quiet room with her husband, who clasped his hands behind his back, and gazed out the lead-paned windows.

"What's to do?" she ventured.

Slowly, he replied, "It seems that Father Clarence was connected to the Clarences, of Yorkshire."

A bit impatiently, Doyle crossed the room to stand beside him. "I'm not your mum, Michael—thank God fastin'—and so I've no idea why you're so wonderstruck by this. Who are the Clarences of Yorkshire?"

"A very wealthy Roman Catholic family, with roots that go back to the War of the Roses."

She lifted her brows, thoroughly surprised. "Oh. Well, that's of interest, and small wonder he was so interested in that time period. But that's neither here nor there, since there's no such thing as a rich priest, Michael—or at least, there shouldn't be," she corrected.

But Acton continued to gaze out the window, thinking mightily. With a sudden movement, he turned to pick up the envelope, and—after pulling out the tox report—he began to scan it, as though he was looking for something in particular.

Doyle held her tongue and watched him, until he suddenly paused, to lift his head and gaze out the windows again. "High levels of theobromine."

With a strong feeling of disquiet, she asked, "What's that, Michael?"

With a deliberate movement, he slid the report back into the envelope. "Theobromine is a toxic substance, found in certain kinds of chocolate. Under ordinary circumstances, it is difficult to consume enough to bring on death."

Doyle stared at him in surprise. "Death by chocolate? I'd no idea there was such a thing."

"Very rare," he advised.

Bewildered, Doyle ventured, "What does it mean, though? Tell me why you're all on-end."

He drew a long breath. "I would not be surprised if Father Clarence held a tidy fortune in trust. And I would not be surprised if his heir was recently changed to the Trestles Foundation."

She blinked in amazement. "Never say you've fallen into another fortune, Michael? Faith, but sometimes I think the universe is laughin' at me."

He turned his gaze toward her. "No—not I. You are forgetting that my mother is the trustee, for the Trestles Foundation."

The penny dropped, and Doyle stared at him in abject astonishment. "Holy *Mother*, Michael," she breathed. "*Holy Mother*, but there's a motive. D'you think they set it all up to kill him, your mother and Sir Stephen?

He tilted his head. "It would be very difficult to prove. The decedent was known for over-indulging in rich food, and he'd gained quite a bit of weight, in a relatively short amount of time."

"Holy *Mother*," she repeated in amazement. "So, your hands are tied?"

He turned to meet her eyes in surprise. My hands are never tied, Kathleen."

"Sorry; I forgot what's what, for a minute. What will you do? I imagine you'll not put 'em in the dock for murder—as much as you'd like to."

With a thoughtful nod, he agreed. "No; there would be a great deal of unpleasantness, if I were to make such an accusation, with so little evidence to back it up."

"Aye, that," she conceded. Poor Acton, she thought; a golden opportunity to roll-up his awful mother and cousin, but it would come at too great a cost.

As though coming to a decision, he dropped the envelope

on the table. "Nevertheless, I can bring pressure to bear. Perhaps hold a meeting, to discuss my grave concerns."

Doyle could only approve. "At the very least, they shouldn't get the money, Michael; we can't give the go-by to a murder in material gain—especially if it's your wretched relatives."

"Yes," he agreed, but he said it rather absently, and she could see that he was turning over strategies in his mind.

CHAPTER 31

"I'm worried he's goin' to go all medieval," Doyle said to the ghost, that night.

The ghost seemed to find this amusing. "Oh? And he hasn't, as yet?"

She explained, "It's just that he tends to get himself into trouble, when he does."

With a desultory gesture, the ghost bent to run a finger along the edge of a frayed cuff. "Bertie would get himself into trouble, but then he would just buy his way out, again. It gives you immunity, when you've so much money."

"It's exactly the same, nowadays," Doyle advised.

"Well, he knew how to spend it. He loved his light-skirts, loved his hunting-pack."

She sensed a certain bitterness, behind the words, and so offered gently, "He must have loved you, too. He wanted you here with him, at Trestles."

"He loved my paintings," the ghost agreed, in faint praise.

"At least, he didn't go off, and leave you to your own

devices." Fighting off her own stab of bitterness, Doyle added, "It's beyond me, how anyone can't cherish their own children."

"Even that Frenchman does," the ghost offered, with a hint of derision.

"You shouldn't be so prejudiced," Doyle scolded. There's a Parable about it."

He cocked an amused brow. "Tell that to the knight."

Doyle could only acknowledge the truth of this.. "No—he doesn't like Savoie very much, and positively hates it, when he's visitin' here. He holds a grudge against the French—something about a famous battle, way back when."

"Waterloo?" the ghost suggested.

Doyle gazed at him in surprise. "No; that's not it—that's a railway station, in London."

"Ah."

Recalled to their conversation, Doyle offered, "I know you feel that Bertie should have seen to it—seen to it that you were taken care of, after he died. I'm just not sure that havin' piles of money would have been the best thing for you." Belatedly, she realized, "Although dyin' in prison wasn't the best thing, either, I suppose."

But—in a bitter tone—the ghost informed her, "No—Bertie arranged for me to have a stipend, outside his will. But the heirs played me a trick—lured me to a meeting at Leadenhall, and then had me thrown right into the Fleet, from there."

Outraged, Doyle exclaimed, "Is that so? Why, that's a terrible trick to pull."

"I certainly thought so, at the time. I had the shakes, though—something terrible—and so I couldn't muster up much of a fight."

"I'm that sorry for it," Doyle replied, and—with a mighty effort—resisted the urge to say something judgmental.

With a sigh, the ghost absently fingered his cuff, again. "So am I."

Thoughtfully, she mused, "You know, nothin' much has changed, has it? Greedy relatives are still doin' their greedy thing, and the Slough Field is still turnin' up corpses."

"There is nothing new, under the sun." He paused, and then clarified, "Although, there's no hunting-pack, anymore."

Doyle knit her brow. "Well, no—and that's just as well. Although, there is the one dog."

The ghost glanced up at her. "The stableman lets him roam, at night."

"Does he?"

But Doyle found she was wide awake, and staring into the darkness of her bedroom. Of *course,* she thought; and you're a dimwit, indeed, not to have thought of it sooner.

CHAPTER 32

Slowly and carefully, Doyle slid out of bed. Her husband—ever the light sleeper— lifted his head. "All right?"

"Yes," she whispered, as she pulled on her robe. "I just have to get up—sorry to wake you." Fortunately, pregnancy provided an excellent excuse for having to get up at night, and so he lowered his head once again to his pillow. Hopefully, he'd go back to sleep, and wouldn't notice that she didn't go into what they referred to as the "retiring room," but instead slipped out the door, and into the hallway.

Once outside the room, she paused for a moment, getting used to the darkness and listening—there was a night watchman, who patrolled the halls—but she didn't hear anything, and so she crept in her slippered feet down the servant's stairs, and then carefully let herself out by way of the kitchen's back door—the hinges were well-oiled, so they didn't make a sound.

Once outside, she swiftly moved across the gardens toward the stables, the wet ground soaking through her slippers as she tried to remember whether anyone had ever shown her where the old dog kennels had stood. The ghost kept bringing up Bertie's hunting-pack, but there was no hunting-pack, anymore, because the kennels had burned down. That was the thing that had changed—Acton had burned the kennels down, years ago. The kennels, where Acton's horrific father had done his horrific deeds, until he'd received a full measure of medieval justice, in true Trestles-style.

So; the ghost must have hid the axe in the kennels, to be retrieved at a later date, only to be thwarted in this aim, and then—many years later—the building had been burned down, for good measure. It would be a wonder, if the axe had survived, but Doyle figured that the knight wouldn't be leaning on the poor ghost unless it was retrievable, and so retrieve it she would.

Briefly, she wondered why it would be so important to the knight; Reynolds had said they'd found more than one of these jade axes—in ordinary graves—and that the scholars weren't sure of their purpose.

She came to the edge of the garden, and then stood for a moment on the pathway that stretched toward the stables, trying to decide which direction to go. It stood to reason that the kennels would be out near the stables, but there was too much ground to cover, and she hadn't the faintest idea where to start.

And then, unexpectedly, Grady's dog appeared, illuminated by the moonlight, about fifty feet ahead of her. He paused, staring at her, and for once—thank God fastin'—not barking his fool head off.

"Where were the kennels?" she asked softly, and then, thinking she needed to be more specific, she added, "Fetch the axe."

The dog wheeled, and ran off, disappearing into the darkness, and she hurried along after him, as best she could on the uneven ground, wrapping her robe tighter around her as she went—it was cold, and heaven only knew what someone would think, if Acton's madwoman of a wife was caught wandering around the grounds in her night-clothes.

As she scanned the darkness ahead, trying to catch a glimpse of the dog, she thought about the dreams, and the ghost, and decided that there must be more to all of it than just this stupid jade axe, but she was at a loss as to what it was.

It all had to do with—with money, and promises, and—and opium, of all things—although how that factored-in was a mystery; the only person Doyle knew who'd been addicted to drugs was Officer Gabriel, and she was fairly certain that he was clean, now.

The subject of ancient feuds had come up, too, but the only ancient feuds she knew of tended to feature the Trestles ghosts, who'd feuded with nearly everyone they'd met—although the Trestles knight hated the French with good reason, because they'd been doing their best to kill him, once upon a time.

Although she was forgetting, of course, that the master-feuder was her own husband, the illustrious Chief Inspector, who'd decided—no doubt as a result of his experiences with his father—that he would embark on a bloody feud with London's underworld, so as to mete out a rough justice, Trestles-style, instead of by-the-book, like police officers were supposed to. He was a take-no-prisoners throwback to the old days, and it worried her, that he'd come a cropper, some day—that his very boldness would be his downfall.

The poor ghost was the opposite of bold, and no doubt Acton would have as little patience for the fellow as the Trestles knight did; to their way of thinking, any perceived weakness was to be scorned. For example, Acton would never in a million years walk into an ambush, like the poor ghost had done, and allow them to toss him into prison— faith, Acton would have razed the place to the ground, first.

Her scalp prickled, as she paused to peer into the darkness, having lost sight of the dog. What? she thought, a bit perplexed; Acton is a one-man vigilante force—or he was, before she'd come into his life, and tried to steer him toward a better path—and he tended to bend justice to suit his own notions. Which was not a good thing, but she may as well be whistling in the wind, to try and change that thousand-years mindset.

And, as a perfect example, one need look no further than the skimming rig at the prison; Acton wanted to handle it himself—he didn't want the Met to catch wind of it, because the publicity might hurt the DCS, and Acton owed the DCS a blood-debt; the man had helped save the fair Doyle's life, once upon a time. Not to mention that Martina Betancourt was a Doyle-friend-of-sorts, and if she was the whistleblower, then he'd feel obligated to protect her, too.

She paused to catch her breath, and suddenly found herself frowning into the darkness. Although—although, wait a minute; wait a blessed minute. Faith, she was forgetting something that made no sense; Acton had sent the fair Doyle in with a listening device, but Martina had a jammer—which she must have got from Acton, right? Where else would she have got one? If Acton was trying to listen-in to the villains, and Martina was the whistleblower, why would Martina have a jammer?

Perplexed, she lowered her head to contemplate the ground before her. Mayhap the jammer was so that Martina could hear or pass along information, without being overheard? After all, Acton had ventured into the prison, last time, when he'd tried to swing a commutation for the DCS. But it still didn't make much sense—even though he'd gone into the building, Doyle didn't see how he could manage to meet up with Martina, in the process. Acton had gone to meet the Men's Warden, on the men's side. Not to mention that—even if Acton could meet-up with Martina, somehow, he'd be the one to take care of any and all jammings, Martina didn't need to worry.

Oh, she realized, her brow clearing. Martina's jammer must be for when she needed to hear or pass along information from someone else, then—probably the DCS. Acton must have gone into the prison to have the DCS pass along his instructions to Martina—Martina would be in contact with the DCS on a regular basis, because she was working with the Ministry.

So; this all seemed to fit, and would explain why Martina had a jammer—problem solved.

Except—except there'd been one more thing; for some reason, Martina had implied that it was Acton, who was skimming money from the Ministry. She'd suggested that Doyle stay well-away, because her own husband was behind the scheme—although to be fair, she hadn't accused him in so many words.

But when Doyle had confronted Acton about Martina's

accusation, her husband said he was not involved in the rig, and it was true. And—even more strange—Acton hadn't used that opportunity to explain to her Martina's role as a whistleblower, which you'd think he would have. Instead, he'd said nothing. Instead, he'd sent-in Reynolds, as another listening post. Reynolds, who'd always been careful to stay a fair distance away from Martina, and her jammer.

"Martina," she breathed aloud, in abject dismay. Could Martina be one of the villains, in this mess? It would explain why Acton wanted to leave Doyle in the dark—she and Martina were friends. Faith; Doyle had even saved the woman from Acton's tender mercies, which was why she now serving such a soft sentence, for her crime.

I'll not believe it, she thought in bewilderment; Martina was miles more likely to bring down the skimming rig, rather than aid and abet it.

After a moment's thought, though, she conceded, with some reluctance, that Martina's involvement would also explain why Acton was taking such pains to make sure that the wife of his bosom didn't find out what was afoot. That was another puzzler—after all, she and Acton had teamed-up to take down many a villain, and you'd think he'd want the fair Doyle to be asking questions inside the prison, and nosing out who was lying like a lying liar. But he hadn't; instead, he's sent her in, like a lamb amongst the vipers—or whatever it was—but he didn't want her to know what she was walking into. It was very unlike him, truth to tell, which only told her that matters must be very grave, indeed.

"I need to speak with Martina, face-to-face," she said aloud. "I need to find out what's what."

This pronouncement was met with a low whine, and she

lifted her head to see that the dog was impatiently waiting at a small distance.

"Sorry," she said. "I'm comin'. And I do appreciate it; between this and Edward's dinosaur, I'm beginnin' to think that you're more friend than foe."

The dog promptly lifted a lip to growl at her.

"Got it," she amended. "We're only to have a temporary truce, due to more important matters. Mother a' mercy; but you're Trestles-bred, through and through."

The dog wheeled and ran for a bit further, and then he halted in a small, clear area, and began digging at the loose dirt. Doyle cautiously stepped forward, and peered at the muddy, leaf-covered ground between the dog's paws. Looking around for a stout stick, she began to pry at the area, bringing up great clods of earth, as the dog continued with his scratching. Finally, her stick hit a solid object, and she pried loose what appeared to be a large, dirty stone.

The dog had stopped his digging, and retreated a small distance to sit and watch her. Tentatively, she rolled the object with her stick, and ventured, "That doesn't look much like an axe, my friend; I think that's a rock."

The dog lifted a lip, and growled again.

Thinks I'm stupid, she thought; and mayhap I am. Cautiously, she crouched down, and examined her find. Was this truly the axe? It didn't much look like an axe—only a piece of stone about the size of a man's hand, and shaped rather like a slender triangle. With the corner of her robe, she brushed it off a bit, before lifting it—it was quite cool to the touch—and saw that under the dirt, it did look to be a deep green color, although it was hard to tell, in the moonlight.

Gingerly, she closed her fingers around it, and then she was almost overwhelmed by the sudden sense she had—of the many, many nameless men, who'd held this axe in just the same way.

"Oh," she breathed aloud, blinking back tears. Small wonder the knight was so unhappy that the wretched artist had filched it. It was not meant for someone like him, at all.

CHAPTER 33

*A*fter carefully securing the axe in her robe's pocket, she looked up to note that the dog had disappeared —not a surprise, since his task was completed, and he didn't want to abide with her any more than she wanted to abide with him.

She began to trace her steps back to the manor house, visible in the distance, and looking much like the setting in a gothic story, with its gabled roof, and the moonlight glinting off the tiles. I'm the heroine in my very own gothic story— complete with buried treasure, she thought with some amusement; and who would have thought it, back when I was slinging fish, at the fish market? How very strange, life is —in all things, give thanks.

She'd only gone a few steps, before she glimpsed a familiar figure, making his way toward her with a lighted torch; small chance that Acton-of-the-all-seeing-surveillance was not going to know where his wife was, at all times. He's a bit nicked, she acknowledged with a fond smile. Now, I've only got to somehow convince him that I'm not.

"Kathleen," he said in a mild tone, as though they were at the kitchen table at home. "I'd wondered where you'd gone."

"You'd never believe me if I told you, Michael," she replied in all honesty, and linked her arm in his, lifting her face for his kiss. "So instead, I'll just say I thought I'd take a walk."

He tilted his head. "Perhaps next time, I could accompany you?"

"Perhaps," she said, in the tone she used with Edward, when there wasn't much of a chance.

"You're cold." He opened his own robe to enclose her in it —no doubt he wanted to relinquish it to her, but since he didn't wear anything to bed, he was forced to compromise, lest the night watchman get an eyeful.

"I am, a bit," she acknowledged, and then turned her head to gaze upon Trestles, as she drew in a deep breath of night air. "It's a fine sight, isn't it?" She pronounced it "foine," so as to tease him.

"Yes," he agreed. "Shall we return?"

"We shall," she agreed. "Forthwith."

She put an arm around his waist as he tucked her under his shoulder, and they began their walk together, toward the main house

"I'm not havin' a relapse," she assured him. "My hand on my heart."

"No," he agreed. "But can't you tell me?"

Regretfully, she shook her head. "I'm afraid 'tis a secret, 'twixt me and Grady's dog."

He lifted his head in mild alarm, and scanned their

surroundings. "Grady's dog is out here? He didn't bark at you?"

"He didn't dare."

"I see," he said, although he didn't see at all.

Poor man, she thought fondly, as she squeezed his waist; I'm constantly oversetting his card-table. Or his chess-table, more properly.

"Are you hungry?" he asked, leaning his head down to hers. "I know where Cook keeps the biscuit tin."

She laughed. "Do you? I am amazed—did you stumble on it, when you were searchin' for the kale?"

"I enjoy the occasional biscuit," he protested.

"Then lead on," she replied.

And so, a short time later, they were seated at the kitchen's massive work table, eating out of the biscuits tin after having deciding they couldn't make cocoa, because neither one of them knew how to light the stovetop.

"We've left muddy footprints," Doyle noted, as she reviewed the floor. "Cook's goin' to know we were the perps."

"We will plead for mercy," he decided, and lifted another biscuit from the tin.

Doyle made a face. "There's truly no need, Michael; not only will she will forgive you in a heartbeat, she'll tell everyone who will listen how wonderful the thievin' aristocracy is."

He smiled. "You are harsh, Lady Acton."

"Only a keen observer of facts, my friend."

"Sir?" The night watchman stood at the kitchen doorway, shielding the light from his lamp as soon as he realized who it was. "I'm sorry to interrupt; is everything all right?"

"D'you know how to light the stovetop?" asked Doyle.

Barely hiding his bemusement, the watchman set down his lamp, and dutifully lit the stovetop, before tipping his hat, and continuing on his way.

"Another one, who will happily tell this tale tomorrow," Doyle observed, as she began to stir the cocoa in the pan. "It must be nice to be you, and immune from all criticism, or repercussions. Although not all of your ancestors had it so easy; a few them had to pay off the King so as to avoid prison, back when that was somethin' you could do."

He tilted his head. "You are a bit naïve, perhaps, to think it doesn't happen today."

"Mayhap," she agreed. "But true justice will be dealt-out, sooner or later. It may take a bit longer, is all."

He was silent, watching her stir, and she offered, "I know it gave you the willies, Michael, but I had good reason to wander the moors, tonight."

Slowly, he replied, "I hope I have not given you the wrong impression; it is not that I don't want to hear about—about your visions—"

"Liar," she said amiably, as held the pan handle with a dish towel, and carefully poured the cocoa into the cups.

He ducked his head in acknowledgement. "Yes. I confess that the topic makes me uneasy."

She set the pan back down, and glanced over at him. "Me too, my friend. But I've learned to live with it."

"Then I should do no less," he said quietly.

With a smile, she carried the cups over. "That's very sweet, Michael, but I think we've already sorted this out, over many a semi-discussion; I can only tell you so much, and you can only tell me so much. We're not like an ordinary couple, who can unburden their bosoms, and such."

"Very true," he agreed.

Thoughtfully she cradled her cup in her hands, as she leaned against the table. It seemed an opportune time to voice her suspicions about Martina, but she decided to hold her tongue, instead. Better to confront the woman, herself—go straight to the source—and anyways, Acton didn't want her to know, and so it was probably best that she not tell him she'd figured it out—let him think he was protecting her from bad news. It seemed only right, after all the trouble he'd gone to.

He said, "I may need to go into the City for a brief time, tomorrow."

This was of interest, and she perked up. "D'you need me to come along, and listen-in?

"No, but thank you."

She nodded, and decided he must be going in to do whatever he was going to do, so as to roll-up the skimming rig, and make this whole mess sink from sight. It was just as well; she wanted to nip into the prison to speak with Martina without Acton's listening-in, and this would give her the perfect opportunity.

"The new painting has been installed in the dining room. Would you like to go see it?"

"I would," she agreed, and noted with some amusement that he couldn't bring himself to call it a Rousseau. And since she couldn't very well tell him that it was an even more valuable Benedict, they were at a standoff. With a quick movement, she snatched one last biscuit, and followed him out.

They walked up the servant's stairway to the dining room, where he shone his torch on the new painting that adorned the wall, in the place of the ship's painting.

"Oh," she breathed, with sincere appreciation. "It's truly

lovely, whether it's a forgery or not."

"The hills look a bit like Ireland," he observed.

She nodded, and didn't have the heart to tell him that this tranquil country scene was not like any Ireland that she would recognize; instead, cramped streets and fish-barrows were more in line with her own memories.

He's being extra-sweet, she thought, as she leaned her head on his shoulder, because I gave him a scare, this night. Such a shame, that I'm going to jump right over the traces again, tomorrow.

CHAPTER 34

The next morning, Acton left for London after breakfast, and Doyle asked Reynolds to accompany her, as she embarked on her usual morning walk with Edward and Callie.

After they'd cleared the gardens, she signaled to his cuff, and almost imperceptibly, he shook his head in the negative.

She informed him, "I'm that glad you told me about the listenin' device, Reynolds. It made me realize somethin' important, and I'll need you to nip me over to the prison this mornin', for a quick visit to the Ministry Office."

Reynolds could not quite hide his extreme disquiet at this pronouncement. "Does Lord Acton know you will be making the visit, madam?"

"No, Lord Acton does not, and it's important you not tell him, Reynolds. Or, leastways, not yet," she amended. "Instead, we'll say we're drivin' over to the village, or somethin'."

Reynolds was understandably dismayed, despite his

wooden expression, and since he seemed unable to find his voice for a moment, she assured him, "You'll come into the prison with me, of course; I'd not go in there again without back-up—now, there was a lesson learned."

Thoroughly alarmed, he asked, "Never say you expect violence, madam?"

"No—no, I was just jokin' my friend. But I do need to find out somethin', on the sly—please don't worry, I'll not interfere with Acton's plans," she assured him, and hoped that this was true. "But there's somethin' here that I'm not sure he realizes." Carefully, she added, "Sometimes Acton needs to be saved from himself, and this may be one of those times."

This was an oblique reference to the other, memorable occasions where the fair Doyle had managed to talk the servant into skirting the hierarchy-rules, and since those occasions had resulted in beneficial results all-around, Reynolds managed to nod, despite the uneasiness he entertained within his breast. "Very well, madam."

She smiled at him. "Cheer up, Reynolds; we haven't shared a decent adventure in some time, you and me."

"Indeed, madam."

They abandoned their walk to the others, and returned to the house to call for the spare car, with Doyle making a vague reference to an errand she wanted to run in the local town. As she stood on the portico and waited for the car to come around, she realized that she was very much looking forward to getting out on her own, and having an adventure —she'd missed that feeling. It was similar to the feeling when there was a new assignment at work, and she was called upon to move quickly, so as to outfox the villains. Truth to tell, she was sick to the gills of all the peacefulness, here—it was not something a body could bear, in long stretches.

Although, they'd their very own homicide here—lest she forget—with the Slough Field claiming yet another victim. And, to be fair, Trestles hadn't been much of a place of peace until just recently—for much of its history, it was more along the lines of a fortress.

Thoughtfully, she gazed at the front façade of the place— so unassuming, despite the fact there'd been bloody battles fought right here, where the entryway now stood.

Her eye was then caught by the little black boy, who peeped at her from around the corner of the building. Sweet little thing, she thought; and was reminded that she'd got no further in figuring out whatever it was she was supposed to be figuring out about him. He was waiting for his mum, the ghost had said, but she still hadn't a clue who he was. Mayhap she'd got hold of it from the wrong end of the stick, though; mayhap instead of trying to discover who he was, she should be trying to discover who was his mum, and why was she slated to die.

Marcelin, she thought suddenly; could his mum be Marcelin? The prisoner was Haitian, but it stood to reason that there weren't many redheads in Haiti, either. The other prisoners weren't treating her very well, and Harrison had already been murdered, for her sins.

With a pang of alarm, Doyle made a mental note of yet another thing she should try to sort out, whilst she was over at the prison. Although, even if she decided the young woman was in danger, she was not sure what could be done; it seemed that Acton himself was stepping very carefully, as though his hands are indeed tied, even though he'd assured her that his hands were never tied.

They loaded-up and were away, and as Reynolds drove the car down the drive, Doyle frowned out the window. Despite his assurances, there seemed little doubt that Acton's hands *were* tied—or at least, when it came to the DCS. Her husband had been telling the truth, when he'd said the DCS wasn't interested in a commutation of his sentence, and he'd been genuinely frustrated by the man's attitude.

No doubt the DCS is in danger, too, she realized; that's why Acton wants him well-away from that place. After all, if the DCS could grass on the people who were skimming money from the Ministry, then—like Harrison—his life was at risk. They'd seen it often enough in their business, and it almost didn't matter whether the sum was large or small— people were willing to do terrible things, if it would lead to material gain; only look at Acton's wretched relatives, and the poor dead priest.

Not to forget the poor ghost, too—he was another one who'd discovered this unfortunate truth the hard way; faith, he couldn't stop talking about how he'd walked into that meeting, all unaware that they were going to throw him into prison, rather than give him a stipend. The poor fellow was still smarting about how unfair it was—it happened at Leadenhall, he'd said. Of course, nowadays, Leadenhall was a market—who knew what it was like, back in the ghost's day. As a matter of fact, they'd once had a tit-for-tat murder, in Leadenhall—two villains had very helpfully murdered each other in an alley, so that a nasty case was closed. Only— only, it wasn't truly a tit-for-tat, at all; instead, the real killer had set it up to look like a shootout, but in truth, he was murdering off his loose ends. As a matter of fact, the true killer was Philippe Savoie's little brother—the *raving* lunatic.

Her scalp prickled, and she wished it hadn't, because the

last thing she wanted to think about was how she'd walked into an ambush, once, with Savoie's lunatic little brother intent on putting a period to the fair Doyle. Mother a' Mercy, but that was right up there with this most recent ruckus at the flat, in terms of traumatic memories, and it was a wonder she didn't flee in horror from the place. Acton had suggested they move, and more than once, but she didn't mind the memories, because in the end, she'd managed to save the day.

And—come to think of it—she'd saved the day in similar fashion on both occasions; she'd managed to talk the villain into putting down his guard, for a moment—long enough to turn the tables. It was truly a talent, that she could blather on and on, and make people forget to pay attention. Another point to the Irish.

With a small shake of her head, she moved away from these disturbing memories, and decided to concentrate instead on what she should say to Martina. Best keep her attention on the task at hand, instead of dwelling on long-ago confrontations, just like the poor ghost did. Unhelpful, is what it was.

CHAPTER 35

*O*nce at the prison, Doyle headed toward the Infirmary, with Reynolds in tow—the servant trying to mask his uneasiness with only moderate success. And small blame to him, after all; there was little chance that Acton wouldn't find out about this little side-trip.

Because her husband tended to keep tabs on her through her mobile phone, Doyle had left hers at home, but she figured that if she asked the same of Reynolds, it would have been a bridge too far, and he'd balk. Therefore, she knew that it was only a matter of time before her husband wondered what Reynolds was doing at Wexton Prison, and suspected that the servant had not ventured forth all on his own. It wasn't so very strange that she'd come here, of course—given that she was teaching the class, and all—save for the fact that Doyle wouldn't go anywhere without telling him. He knew she knew that he'd work himself into a fret, if she wandered off, and so she tried to keep all wanderings-off to a minimum.

No matter; hopefully she'd have enough time to buttonhole Martina, and find out why in heaven's name she was throwing-in with the blacklegs. Mayhap she was being threatened, or something, but this seemed unlikely; Martina was not the type to feel threatened by earthly threats.

Fortunately, they found Dr. Okafor was working in her medical office, and so Doyle greeted the woman rather briefly, and then bluntly asked, "Would it be possible to call-in Martina to your examination room, so that I could speak with her privately? I'm sorry to pull you about, but I think it's important."

Dr. Okafor's serene expression did not change, but Doyle had the impression she waited a beat before saying, "Of course; I will call her in, Kathleen."

She did so, and Doyle thought to assuage any alarm she may have caused the good doctor by making casual conversation. "What's the subject for my next class? I'm half-afraid it's goin' to be Bathsheba at her bath—or Susanna at hers— and with this lot, I'll never hear the end of it."

But her joking manner did not inspire a similar response, as Dr. Okafor only replied, "I'm afraid I do not know; Edwin will handle your next assignment."

Doyle admitted, "If we're talkin' about the DCS, I can't call him 'Edwin,' without feelin' as though I'll be brought up before Professional Standards."

At this, Dr. Okafor smiled, slightly. "It must seem to you that he had changed quite a bit, since the time you knew him from before."

"Indeed, he has," Doyle agreed, and decided to leave out any hair-raising details; the man had truly turned over a new leaf, and she was more than willing to leave the past behind.

They were interrupted when Martina tapped on the door, and then Doyle stood to escort her into the examination room, leaving Dr. Okafor and Reynolds behind in the office.

Understandably alarmed by these maneuverings, as soon as the door closed behind them, Martina asked in some alarm, "What is it? Are you all right?"

Doyle lowered her voice. "I asked for you to be called-in so that I could speak with you in private. D'you have your trusty jammer? I don't have mine, today." Not that I ever had one, thought Doyle, a bit grimly—stupid Acton and his stupid button.

"Of course, Kathleen; what is on your mind?"

Doyle had already planned her strategy—much like you planned your strategy when questioning a suspect—and so she started in a roundabout way, so as not to raise immediate alarm. In a low voice, she began, "I was thinkin' about Harrison—about how she died, and I wonder if it was because she was speakin' about the skimmin' rig too freely. If that's the case, then I'm worried you might be in danger."

But the other woman's answer was unexpected. "No, Kathleen—although I appreciate your concern. Harrison died of—of other complications." Martina paused, and then added in a grave tone, "They believe it was malpractice, on Dr. Okafor's part. It's a shame, but the doctor is going to lose her job. In fact, she may well lose her medical license."

Doyle stared in surprise. "Oh; oh—saints; that's terrible. I hadn't heard." After deciding this seemed a little too convenient, she asked with a show of concern, "D'you suppose it's true?"

"No," Martina readily replied. "I think they want Dr. Okafor away from here—she knows too much."

This was the truth, and Doyle could only be relieved; it seemed that Martina knew what-was-what, and wasn't trying to pull the wool over the fair Doyle's eyes. It would have been hard to believe—that Martina was one of the blacklegs; the woman answered to no one but heaven, and heaven would not have been at all happy about what was going on, here at the prison.

But the young woman's next words were unexpected, as she leaned forward and offered in a sincere tone, "It is for the best, Kathleen. And she will manage—Charbonneau will see to it that Okafor gets another job, in the private sector."

Oh-oh, thought Doyle in deep dismay; I spoke too soon—the plot thickens, yet again.

Feigning puzzlement, she asked Martina, "I thought that you didn't like Charbonneau, much—the two of you are always bickerin'."

Martina lowered her gaze, for a moment. "Yes; you must think it strange. But it is a case of the ends justifying the means. I am afraid that as—as a result of Antonio's death, my Order has lost a great deal of its funding." She raised her gaze to Doyle's, again. "You, of all people, understand how important my work is."

With dawning comprehension, Doyle stared at the other woman in dismay. Her first instinct was correct, then; Martina was a part of this rig, as unbelievable as it seemed. And the reason had now revealed itself; in killing her husband, she'd destroyed the main source of revenue for her Order, and now she wanted to make up for it, in any way she could.

Slowly shaking her head, Doyle breathed, "You can't be stealin' from the Prison Ministry. For heaven's sake, Martina— it's like that sayin'—it's stealin' money from Peter to pay Paul."

"No—it's not the same at all, Kathleen. These people are heretics," Martina pointed out gently, as though she were speaking to a child.

But Doyle wasn't having it, and scolded, "Well, St. Paul wasn't a heretic, and he said we can't do evil, just because good will eventually come of it—the ends can't be used to justify the means. Not to mention there's a Commandment that says no stealin', plain as day."

A bit irritated, Martina replied, "You mustn't cite scripture to me, Kathleen. And no one is 'stealing,' instead the money is being redistributed for a better purpose." She paused, as though deciding what to say. "This embezzling operation was already underway, when I arrived, with much of the money going to a far less worthy cause. In truth, I have righted many wrongs."

"The Warden was in on this rig?" Doyle asked in surprise. She found this hard to believe, because the Women's Warden didn't strike her as someone who could mastermind her way out of a paper bag.

But Martina nodded in affirmation. "Yes. He was looking the other way, while some of the donations were being siphoned off to pay for fentanyl, which was then sold through the prison's Infirmary."

"I see," said Doyle, who processed the unsurprising fact that it was the Men's Warden, who was the corrupt one. And no doubt Acton was aware of this—what with his meetings, and such; it all made sense, now.

Martina continued, "They were using Dr. Okafor's office as a front, to process and distribute the fentanyl." She paused, and then said with some emphasis, "Charbonneau assures me that as soon as Dr. Okafor is removed, the drug-smuggling will be put to a halt, though; I told her I would not lend my talents, if drugs were involved."

But this proffered fig-leaf only served to infuriate Doyle, who retorted angrily, "However pure you motive is, you are still stealin' money from people who are fightin' the good fight. Shame on you, Martina."

With a small shake of her head, her companion replied in a level tone, "You wouldn't understand, Kathleen— everything is not always so simple. You haven't seen what' I've seen—seen what evil there is, in the world. My work is important, and sometimes we have to weigh what will serve the greater good." Reading Doyle's expression aright, she added, "And I will remind you that the Ministry here is heretical; they shouldn't have equal footing."

Doyle could feel the heat flush her face, as she struggled to hold onto her temper. "Holy *Mother*, Martina—Holy Mother; listen to yourself. You're like the older brother, in the Parable—self-righteous, and judgin' everyone else as a lesser bein'. Faith, you're the Levite priest, too—lookin' the other way, even though people are bein' murdered—"

"Stop it, Kathleen," Martina said sharply. She then took a long breath, and continued in a more conciliatory tone, "I understand that you may not agree with my tactics. Believe me, it is not something I do lightly."

There was a small silence, and in the face of such implacability, Doyle decided to change her own tactics. "All right, then; I'll concede that I don't know the facts on the ground as well as you do, but I'm still concerned about your safety, Martina. I don't know as I would trust Charbonneau to do what she promises—or the Men's Warden, either—and they may decide you're the one who knows too much."

"Thank you for your concern, Kathleen. I don't trust

anyone, except for God, but I cannot overlook this opportunity—it is a windfall, and I cannot help but think I was placed here for just this purpose. I am sorry you are upset with me; I was hoping you'd not find out."

Aye, I'll bet you were, thought Doyle. And—for that matter—so was Acton. Small wonder, that he wanted to keep it secret from the fair Doyle, if Martina was involved in this unholy scheme.

Hard on this thought, however, Doyle paused in confusion. Despite his benign words, there was literally no chance on earth that her husband would exercise any kind of restraint when it came to Martina—instead, Acton would harbor a blood-feud against the woman 'til the crack o' doom, and then some. And, even though Doyle might consider Martina a friend-of-sorts, Acton knew his bride would not look kindly upon this rig, that was stealing from the Ministry so as to turn a profit with drugs.

In fact, this rig was custom-made to be rolled up by the CID—faith, they'd rolled up more than a few, just like it, with one being right here at the prison, when Savoie was cooling his heels. So, it only begged the question; why was Acton stepping so carefully? Why was he being so secretive, and working hard to keep his take-down of this rig off-the-record, and under-the-radar?

Although—although, to be fair, it wasn't very under-the-radar, in truth, because the poor man's execution had been a bit clumsy. These dullards would have to be very dull indeed, not to have twigged on to the fact that Acton had them under surveillance in the parking lot—not to mention he'd come in personally, to strong-arm the Men's Warden. And that was apart from the red flag that must have been raised, when his

Scotland Yard wife started coming in on a regular basis, to teach a class.

The penny dropped, and Doyle shut her eyes briefly, thinking that this was exactly what she deserved for letting her brain get so rusty, from all the lolling about and peaceful living. Acton may be many things, but clumsy was not one of them.

CHAPTER 36

With some concern, Martina asked, "Are you all right, Kathleen?"

"I am," Doyle replied, opening her eyes, and then, improvising, she added, "I just wanted to pray that you'll stay safe, and come to no harm."

"Oh—oh, thank you, Kathleen. May I join you?"

The offer was exactly what Doyle had expected, and it gave her a few blessed minutes to assess the situation, because—despite the fact she'd now realized that Acton was running some sort of misdirection play—she'd no idea why he would do such a thing.

There's something I'm missing, here, she thought in some bewilderment; because nothing makes much sense. What was Acton's aim, in all this heavy-handed stomping about? Was he trying to make them stand down, short of arrest? How strange—her husband was not someone who moderated his actions, especially when it came to villains like these, who were stealing money from the Ministry. Faith, they were stealing his money, too—Acton donated to the Ministry—which presented another good reason for a scorched-earth blood-feud.

And even worse, the villains were using the donations to run drugs. You'd think that such a thing wasn't possible, in a prison, save that it was actually commonplace; drugs and weapons were often smuggled-in and sold at the prisons—it went with the territory, considering the type of people who resided there. Faith, you need look no further than the fact that someone like Savoie was practically appointed mayor, when he'd been serving his time.

The light suddenly dawned, and she opened her eyes to stare at the far upper corner of the little exam room. That's it, she thought. Mother a' Mercy, that's it.

The reason Acton was stepping so carefully must be because it was Savoie, himself, who was behind this skimming-and-drugs rig. Savoie, who'd had the run of the place, last time he was here, and had no doubt taken a keen interest in the DCS's profitable Ministry, being as he was Savoie, and rather Acton-like when it came to dipping his fingers in any loose cash that was washing about.

She'd been completely on the wrong track, thinking Acton was trying to protect Martina; Acton owed Martina nothing—he'd said so himself. But Acton owed Savoie everything—the man had saved the fair Doyle's life, and more than once. It was a blood-debt—a debt of honor. He'd made a promise, the ghost had said; Acton must have promised never to come after Savoie—and it made sense that Savoie would extract such a promise from the man; he knew Acton would never renege—it was in his blood.

So; the pieces were all falling into place; Acton was working on it, and taking steps to make the blacklegs shut it all down, short of putting Savoie in the dock. And he didn't want the wife of his bosom to know about it, because she wouldn't approve of Acton's skirting the law, in such a way. Not to mention that she was friends-of-sorts with Savoie, and —lest we forget—in a moment of weakness, she'd agreed to stand-in as Emile's guardian, and next-of-kin. Acton wouldn't be at all eager to house the boy again—Emile was the antidote to peaceful living.

Her scalp prickled, and she paused in surprise, wondering why it would. Emile was a handful, and even more reckless than Edward, if such a thing was possible; Acton couldn't be blamed for seeing to it that the two boys wouldn't be raised in the same household.

So; she should be relieved by this Savoie-epiphany, and trust her husband to straighten everything out. There was one problem, however, and it was a big one; she'd a ghost, annoying her, and when a ghost annoyed her, it was always a call to action—there was something, here, that required her attention.

Mentally girding her loins, Doyle decided that there was nothin' for it; she needed to ask a few pointed questions of Charbonneau, who seemed to be at the center of all this, and hear what she had to say for herself.

With this in mind, she said to Martina, "I'm glad you warned me off, but I do want to sound-out Charbonneau, because I'm not so sure you should ally with her. Let me see if Dr. Okafor will call her in."

But Martina shook her head. "Not today, Kathleen; she is in London."

Doyle blinked. "Charbonneau's in *London*? Isn't she a prisoner?"

"The Warden allows her privileges."

Just like Martina, Doyle realized. Apparently, Mary had not been mistaken, when she said she'd seen Martina talking with Savoie, at the park.

It was on the tip of her tongue to confront Martina about her meeting with Savoie, but she held back; Martina's view was a bit skewed by the prospect of the money, and so she wasn't thinking clearly. A compromised witness, they would call her at the CID—unwilling to admit something that might make her look bad. And she and Savoie were friends, too—Doyle had almost forgot. Savoie had rescued Martina, once—although Doyle didn't know the particulars—and now Martina was protecting him; only see how she hadn't once mentioned his name, even though she must know that he was behind all this.

So, it seemed the fair Doyle was stymied; Charbonneau wasn't on-site, and—as much as she'd like to start some meaningful interrogations with either or both Wardens—she probably shouldn't interfere with whatever plan Acton had hatched. Best to retreat from the field, confront her husband with her new-found knowledge, and hear what he had to say.

In the meantime, she needed to make Martina believe that she'd stand down—faith, she may already have already gone too far to credibly retreat, but she'd give it a try. In a constrained tone, she offered, "I'm that glad you told me, Martina—and I'll say nothing more. It's all a bit shockin', truth to tell."

Martina smiled in relief, and laid her hand on Doyle's. "I am sorry to have shocked you, but you aren't as used to fighting evil, as I am."

Not so sure that I'd agree with that assessment, thought Doyle, as the two women rose to leave, but she only thanked the other woman again for her honesty, and returned to Dr. Okafor's office.

CHAPTER 37

*D*oyle now understood the sense of graveness she'd perceived, beneath Dr. Okafor's serene manner; the poor woman was about to get railroaded out of a job—and mayhap her profession—because she'd been in the wrong place at the wrong time, and had witnessed too much.

Doyle wished she could offer some assurance, some clever hint that would tell the doctor to fear not—that Acton would right all wrongs—but then realized that she wasn't at all certain that this was the case. After all, the ghost was worried, and the ghosts never worried without good reason, even ones who were vague, and drug-addled.

And so instead, after she'd thanked the woman again, she pivoted to the other task on her list, and asked, "How does Marcelin? I hope you can put her in that job-trainin' program, soon—everyone picks on her, poor thing."

"We will do our best, Kathleen; I do think she will thrive in such a program—it will give her some confidence."

"Do we know of any family?"

239

Dr. Okafor shook her head. "None that she speaks of, Kathleen."

With a casual air, Doyle pressed, "Does she have any children, d'you know?"

"No—I do not believe so."

Doyle's scalp starting prickling, and she paused in some confusion, because Dr. Okafor's words were true. Slowly, she mused, "Mayhap she'd a child who died, in her old country."

But her companion remained skeptical. "I do not think so; we pray together, and she makes no mention."

But Doyle's intuition was practically beating her over the head with a brick-bat, and she found herself staring with dawning comprehension at the Nigerian woman. "But you did. You had a child, who was gathered-up."

Dr. Okafor smiled her soft smile. "Yes—in my old country. A little boy. He was the reason I decided to become a doctor."

Another penny dropped, and involuntarily, Doyle reached out to grasp the other woman's arm. "Holy Mother—you're in danger."

Calmly, her companion agreed, "Yes, Kathleen; I know."

Of course, she knew, and she didn't care. The reason the villains were so intent on framing-up Dr. Okafor was because she was Howard's source; she was the whistleblower, for Howard's mysterious project. And Dr Okafor was not one to quail before the forces of evil—after all, when Doyle had first met the woman, she was fearlessly grassing-out a different set of villains. And, with Acton closing his net, she'd no doubt been slated to die alongside Harrison, until the villains had made the startling discovery that she was a friend to the House of Acton—it was just as the ghost had said; Doyle was protecting the whistleblower. And so, as a back-up plan, the villains were now in the process of ruining her credibility.

Coming to a decision, Doyle announced, "I'm takin' you out of here. I can't trust Martina not to squeak on me, and if she does, the boom will be lowered, and no mistakin'."

Dr. Okafor spread her hands in confusion. "I cannot leave my patients, Kathleen. It would look very strange."

"It doesn't matter how it looks, if I march you out of here, there's not a soul who'd stand in my way; I've a stupid title— two stupid titles, in fact. And I'm somethin' of a legend, here —it's a long story."

There was a small pause, whilst the doctor considered this. "If that is the case, we must take Edwin with us."

With some exasperation, Doyle bit back a refusal, and decided that—all in all—this was probably a good idea, since if Doyle made an unannounced departure with Dr. Okafor, the villains would be quick to realize the jig was up, and then dispatch the DCS with no further ado.

"Aye, then; we'll take him, too—I'll make up some excuse."

Dr. Okafor reached for her purse and coat, but Doyle cautioned, "You mustn't take anythin'; I don't want anyone to guess that we're makin' a break for it."

The other woman nodded. "Where will we go?"

Grimly, Doyle advised, "Well, I'm not about to instigate another shoot-out at this wretched place, so thank God fastin' that I've my very own fortress, close at hand. Let me pull Reynolds in, and tell him what's up."

As she opened the door and signaled to Reynolds, she realized she was actually very much relieved by this latest revelation, and she'd been dim-bulb indeed, not to have realized that the little ghost's shy presence was somehow connected to everything else. Dr. Okafor's son was indeed waiting to see his mum—not because she was going to die, but because she was coming to Trestles, for safekeeping. And since the place had stood firm for nearly a thousand years, good luck to anyone who thought they'd be able to pry the woman out of there.

Reynolds was down the hallway, listening politely to the guard at the security checkpoint, who was in the midst of telling some story that required him to wave his hands around a lot. Doyle interrupted, "Reynolds, would you come in for a minute?"

With discreet relief, Reynolds bid farewell to the guard, and approached. "Certainly, madam. And by a happy coincidence, I saw Mr. Savoie, just now. He tells me he is her to pick up a packet from the Warden, before he returns to London."

Incredulous, Doyle exclaimed, "Savoie is *here*?"

"Yes. He was very civil to me, I must say."

It wanted only this, and with a mighty effort, Doyle refrained from making a smart remark about why Savoie and Reynolds would get along like old friends. Instead she ushered him into the office, asking in a low tone, "D'you have your gun, Reynolds?"

The butler raised his brows in dismay. "Certainly not, madam. It would not be allowed past security."

She made a sound of extreme impatience. "For heaven's sake; Savoie himself is probably walkin' about, armed to the teeth." Suddenly struck with an idea, she asked, "Phone him, if you will; I've a mind to give him my regards, too." This may actually be a stroke of luck; if she could enlist Savoie in her effort to get the DCS out, no one would dare lift a finger to stop them.

I'll talk him into it, even though it's not in his own interests, she decided; after all, I've done as much before.

CHAPTER 38

a discreet knock on the office door announced Philippe Savoie, and Doyle smiled and stepped out into the hall to join him, closing the door behind her.

"Hallo, Philippe, how nice to see you again." In a teasing manner, she noted, "Reynolds told me you were here—he tells me you're runnin' errands for the Warden, now. How the mighty have fallen."

"*C'est vrai*," the Frenchman readily admitted, and offered nothing more. She could sense that he was hiding a low-grade anxiety, however, which in turn gave her a high-grade anxiety, but before she could frame another question, he asked his own. "You are well, yes?"

He glanced at the medical office door, and she realized he was worried about her health—he'd always had a soft spot for her, had Philippe Savoie, and—with a pang—she immediately decided to take ruthless advantage of it.

"Oh—oh, yes—I'm goin' grand. I'm just visitin' with Dr. Okafor, to talk about my Bible class." She decided to add in a casual tone, "Acton is meeting with the Men's Warden about the DCS—he's getting let out of prison, today."

"Ah," Savoie said, and she sensed he was amused, for some reason. He then placed the tip of his finger on her nose, which was something he'd never do, if Acton was anywhere within ten miles. "*Eh bien*; I am glad you have the *grande*. I am glad I will not be needed to deliver *le bebe*, again."

"You didn't deliver the last one, and there's a day I'd rather not repeat," she retorted a bit crossly, and then remembered that she was supposed to be enlisting him on a prison break, and so probably shouldn't bicker about who delivered whom.

Instead, she mustered up her most beguiling smile. "Here; walk with me over to the Ministry Office, if you would—I need to pick up somethin', and then we can have a nice visit, and walk out together." Belatedly, she realized it would seem strange that she wasn't waiting for her husband to walk her out, but decided she'd think of something, once they'd got hold of the DCS.

But her companion glanced at his watch, and explained with regret, "I cannot stay; must go home—I have the meeting."

Beneath his grave manner, Doyle caught the glimpse of amusement, again, and suddenly knew—in the way she knew things—that he was going to meet-up with Acton. So; Acton's meeting in London was with none other than Philippe Savoie, and it only served her right, for fibbing. She was not very good at subterfuge, and so she should never even make the attempt, mental note.

As she said her goodbyes, she concluded that—all in all— this was another revelation that brought with it a sense of relief; no doubt Acton was going to meet with Savoie so as to comb him over the coals, and put paid to any and all nasty schemes. Acton was probably the only person on earth who could rein-in Savoie, because the two men had their own murky doings, and Acton could threaten to cut him off, if he was to continue doing side-schemes that might interfere with their mutual-schemes.

She turned to open the office door again, and decided it was a shame that Acton couldn't rope-in wretched Charbonneau, while he was at it, since she needed coals-combing just as much as Savoie did. Although—mayhap he was planning on it? The woman was in London, after all, even though she was supposed to be a prisoner, for the love o' Mike. But it seemed unlikely that a wily one like Charbonneau would walk into a trap—she was too smart, to show up for a brow-beating; not like the poor ghost, who'd been easily led into Leadenhall, and to his doom.

Suddenly, she stilled, and nearly gasped aloud. Holy Mother of God, that's it, she realized, her mouth going dry. Holy Mother, that's why the ghost kept bringing up Leadenhall; Charbonneau was indeed going to their meeting, but she was going to stage a tit-for-tat, and kill the other two.

Acton was nosing around the prison, and so the blacklegs knew that their scheme had attracted his attention. They were probably not sure whether he was going to roll them up, or muscle-in on the proceeds, but neither scenario would be welcome to them, and so Charbonneau was going to stage a shoot-out, just like that double-murder case at Leadenhall. Their skimming rig might wind-up exposed, but all the blame could then be pinned on Savoie, who'd be conveniently dead, and was probably taking the lion's share, anyway.

"Reynolds," she whispered, as she opened the medical office door again. "Quickly, Reynolds, I need your help."

ANNE CLEELAND

"Certainly, madam," the butler responded, unable to hide his alarm. "Are you quite all right?"

"No," she advised bluntly. "And unless we move fast, it's all goin' to wind up like it did in that stupid play, with everyone killin' each other."

"Which play is this, madam?" asked Reynolds, at sea.

Impatiently, she explained, "You know—that famous play, where everyone dies, in the end—although I suppose that describes most of them. The one where the father is a ghost, and wants his son to murder his murderer—faith, but the stupid son shouldn't have listened to him; talk about a poor role-model." She paused, suddenly, her scalp prickling like a live thing.

"*Hamlet*?" Reynolds ventured.

"Aye," she said absently, and then closed her eyes briefly, trying to understand whatever it was she was supposed to be understanding.

Watching her, Reynolds offered with some concern, "Should you sit down, for a moment, madam? Dr. Okafor, I believe Lady Acton requires some assistance—"

Suddenly, Doyle lifted her head, her gaze resting on Savoie, where he'd paused at the security check point. "That's it," she breathed. "Faith, it's about the sins of the father—it's all *kinds* of biblical."

Reynolds offered, "I believe the playwright drew from the Bible quite often, madam."

Coming to a decision, Doyle replied in a firm tone, "Well, so will we; we'll be like the wily Magi—the villains can't very well pull-off an ambush, if no one shows up for it."

"I beg your pardon, madam?"

But Doyle was issuing orders, and didn't have time to explain. "Listen, Reynolds; you're to call Acton right now,

246

and tell him I've run mad, and I'm at the prison, springin' the DCS."

There was a small, dismayed pause. "Perhaps you could be the one to call Lord Acton, madam."

"No—you need to act all concerned. And don't hang 'round, waitin' for questions; pretend you've been cut off." She paused, thinking. "Don't toss the phone, though, I'll need him to see where we're goin'."

Reynolds swallowed. "Is there any particular reason, madam—any particular reason why you cannot simply explain to Lord Acton what you have planned?"

With grim determination she replied, "Yes, there's a very good reason. I'm needed to save the day, yet again, and there's a little boyo, at stake."

Mentally, she added, and now I understand why my poor pathetic ghost was the one who'd been commissioned; there is indeed a little boyo, at stake. And I was wrong, in thinking that Acton was the only person in the world who could rein-in Savoie—he's the only person in the world, save me; I'm the grand master, at reining-in Savoie.

With a show of stoicism, Reynolds lifted his mobile. "Very well, madam." In a quiet tone, he relayed the urgent message, and then quickly rang off.

Glad I don't have a phone, Doyle thought, as almost immediately, Reynolds' mobile began to ping in his hand. "All right; we'll get the DCS, walk out to the car, and you'll drive both the DCS and Dr. Okafor to Trestles."

Reynolds blinked in alarm. "And—and where will you be, madam?"

"Don't worry—I'll be drivin' there too, only I'll go with Savoie."

With some puzzlement, the butler reminded her, "I believe Mr. Savoie is due in London, madam."

"He's comin' with me to Trestles, instead," she advised, in a grim tone. "Once you get there, march the other two straight into the keep, and bar the door from the inside."

Confused, the servant asked, "Do you refer to the archives room, madam?"

Doyle pressed her palms to her eyes. "Mother a' mercy, Reynolds; just *do* it. "Don't answer any questions, and don't open the door for anyone, save me."

Pale of lip, the butler protested, "If—if Lord Acton seeks entry, madam—"

"Don't open," she ruthlessly commanded, "even for him. Now, go. Have them duck down in the back seat, when you go through the gate—although the DCS is one canny gombeen, and he'll know what's best to do."

"Madam—"

But Doyle had already turned away, and was hurrying down the hall to catch up with Savoie.

CHAPTER 39

*R*ather breathlessly, Doyle caught up to Savoie, who'd heard her coming, and had turned to wait with raised brows. She hoped he'd his own jammer, but decided there was nothin' for it; besides, even if their conversation was monitored, it was unlikely that either of the Wardens would dare stand in Savoie's way.

"Listen, Philippe, I haven't been exactly honest with you, and I need your help. Truth to tell, I'm stagin' a prison break for the DCS, and so I'll need to borrow your weapon."

He stared at her in bemused alarm. "*Que?*"

She continued, "I think I can probably just walk him out of here, but I'd like a weapon, just in case he balks."

There was a small, still moment of silence. "Acton, does he know of this?"

"Indeed, he does." Best not mention that he was probably having an apoplexy, right about now.

Savoie lifted his head, to take an assessing glance down the hall. "*Eh bien*, I will help you—I will come with you."

This reaction was exactly as she'd hoped—Savoie wasn't about to allow her to walk into whatever trouble she was walking into alone.

"Oh, thanks, Philippe—there shouldn't be any trouble, save that I'm worried the DCS, himself, will balk. I'd like a gun, just in case I need to show it—he doesn't know I'm comin', and he may not cooperate. I don't have time to talk him 'round."

Savoie's skeptical expression indicated that he was not inclined to comply—he hadn't survived this long by taking lame explanations at face value—and so she added with some exasperation, "For heaven's sake, you still have your stupid knife, right? Don't be selfish, and hoard all the weapons for yourself."

Instead of complying, he lowered his head to hers and asked in a quiet tone, "What has happened, that you must do this now?"

Small wonder, that he was wary. "I'm worried that he's in danger, but I can't say more. Just turn it over, and I'll put it in my pocket—hopefully I won't need it, and he'll be willin' to come along. Quickly, now."

She could see him weigh his options, and then, rather reluctantly, he drew his pistol from its armpit holster, and handed it over to her. She duly noted that he didn't seem over-concerned about this action being caught on surveillance tape, and decided that this was probably a good thing—it meant she'd guessed right, and that he controlled the Wardens, here.

"Thank you," she said, and slipped it into her coat pocket. "Now, let's go nab the DCS. Let me do the talkin'; he probably doesn't trust you as far as he could throw you."

She glanced down the hallway, and Reynolds and Dr. Okafor took their cue, and stepped out so as to follow them.

"If you would go to the car, Reynolds; I need to stop by the Ministry Office," Doyle said in a casual tone. "I'll be out in two shakes."

"Very good, madam," said Reynolds calmly, even though he was emanating all kinds of nervousness.

"I believe your phone is ringing, Mr. Reynolds," Dr. Okafor said in her soft voice, as she accompanied him toward the security point.

"A sales call, only, Reynolds explained. "They are very persistent."

After checking through security—no problem at all, with Savoie by her side—Doyle then walked at a brisk pace toward the Ministry Office. Her companion didn't say anything, but Doyle could sense his wariness. He knows I'm up to something, she thought, with a small pang of conscience; but in the end, he trusts me—not to mention that he's worried I'm doing something stupid, and not without good reason, of course. He's a bit like me, in a way; we can't *not* rescue someone, if rescuing is called for. In a strange way, it's our saving grace.

The DCS was prepping for his podcast, when Doyle used her entry card and came through the office door with Savoie. The other man said nothing, but his gaze moved between them thoughtfully.

"We're bustin' you out," Doyle announced. "It will be like old times, save without all the horrible labor pains."

"What has happened?" he asked, unmoving. "Where is Dr. Okafor?"

"She's comin', too, and I'd rather not say any more. Mr. Savoie, here, has graciously consented to ride shotgun."

"I am not certain," the DCS said slowly, "if that is the best strategy, Sergeant."

"He cannot trust to throw me," Savoie agreed fairly.

But Doyle continued in a firm tone, "Look; I canno' argue with you, right now; only know that we've a Code Five, and you're comin' with me, even if I have to perp-walk you straight past the front desk."

The police code referred to an undercover situation, where uniformed officers were not to interfere, and she could see it gave him pause. He'd not know what she meant by it, only that there was more to this than met the eye. Fortunately, he seemed to decide that he'd see where it led, as he placed his hands on the desk to rise. "Very well, then."

They walked at a brisk pace toward the front desk, and Doyle turned over her strategy in her mind. Hopefully, Reynolds was at the car by now, and watching to pick up the DCS as soon as they emerged; the tricky part would be getting him past the guards at the front desk, although Doyle wasn't at all certain they'd even notice there was a break-out in progress—the guards here weren't exactly the best and the brightest.

In this, however, she was mistaken, as one of them scowled at the DCS, and straightened up in his chair. "Hey— wait a minute; aren't you a prisoner, here? Where are you going?"

"He has privileges," Doyle explained. "He's needed for— to testify, before a Committee, in London. There's a prisoner named Charbonneau who's already there—remember?"

But the fellow only frowned in puzzlement. "I don't know anything about a prisoner named Charbonneau."

"Oh; well she's on the women's side."

Still frowning, the guard pulled up to his desk computer. "How do you spell her name?"

Doyle considered this. "I haven't a clue."

The DCS stepped in the breach, and spelled-out the name, whilst Doyle duly noted that Savoie had not offered a word, during this confrontation—and you'd think, if all the guards here were bent, he'd have done so. Little point in enlisting a criminal kingpin to get them past the checkpoint, if no one seemed to realize he was a criminal kingpin, in the first place. Unless these two weren't bent, in which case she'd best re-think her strategy, here.

"No prisoner with that name," the guard announced.

There was a small silence, whilst Doyle blinked. Charbonneau was not listed as a prisoner, here? Of course, she was a CI—was she here on some sort of assignment? It all made little sense.

In any event, it seemed that the fair Doyle would be called upon to change her tactics, and she weighed whether it would be best to be a police-hero, or an aristocrat, in this situation. After deciding that the aristocrat had the edge, she mustered-up her most Countess-like attitude, and declared with no small annoyance, "I've got the name wrong, then, but Lord Acton is waitin' for us at Parliament, and we shouldn't keep the MPs waitin'."

This seemed to turn the trick, and the two exchanged uncertain glances, as the first fellow reached for the phone. "Oh—oh, I see. Let me call the Warden, then, just to double-check."

There was nothin' for it, and Doyle could only make a show of extreme impatience, as the guard raised the Men's Warden, and put him on speaker-phone.

"Sir, I have Lady Acton here, and I wanted to double-check whether she can take the Minister off-premises, for the hearing in London."

Before the man could respond, Savoie spoke up, "*Vite, s'il vous plaît*; we are late."

There was a small silence. "Certainly," said the Warden.

Good one, Savoie, thought Doyle. At least the Warden was bent, and recognized a criminal kingpin, when he heard one.

Her relief was short-lived, however, as the Warden then said, "Which hearing is this?"

"The Public Accounts Commission, with Nigel Howard," Doyle replied, thinking to put the fear of God into the man, but instead there was a small, profound silence.

Oh-oh, she thought in abject dismay; now, there was a blunder—I shouldn't have mentioned the Commission; that's going to put the cat amongst the pigeons.

"We should go," said the DCS, who probably felt the same.

"*Oui*," said Savoie, a bit grimly, as the guard buzzed them out the door.

CHAPTER 40

Thankfully, Reynolds drove up to the kerb straightaway, and the DCS quickly ducked into the back of the car, alongside Dr. Okafor.

"Follow instructions; we'll be right behind you," Doyle advised the servant, and then she turned to Savoie, who was now a toxic mixture of surprise and rage.

"I'm not double-crossin' you," she said immediately. "I just had to get us out the door. I'll explain, whilst we're drivin'."

"*Non,*" he said, and abruptly turned to walk toward his car.

She trotted after him—faith, he was simmering, and nearly a'boil. "No time to argue; you're to come with me," she said, and drew his gun from her pocket, so as to direct it toward him under her arm, where hopefully the CCTV cameras couldn't see. "I'd hate to have to perp-walk you, but I will." Unsaid was the obvious truth that she wasn't about to shoot him, and that there was little chance she would prevail, if it truly came down to hand-to-hand, being as she was pregnant, and a bit ungainly. To gloss over these disadvantages, she advised in a firm tone, "Where's your car?"

But he was still wary from her mention of the Commission, and stubbornly shook his head. "*Non*, I do not come with you."

With some exasperation, Doyle trotted along beside him. "You *have* to drive me to Trestles, Philippe. It's very important —I'm not going to lead you into a trap; instead, I'm tryin' to keep you out of a trap—you mustn't go to London."

Still no response, as he strode along, and—since it seemed clear he was not inclined to cooperate—she turned his gun around, and offered it back to him, hilt first. "It's me, Philippe," she pleaded in a quiet voice. "Please, please trust me. I have to speak with you privately, it—it has to do with Emile."

This surprised him, and he stopped to accept his gun, and re-holster it. "Emile? Yes? He is safe?"

"He's fine, but I have to talk with you about him." She drew a breath. "It's my turn to be the St. Bernard, this time." She glanced toward the guard gate, and saw with some relief that Reynolds' car had cleared it, and was headed out toward the main thoroughfare. "Let's go, please."

He nodded. "*Bien.*"

After they'd cleared the gate themselves, he continued silent, and—since Doyle wasn't yet certain that he was actually going to cooperate, as opposed to leave her on the side of the road, somewhere, she teased lightly, "We'd a car drive once before, remember? We should stop and pick up some fruit pies, just to relive old times."

At her words, he drew-up a corner of his mouth. "You said '*non*' to me."

This seemed encouraging, and so she semi-scolded, "I did indeed, and shame on you for askin', since I was a married woman. Never fear, Philippe; you'll find someone—someone who's just right for you." Diplomatically, she didn't add that his 'someone' would necessarily have to possess nerves of steel. It was a shame, truly, that Acton had already paired-up Lizzie Mathis with Williams, since Lizzie would have been just the right person, to trim Savoie's sails.

But apparently, her companion wasn't much interested in discussing his love life. "Tell me of Emile."

Here goes, she thought; start talking, Doyle—do what you do best. "If you want Emile to have any kind of a decent life, you have to step back, and start mindin' yourself. You can't be dabblin' in drugs."

He was offended, and turned to frown at her. "I do not take the drugs."

"But you're runnin' them—don't deny it. And Emile may think it all a big lark, when he finds out about it—he's a clever little boyo, and he will, sooner or later. You don't want him to wind up—" she paused, because she didn't want her voice to break, "—to wind up a shamblin' shell, like the drug addicts that we see, in our lines of work."

Incredulous, he glared at her. "*C'est ridicule*; why do you say such a terrible thing?"

"I don't want to say it, believe me, but I'm—I'm just worried about the possibility. He loves you so, Philippe. He wants to be just like you. You have to make sure that he's copyin' somethin' worthy."

"I am the worthy," he angrily advised, and slapped his palm to his chest.

"Not on the path you're treadin', my friend." She paused, trying to decide how to best explain what she wanted to explain without invoking ghostly visitors. "I understand how it feels—faith, there's probably no one else who understands it quite like I do—because I'm Acton's lodestar. I'm Acton's lodestar, but I shouldn't be—that's too much pressure, to put on any livin' person. Emile's your lodestar—and I'm not sayin' that you shouldn't love him; of course, you should. I'm just sayin' that he represents somethin' more to you, than just your son."

He fell silent, and thus encouraged, she continued, "You're tryin' to right all past wrongs, because you see yourself in him. If Dr. Harding were here, he'd explain it better, but I can use Acton as a comparison, because you and Acton are very much alike, in a way. He keeps tryin' to give me things, but I don't want things; all I want is him. People are miles more important than things; you're like the Foolish Farmer in the Parable, thinkin' that just one more silo-full— one more lucrative rig—is goin' to protect Emile from life's heavy blows. But it won't—it can't; that's not the way it works. Instead, it's how he reacts to those blows that's important; he has to learn that you don't numb yourself, to avoid sufferin'. It's miles better to weather the heavy blows, and come out stronger—just like you and I have done."

Watching him, she fell silent, and thought, I had this exact same conversation with Acton, once—although I'm not certain I made much of a dent. Here' s hoping.

Since he still made no response, she ventured, "D'you understand what I'm tryin' to say? Money gives you entry everywhere save heaven, and gives you everythin' save happiness. Not to mention you shouldn't get into a knife-fight with Acton; you saved my life, and so he'd really regret rollin' you up, but roll you up he would, my friend, if push came to shove."

With sudden clarity, she realized that this was the whole point of Acton's operation. He'd sent his wife into the breach, because he knew what Doyle meant to Savoie, and the message was unmistakable: *Remember what's at stake, and stand down; don't make me do this.*

With absolute conviction, she continued, "Your poor bones would only wind up in the Slough Field, if you don't do as he asks. The nobs have murder-in-the-blood, and it's a shame, but there it is."

"*C'est vrai*," her companion agreed.

"You don't want Emile to grow up without his Papa—so don't put Acton in such a cleft-stick."

He tilted his head in inquiry, and she explained, "It means that you're stuck, and there are no good choices."

Savoie nodded, and then confessed, "Yes. Acton, he has already put me in the clef-stick."

She lifted her brows. "Has he? I suppose I'm not surprised, he's good at it—he's subtle as a serpent, and twice as guileful. So please, please don't push him into doin' somethin' he'd rather not—he's honor-bound to you, and that's a good thing, all in all."

She paused, and gazed out the windscreen thoughtfully. "Ironic, is what it is; you're The Good Samaritan, despite your wicked ways. You've made a habit out of savin' people, and in the end, you've wound up savin' yourself."

CHAPTER 41

They entered the gates at Trestles, with Savoie having said little else during their drive. She could sense his overall concern, though—he knew she wouldn't give him such a lecture unless there was good reason—but thus far, he hadn't asked any questions.

They pulled up on the circular drive in front of the main house, and he asked, "Acton; he is here?"

"Probably not yet, if he was comin' from London, but I imagine he'll be here soon. We'll go in, and wait for him."

"*Non*," said Savoie, as—with a decisive movement—he shifted the gearshift into park. "*Bien*, we wait here."

Doyle blinked. "We do? I promise you, Philippe, that nothin' goin' to happen, save for a bit o' talk—and mayhap a scoldin', or two. I was just kiddin', about the Slough Field."

"We wait here," he repeated, and waved the confused footman away from the car.

Nonplussed, Doyle decided that she truly couldn't blame him, all in all; he'd no real assurance that she wasn't leading him into a trap, and she'd already demonstrated that she knew more about his doings than he could be comfortable with. That being said, however, it didn't seem very wise to present Acton with a situation where it might appear that Savoie was holding the fair Doyle against her will. To say that Acton would not be amused would be to understate the matter by orders of magnitude.

After a small space of time, Hudson descended the steps, in his dignified manner, and approached the vehicle, taking a moment to meet Doyle's eyes for a significant moment. She nodded, slightly, to affirm that she was not alarmed, and so the man then trod on the gravel over to the driver's side— apparently, Hudson had determined that this strange situation should be handled by the Steward of the Estate, personally. It was probably in their handbook, or something.

At Savoie's window, he respectfully bowed his head, and Savoie opened the window about two inches.

"*Monsieur,*" said Hudson politely. "Is there anything you require? *Puis-je vous aider?*"

"*Vous aurez des visiteurs. Vous avez besoin de fusils, au sud,*" said Savoie. "*Éloigner l'enfant.*"

"Very good," said Hudson, and with a measured tread, he mounted the stairs to the portico, where he promptly signaled to a footman.

"What did you say?" asked Doyle suspiciously. "You shouldn't alarm poor Hudson, like that."

"We wait," Savoie informed her, as he shifted his shoulders so as to watch the entry drive. Then, with a casual gesture, he pulled his pistol, and set it on his lap. "You are the hostage."

Frowning, she stared at him; there was no question that he was keyed-up, but it seemed unlikely that he'd completely lost his mind. "Acton's not goin' to be happy, Philippe. What are you about?"

But the answer soon presented itself, as another car—not Acton's—could be seen, traveling up the long drive at a rapid pace. Doyle peered at it. "Who's that?"

Savoie didn't look at her, but instead watched the vehicle, his face a grim mask. "Stay quiet, little bird; a few more minutes."

The other car slowed, and then came to a stop, about fifty feet away, down the drive. The door opened, and a man cautiously stepped out, to stand behind his open door. "Savoie!"

"Is that the Warden?" asked Doyle. It sounded like the same voice—faith, she'd been a fool to mention the stupid Public Accounts Commission, and unleash their panic, down upon their heads.

Savoie did not respond, and so the Warden shouted, "What's going on? We need to talk!"

Savoie lowered his window, and angrily called out, "You did the double-cross. I make you pay."

"No—no; this isn't my doing! I swear!" Aghast, the man was no doubt contemplating the firestorm that would erupt if the pregnant Lady Acton were murdered by his cohort.

The passenger door to the Warden's vehicle then opened, and Martina Betancourt stepped out, her manner calm and contained. "Philippe," she called out. "Please—you are frightening Kathleen."

"Oh—oh; should I look frightened?" Doyle whispered to Savoie, but her companion ignored her, and instead brandished his pistol in her general direction.

"I will kill you all, before I go to the prison, *encore*—I will make you pay," he shouted.

"Come on, now; it wasn't such a terrible hardship," Doyle observed in a low tone. "Between the larkin' about, and the cigarettes."

"Me, I would like the cigarette, *maintenant*," her companion replied, without looking at her. When Martina cautiously stepped forward around her door, he turned the pistol away from Doyle and aimed it at the other woman, barking, "Stay back—stay back."

With her eyes fixed on her companion, Doyle carefully raised her hand to the passenger window, where it faced Hudson and the footmen, and spread her fingers in what she hoped was a reassuring message. Stay back. Stay back.

"Please, Philippe," Martina pleaded, as she slowly began to step toward his car. "You mustn't hurt Kathleen— Kathleen, are you all right?"

"Stay quiet," Savoie commanded Doyle.

"Good luck with that," Doyle advised him. "Better men than you have tried." To Martina, she shouted, "Get back, Martina; he's goin' off half-cocked."

"*C'est quoi, ça?*" asked Savoie, who turned to her, much affronted.

"It doesn't mean what you think it means," Doyle replied. "Pay attention—Martina's sneakin' up on you."

"You must put the gun down," shouted the Warden, but he was a crooked bureaucrat, and therefore had little experience in issuing imperative commands.

From behind them, Doyle could hear Hudson say in a carrying voice, "*Prêt.*"

Everyone speaks French, save me, thought Doyle crossly. What's afoot?

But she had her answer, as suddenly Savoie swung his

door open, and crouched down behind it, aiming through his open window at Martina.

"Come no closer. You did the double-cross."

"No—no I didn't, Philippe."

But Savoie was now addressing the Warden. "She gives the information. She double-crosses you, too."

"*What*?" asked the Warden in abject horror. "Martina?"

Turning the blacklegs against each other, Doyle noted with approval. The man must have taken notes from Acton.

Martina paused, exposed in the open area, and turned to lift a reassuring hand to the Warden. "No—no, it's not true—can't you see? He's trying to turn you against me."

"She lies," Savoie shouted.

There was a moment of profound silence, as the Warden froze in place, clearly trying to decide what was best to do. "Then we can deal with her," he shouted to Savoie, obviously afraid to say too much before their audience.

Hearing these words, Martina abruptly whirled around, and began racing toward Savoie's car.

That's what I'd do, thought Doyle, as she watched with bated breath; throw yourself on Savoie's mercy—he's got a soft spot, for women in peril.

But then, several things happened almost simultaneously; Savoie fired, and the Warden's windscreen shattered. In a panic, the Warden raised his own weapon to return fire, only to be immediately gunned down by a volley of gunfire that erupted from the tree-line, along the drive. Doyle gasped, as she watched both the Warden and Martina crumble to the ground.

In the sudden silence, Savoie hurried over to inspect the fallen, holding his pistol at the ready, and—nothing loath—Doyle scrambled to follow. She glanced over, to ascertain the origin of the gunfire, and saw that Grady and two footmen were emerging from the trees, holding rifles, and advancing toward them.

Doyle decided she'd best make certain no one got the wrong impression, and so she said in an urgent tone to Savoie, "Let me take you down; they're all in battle-mode, so we should take no chances."

"*Bien*, he said briefly, and—after relinquishing his pistol to her, lowered himself, spread-eagle, face down on the gravel.

"Don't move," she advised, as she held his gun on him, and signaled to the others to approach.

"Be careful," he warned.

"Be careful, yourself; you should get somethin' with a safety, now that Emile's in the house."

He lifted a palm off the ground in acknowledgment. "I keep this one, because it was my brother's."

Oh—the irony is thick upon the ground, thought Doyle, as she contemplated the gun in her hand; this wretched thing gave me a scar, once upon a time. "Hold him here," she instructed one of the footmen, "I've got to see to Martina."

"Lord Acton has arrived, madam," Hudson called out.

She looked up to see that this was true, her husband had pulled up behind the Warden's car, and was now striding toward her.

Savoie got up to dust himself off, and—upon seeing this—Grady promptly raised his rifle on the Frenchman, walking forward in a menacing manner, as his dog ran in excited circles, barking.

"You may stand down," Acton called out to the Irishman. "Thank you."

"Stop it," Doyle addressed the dog crossly. "We're weapons-free, and don't think I'm not lookin' for an excuse."

CHAPTER 42

*D*oyle's husband took a long, assessing look at his wife. "You are all right?"

"I am, Michael; it's all over, save for the shoutin'. Let me see to Martina, though."

Together, they walked over to contemplate the fallen woman, who was clearly dead; a bullet wound through her head. Doyle found she had mixed emotions, as she silently viewed what was left of Martina Betancourt. It was a shame, and then again, it wasn't; ever since she'd killed her husband, Martina had been spiraling toward her own destruction, and it seemed as though it was only a matter of when, and where.

I thought she was the older brother from the Parable, Doyle thought; but I think she's more along the lines of that fellow from the play—the one who was so very wracked, and was finding it harder and harder to want to stay alive.

Savoie approached to stand beside them, and Acton raised his head to address the Frenchman in an ominous tone. "You brought this to my home?"

"Fah; it was your wife—she does the kidnap," the Frenchman complained, as he drew out a cigarette, and paused to light it. "And then, when I set-up the—the *embuscade*, the attack—she is the comic, to try to make me laugh."

Acton tilted his head in fair acknowledgment. "I know the feeling."

"I had to bring everyone here," Doyle defended herself. "I had to secure the DCS and Dr. Okafor, since they were in danger, and I had to draw you both away from London because you were in danger, too—Charbonneau was settin' up an ambush. It was all very complicated, I must say, and so I will be the first to pat myself on the back, for a job well done." Hopefully, she could gloss over exactly why the villains had hot-footed it to Trestles.

There was a small silence. "*Bien*, I will go," Savoie announced. "Me, I do not like this place."

"This place doesn't like you, either," Doyle noted.

Acton nodded. "I will be in touch."

The Frenchman then turned and headed back to his car, drawing on his cigarette as though nothing out of the ordinary had occurred.

"I will need a debriefing," Acton noted in a mild tone.

I am a trial to my poor husband, Doyle thought, but in the end, he trusts me—which is a wonder, when you think about it; I barely trust myself. "Are we goin' to process the scene, first?"

Glancing around them, he shook his head, slightly. "Not necessary; it seems fairly straightforward."

With a wry smile, she added, "Not to mention that the bullet in Martina's head might be traced to your own weapon."

"That would be awkward," Acton agreed.

She blew out a breath. "It was a justified shootin'," she admitted. "She was chargin', and you didn't know whether she was armed."

Acton turned to gesture to Hudson, who'd been clearly awaiting such a signal, and said to the Steward, "I came late, but it looked to me as though it was the Warden alone, who sought to harm Lady Acton. A desperate and dangerous man."

"Certainly, sir," said Hudson without blinking an eye. "Shall I call the Coroner?"

"If you would, please."

As the Steward retreated, Doyle offered, "Faith, Michael; you're puttin' our poor Coroner through his paces. Small wonder, that you feed him biscuits, and treat him all gracious-like."

"An unusual year," Acton agreed.

But Doyle only shook her head. "No—not truly. This is more the usual; it's just been awhile, since the bodies have hit the ground, around here—not since the Monmouth Rebellion." She paused. "Whatever that is."

He took her elbow. "Shall we go in?"

But Doyle balked. "Not yet; I should give her Last Rites— we've no priest, close at hand."

Her husband wasn't happy, and said quietly, "She doesn't deserve it, Kathleen."

Doyle contemplated what remained of Martina, lying crumpled on the dusty gravel, her eyes staring sightlessly toward the sky. "Deserve's got nothin' to do with it, my friend."

He began to shrug out of his suit jacket. "Let me put this down for you, then."

"Thank you, Michael." He helped her kneel down upon his folded jacket, and as she did so, Laddie began barking again, over along the trees. Doyle looked up, to catch a glimpse of the Trestles knight, walking away from the battlefield with his sword resting on a shoulder; the little African boy's ghost skipping happily along beside him.

The boy turned to smile back at her, over his shoulder, and she thought; I'm glad you got to see your mum. And you'll see her again—just not anytime soon.

Clasping her hands, she bent her head, and began to recite the ancient ritual.

CHAPTER 43

*R*eynolds was much relieved to hear Doyle give the all-clear, and as the archive's heavy oak door was swung open, the butler immediately informed Acton, "I took some liberties, sir, and I must apologize for it. Lady Acton believed the situation was rather dire."

"Lady Acton was correct," said Acton, who was incapable of gainsaying the aforementioned Lady Acton, especially in front of the servants. To the DCS, he said, "I'm afraid the Men's Warden is dead, as is Martina Betancourt. They were killed here, on the front drive."

Dr. Okafor gasped. "Oh—oh, no—"

"I must ask that you both wait within, while the Coroner finishes his task." He indicated Reynolds. "Reynolds will make certain you are made comfortable, while you wait."

"Certainly sir," said Reynolds, who was dying to show Acton that he couldn't be ordered about enough.

To the DCS, Acton said, "I would advise that you not return to the prison. I imagine an inquiry will be opened

271

immediately, and certain persons will not wish you to be called as a witness."

"Yes," the man agreed.

"You can stay at my flat tonight, Edwin," Dr. Okafor offered.

And they will never be parted again, thought Doyle with an inward smile; love's a wonderment, is what it is.

But—wonderment or not—she was due for a scolding from her own true love, and so, once she was left alone in the archives room with her husband, she made a determined effort to head-off any and all discussions, by winding her arm around his waist.

"Are we headin' to bed?" she asked in a hopeful manner. "Because that's what usually happens, after we've battled it out with the evildoers."

But he proved to be impervious to her wiles, and held firm. "I may have to remonstrate, first."

"I'm lucky I've no idea what that means," she replied. "Because it doesn't sound good, a'tall."

He leaned back against the study-table, and prompted, "Tell me, if you would, what went forward, today."

Now, there's some aristo-speak for you, she thought; I'm in the dog house, and no mistaking.

She straightened up to face him, and in her best support-officer voice, she began, "I thought Martina was the whistleblower for Howard's Commission, and so I wanted to go over to the prison, and ask her a few questions. But then I realized she was a blackleg, herself. Not only that, but that the blacklegs were panickin', and that Charbonneau might be stagin' a tit-for-tat, between you and Savoie, so as to get rid of you both. So, I sent Reynolds ahead with the DCS and Dr. Okafor, and then I commandeered Savoie."

She paused, and added honestly, "I truly didn't realize that the other two would follow in hot pursuit, but obviously Savoie realized they would, and so he set-up the ambush, with a fine assist from Hudson."

Her husband was silent for a moment, since he was a wily one, was Acton, and knew full well she was glossing over some of the more important bits—for example, the reason that the blacklegs had suddenly started panicking.

As the silence stretched out, she decided that the best defense was to go on offense, and so she asked in an accusatory manner, "And why didn't you tell me this was Savoie's rig, husband? You should have kept me better informed."

This strategy turned the trick, because he did become a bit defensive, and seemed to choose his words carefully. "I didn't want you to discover Savoie's plans."

This was true, and with some exasperation, she chided, "Faith, it shouldn't have been such an almighty secret, Michael; it was just a rig, chasin' down money—the same old song, same as it ever was. The shockin' thing would have been if Savoie *wasn't* runnin' some wretched rig. There's no need to coddle me, as though I'd run off to the faintin' couch, or somethin'; I know what the man's capable of—none better."

He bent his head in concession. "Perhaps," he offered, which was an equivocal answer if she'd ever heard one.

Interesting, she thought, as she watched him for a moment; there must be more to this Savoie-business than he's letting on. Mayhap it has to do with Acton's stupid hierarchy-world, again; after all, there was no mistaking that Acton had been annoyed with Savoie—and Reynolds, too—ever since he'd discovered their little side-plot, which was done without his say-so. He was not one to like it, when his henchmen went off plotting things, all on their own.

His head still bent, he took her hand in his, and noted in a mild tone, "I am not so foolish as to walk into a trap, Kathleen."

With some surprise, she stared at him. So—he knew what Charbonneau had planned; and had probably set up a counter-ambush, to boot. "Did I throw a spanner in your scheme, then?"

"A bit," he conceded.

Hotly, Doyle defended herself. "Well, what was I to do? I didn't know what you knew, because you weren't *tellin'* me *anythin'*, remember? And I didn't have a lot of time to think it through, I only knew I should make sure neither of you wound up in London."

"You took a chance that I cannot like, Kathleen. Savoie is often unpredictable."

In spades, she thought; the man can't decide whether he's a ruthless killer, or a Good Samaritan. "He's not goin' to do me wrong, Michael. In fact, that was why I sent the others ahead—I wanted to get Savoie alone, so as to give him a bear-garden jawin'. I'm one of the only people who can—between me and Emile—and Emile's not old enough, so it fell to me. I sorted him out in the car-ride here, and gave him what-for."

This was of interest, and he asked in all curiosity, "Do you think it stuck?"

She quirked her mouth. "Heaven only knows—it's a bit like jawbonin' at you, husband." She took a long breath, and pressed her palms to her temples. "Mother a' mercy; but I'm that tired of singin' the same old song, and railin' like an archwife at all and sundry. It's exhaustin', is what it is."

Instantly, his attitude softened, and he drew her to him.

"No; instead, you are very generous. I only wish you didn't take such chances."

His arms around her, she rested her head against his chest. "As long as you're not castin' me off, I'll count it as a win."

"No worries, on that front."

She smiled into his shirt. "No; you made a promise, and now you're honor-bound to stick with me, through thick and thin. That's the good side, to your stupid aristo-code."

"Yes," he agreed, his breath stirring her hair, and she stood, content in his embrace, and happy to be in his good graces again—not that she ever truly fell out; it was only that every once in a while, she took the bit between her teeth, and gave him a few anxious moments.

She offered, "Speakin' of sortin' out, now we've another unholy scandal at Wexton Prison to deal with. Mayhap we should just burn the place down."

"The Prison Ministry is there," he reminded her.

"Oh—aye; now, there's a light in the darkness." She lifted her head. "I suppose you could frame the story in such a way so as to make the embezzlement rig an evil attack against the forces of good; it would give the DCS some good PR."

Acton, of course, was not so certain that any kind of PR was desirable, since he'd a long history of sweeping things under the rug so that they never saw the light of day. "It may be more beneficial to clear out the administration, there, and say as little as possible with respect as to why."

But Doyle knit her brow, thinking. "Was the Women's Warden in on it, too?"

"Yes. To a lesser extent, but she was aware. She was needed to look the other way, and ask no questions."

Doyle raised her face to his. "I think you can turn this 'round, and do it easily. Put her in charge of the harrowing of the prison administration. She'll do it up a treat, because she's a Zacchaeus."

With some bemusement, he asked, "Remind me what that means."

"Zacchaeus was a bureaucrat, too—and he wasn't a good man, but he was willin' to turn it around, when the right person asked him to. If you make her the hero, in this particular play, I guarantee that she'll never put a foot wrong, ever again." With some cynicism, she added, "And you'd have the female-hero-in-a-world-of-men angle, too; the public would eat it up with a spoon."

"How can I possibly make her a hero?" he asked practically.

She chided, "Fah, husband; I can't believe that you're even askin' me. Do what you always do—finesse it, smooth as silk, and imply that she was instrumental in exposing the evil Men's Warden, and should therefore oversee the reforms. Anyone who knew that she wasn't much of a hero is dead now, anyways."

"It is not a bad idea," he mused. "They have had some difficulties, finding an honest administrator."

"She'll turn into a zealot, mark me," Doyle assured him. "If you can think up an award to give to her, all the better."

"And, speaking of zealots, what would you like done with Martina? Shall we bury her here, at Trestles?"

Doyle drew away in protest, staring at him in disbelief. "Heavens no, Michael; she's a Spaniard, and that's second only to the French, in hated blood-enemies, around here. Send her back to Spain—back to her Order. That's what she'd want, anyways—England is chock-full of heathens. Faith, but she was prejudiced, for bein' such a holy-jane."

"Very well."

He drew her against him again, and as his hands wandered, he ventured, "Perhaps we should indeed go to bed. I will say you need to lie down, after your ordeal."

Doyle eyed him with suspicion. "Not so fast, my friend; you've not mentioned what's to happen to Charbonneau."

With some regret, his hands paused. "She has done nothing illegal."

"Only because she didn't get the chance, Michael. She's not officially a prisoner at Wexton—did you know?"

"That does not surprise me."

I'm getting better at this, she thought. "That does not surprise me" means the same as "yes, I knew," in Acton-speak.

Heavily, she advised, "You will behave yourself, my friend; leave retribution to God—I've told you a *million* times. You don't have immunity to go about murderin' people; it will catch up to you, either in this world, or in the next."

But he deftly turned the subject, which was only to be expected. "Speaking of which, I have planned a meeting with my mother and Sir Stephen, and unfortunately, I would ask that you attend."

So, he needed a truth-detector; no doubt he wanted to know for certain whether his wretched relatives had contributed to poor Father Clarence's untimely death—a nice little tidbit, to hold over their heads, if the need ever arose. "Aye then; what's the protocol?"

"Mainly, I'd like you to sound out Melinda—she wishes to attend, also, and claims to have witnessed evidence of foul play." He tilted his head in skepticism. "She may be a compromised witness, however."

Doyle blinked. "Mother a' Mercy, Michael; d'you actually think she'd lie to you, just to set them up?"

Instead of answering directly, he said slowly, "Melinda is
—she is not grounded, at times."

"Not a news-flash."

"No."

There was pent-up emotion, behind the simple word, and
so she placed her head against his chest again, and embraced
him gently. "Tell me about Melinda, Michael, and why you've
been so annoyed with her."

She could feel him take a breath, his chest rising and
falling. "Melinda ran afoul of my father."

Oh-oh, she thought; Acton's miserable father rears his
ugly head, yet again. "Tell me what 'afoul' means, Michael."

"As you are aware, Melinda and I had—we had a
youthful fling, I suppose you'd say. My father—"

"Who was awful," she prompted.

"Who was awful," he agreed, "—decided to take
advantage of her. By doing so, of course, he'd also inflict
injury upon me."

Doyle closed her eyes for a moment. "He was a monster,
Michael. Poor Melinda."

"Yes. And that was not the end of it; there was a child."

Stepping back a pace, Doyle stared up at him in surprise.
"A child? Lizzie?" But then she answered her own question
and shook her head. "No, Lizzie would be too old."

"Callie," he said.

There was a moment of profound silence, and then Doyle
ventured, "So—Callie's your sister."

"Half-sister, yes. She was adopted by a couple in the local
village. They are not aware of her origins."

And there's the by-blow, Doyle thought; although I've no
idea if that's a good thing, or a bad thing—the ghost seemed
to carry a bucketload of resentment about it, but these kinds

of things are viewed through a different lens, nowadays. "Does Callie know?"

"That Melinda is her mother? No."

Doyle let out a breath. "Melinda's longin' to tell her."

He gazed at the wall opposite. "I confess I feel differently about it, ever since we've had Edward."

"I'm one for daylight, and you're one for darkness," she agreed. "I'll let the chips fall where they may, and you'll try to keep those self-same chips from runnin' amok."

"That is an interesting insight," he replied. "And, perhaps, very apt."

She raised her face to his, because he hated speaking of his father, and he was in need of a distraction, on the quick. "I'll tell you what; let's sort it this one out after I have my lie-down—after all, I need to rest from my ordeal."

"Certainly," he agreed, and needed no further urging.

CHAPTER 44

*D*oyle wandered into the formal dining room, where the meeting with the Dowager and Sir Stephen was scheduled to take place, and hoped that Acton would show up before the guests, so that she wouldn't have to make idle chit-chat with their visitors in the meantime. Her poor husband had been frenetically busy, in the past few days, conferring with various persons on the phone—the Director-General of Prisons, for one—and he'd made several trips into town, for huddled meetings.

It's past time we were back in action, she thought, after drawing her own conclusions. I've the feeling this involves a whole lot more, than a paltry skimming rig at Wexton Prison.

Reynolds was in the process of setting up a demi-tea service, because Acton had said—in no uncertain terms—that no refreshments were to be served. The butler paused, upon sighting her, and ventured, "Madam; I wanted to ask—has Lord Acton—has Lord Acton made any mention—"

Crossly, Doyle replied, "For the love o' Mike, Reynolds;

get over it. You did exactly as you should have, and there's no need to quail—I'm half-ashamed of you."

"I do not believe that I am quailing, madam," the butler returned, very much affronted.

"No—instead you should stand your ground, and spit in his eye, if he gives you any guff. He'd only admire you for it."

In a frosty tone, her companion replied, "Perhaps it is not a joking matter, madam."

With an apologetic gesture, she smiled at him. "No; and I'm sorry for bein' so short with you, Reynolds." Not that she'd been joking, of course, but she had to remember that she could get away with miles more than anyone else could, in the standing-up-to-Acton department, and so she shouldn't scold poor Reynolds, who often found himself in his own cleft-stick.

Their discussion was interrupted when the lord of the manor, himself, entered the room, and announced to her, "Kathleen; you will be pleased to hear that Mary was safely delivered of a baby girl, this morning."

Doyle laughed aloud. "That's *such* aristo-speak, Michael; as though the baby turned up, parcel post, and everybody just skipped over all the blood, and the wailin'."

He smiled, and leaned to kiss her. "Howard tells me everything went well."

"Well, I can't wait to take a gander at the wee lass—and now, Gemma's a big sister." She eyed him. "Mayhap Gemma's adoption will come through, soon."

"One can hope," he replied, and turned the topic. "Our visitors should arrive at any moment. I don't think I have to remind you to be circumspect."

"Not to worry," she declared stoutly. "'Circumspect' is my middle name. Isn't that right, Reynolds?"

"Certainly, madam," said Reynolds, in a quelling tone.

Acton dismissed the butler, "Thank you Reynolds. Please see to it that we are not disturbed, for any reason."

"Yes, sir," said Reynolds, just as Hudson formally knocked on the door jamb, to announce their visitors.

Sir Stephen and the Dowager then filed in, followed by Melinda, and Doyle's mood instantly sobered. Everyone's a nasty mixture of triumph, and wariness, and—and guilt, she thought. I wonder how Acton's going to play this.

She wasn't to wonder for very long, however, because immediately after they'd all sat down, he began, "I am afraid that I have discovered some disturbing information about Father Clarence's death."

He's going in hot, thought Doyle. Wants to shake them up, a bit.

"It is certainly disturbing," the Dowager agreed, in her imperious voice. "To think that the poor man was left as carrion for the animals, with no one to miss him, or care."

"Speak for yourselves; I cared—I cared very much," Melinda offered, and made a show of dabbing at an eye with a scented handkerchief.

"Shocking," said Sir Stephen, who couldn't quite conceal an unattractive smirk, that showed through his solemn expression.

Doyle brushed her hair off her forehead, in the signal she used to inform Acton that this was a lie, and—with a mighty effort—managed to refrain from making a smart remark. I can be circumspect with the best of them, husband, she thought, rather defiantly.

"As it turns out, there is a great deal of money at stake," Acton continued, "and so some questions must be raised about the recently-created Trestles Foundation."

The Dowager regarded him with a false show of affronted dignity. "The man was writing a history, and, since he was a priest, he could not very well keep the proceeds for himself." She turned to Doyle for support. "Isn't that right, my dear?"

"That sounds about right," Doyle admitted.

But Acton continued in an implacable tone, "It appears the Foundation not only would receive the proceeds from his book, the Foundation would also serve as the beneficiary for any inheritance." Acton paused. "And Father Clarence was the beneficiary of a substantial trust, to be distributed upon his death."

"Is that so?" asked Sir Stephen, raising his brows, and barely concealing his glee beneath a mask of wonderment. "How extraordinary—I'd no idea."

Doyle brushed her hair back—twice, for good measure.

"To think, that his death will not be such a tragedy, after all," said the Dowager.

"It's a *terrible* tragedy," Melinda insisted, waving her handkerchief with a graceful hand. "I am utterly *bereft*."

"There, there, my dear Melinda," said the Dowager. "We shall find someone else to give you your religious instruction. Why, perhaps Acton can take up the mantle, and begin meeting with you privately."

Circumspect, Doyle reminded herself. Cir-cum-spect.

But Melinda only waved a vague hand. "Oh—no, ma'am; you misunderstand. I am bereft because I loved him." She paused, lifting her face to gaze off sorrowfully into the distance. "And—and he loved me."

Doyle blinked. "What?"

Melinda sighed. "We fell *madly* in love. A forbidden romance, if you will."

Outraged, Doyle chided, "You mustn't go about seducin' priests, Melinda. That's got to some sort of double-sin."

Melinda turned to Doyle, very much upon her dignity, and pronounced, "No such thing, Kathleen; we did the legal thing, and got married."

This pronouncement was met with the silence it deserved.

Doyle stared at her. "You—you *married* Father Clarence?"

Misty, the other woman smiled. "A secret marriage. So *thrilling*."

With dawning comprehension, Sir Stephen leapt to his feet. "That's a lie," he blustered in outrage. "It cannot be legal."

"Oh, it's legal, all right." Melinda smiled a sad little smile. "And I suppose that makes me his sole heir."

With a curse, Sir Stephen slapped the table, and exclaimed, "This will not stand; I will call my solicitors—"

"Call them," Melinda suggested, with a voice that had suddenly hardened. "We will have much to discuss."

There was another small silence, and Doyle duly noted that her husband was making no comment—because truly, there was nothing left that needed to be said. It was another sheep-raid—just like the people who used to live here, long ago, were constantly doing. Only this time, the sheep was a rather dull priest, and the raider was a wronged woman, who'd seized the main chance and taken her revenge, even though it may have been a few steps removed.

I can't muster up any disapproval, Doyle thought; even though the racking-up of riches is frowned upon. I only hope Melinda can find a measure of solace, in her new-found wealth.

Into the tense, incredulous silence, Acton said, "Let me call for refreshments."

CHAPTER 45

They were finally home, and Doyle was ready to kiss the polished marble beneath her feet, it felt so good to be back to normal. Trestles was bearable in short bursts, but it was very wearing, for someone like her, and she could only hope the over-long holiday break wouldn't be repeated, anytime soon. Acton loved the place, of course, but she wasn't sure she much liked the influence the place had on her husband—it was hard to convince him to temper his actions, whilst the trophies of war were always out on display, in every nook and cranny.

At present, she was sitting on the sofa, and watching him on the telly. He was giving a press conference about the scandalous death of the Men's Warden, who'd attempted to storm his estate in a frenzied attempt to escape justice. The recitation, understandably, glossed over some very pertinent parts, but emphasized the valuable help the CID had secured from the Women's Warden, who stood next to him at the press conference, beaming at the cameras.

At the conclusion, Acton took some polite and respectful questions—many of them asking whether Officer Doyle had been harmed in any way by the encounter—and his thoughtful demeanor made it clear he was acting more in sorrow than in anger, and held no grudges.

"Turn it off," Doyle begged Reynolds. "I can't watch—it makes me want to throw a blanket over my head. And before I forget, I've got somethin' for you, that I want you to have."

She padded over to the bedroom, and pulled the jade axe from where she'd hidden it, rolled up in one of her wool socks. Upon returning, she approached the waiting butler, and handed it over with a smile. "Here; I wanted to give you this."

The axe—now cleaned—glowed deep green in his hand, the jade surface carved with worn markings whose meaning had been lost in time.

Reynolds stared at it. "Great *heavens*, madam."

Doyle explained, "They were given as prizes, long, long ago—faith, it's miles older than your paltry Ming-bowl. They were always given to a faithful servant, for service above and beyond. There was a fellow at Trestles, who was last given this one; he saw a raidin' party comin', and held 'em off at the gate, until reinforcements could arrive."

There was a small, profound moment of silence whilst Reynolds regarded the axe, his head bent. "I cannot possibly accept this."

"Of course, you can, you knocker. I certainly don't want it." She smiled to herself, because—despite his words—she'd noted that he couldn't seem to let go of it.

After a long pause, he asked quietly, "And what was the servant's name, madam?"

"I don't know," she admitted. "Apparently, the fellow didn't think that part was very important."

"Just so," said Reynolds.

Lightning Source UK Ltd.
Milton Keynes UK
UKHW010643131221
395565UK00001B/15